WILDLIFE

WILDLIFE

by

FIONA WOOD

poppy

Little, Brown and Company
New York   Boston

Poppy

Hachette Book Group
237 Park Avenue, New York, NY 10017
Visit our website at lb-teens.com

Poppy is an imprint of Little, Brown and Company.
The Poppy name and logo are trademarks of Hachette Book Group, Inc.

First U.S. Edition: September 2014
First published in 2013 by Pan Macmillan Australia Pty, Ltd.

Library of Congress Cataloging-in-Publication Data

Wood, Fiona (Fiona Anna), author.
Wildlife / Fiona Wood. — First U.S. edition.
pages cm
"First published in 2013 by Pan Macmillan Australia Pty, Ltd."
Summary: Two sixteen-year-old girls in Australia come together at an outdoor semester of school, before university—one thinking about boys and growing up, the other about death and grief, but somehow they must help each other to find themselves.
ISBN 978-0-316-24209-7 (hc) — ISBN 978-0-316-24206-6 (ebook)
1. Teenage girls—Australia—Juvenile fiction. 2. High schools—Juvenile fiction. 3. Bildungsromans. 4. Grief—Juvenile fiction. 5. Friendship—Juvenile fiction. 6. Melbourne (Vic.)—Juvenile fiction. [1. Coming of age—Fiction. 2. High schools—Fiction. 3. Schools—Fiction. 4. Grief—Fiction. 5. Friendship—Fiction. 6. Melbourne (Vic.)—Fiction. 7. Australia—Fiction.] I. Title.
PZ7.W84925Wi 2014 823.92—dc23 2013034979

10 9 8 7 6 5 4 3 2 1

RRD-C

Printed in the United States of America

For AJW

Boys and girls come out to play,
The moon doth shine as bright as day.

William King, 1708

In the holidays before the dreaded term at my school's outdoor education campus two things out of the ordinary happened.

A picture of me was plastered all over a massive billboard at St. Kilda junction.

And I kissed Ben Capaldi.

At least twice a year, my godmother, who is some big-deal advertising producer, comes back to Melbourne from New York to see her family and people like us, her old friends.

Her name is Bebe, which is pronounced like two bees, but we call her Beeb.

She doesn't have kids, so I get all her kid attention, which to be completely honest is not a huge amount. But it's "quality time." And quality presents. Especially when I was little. When I was five, she arranged for me to adopt a baby doll from FAO Schwarz. She took photos of me in the "nursery"—they actually had shop assistants dressed up as nurses—and I showed them at school.

That was when I started being friends with Holly. As she looked at my doll, Meggy MacGregor—who had a bottle, nappies, designer clothes, a birth certificate, and a car seat—I could see her struggling. It was jealousy/hatred versus admiration/envy, and lucky for me admiration/envy won the day. Holly's a good friend but a mean enemy.

We were at the beach house, lounging around in a delicious haze of lemon poppy-seed cake and pots of tea, talking about digging out the wet suits for a freezing cold spring swim, and whether sharks have a preferred feeding time. I was lying on the floor, with my feet up in an armchair. Toenails painted Titanium—dark, purplish—drying nicely.

I'd just put down *Othello* for a bout of Angry Birds. My sister, Charlotte, thirteen going on obnoxious, was laughing too loudly at a text message, no doubt hoping one of us would ask her what was so funny. Dad was doing a cryptic crossword. Mum was answering e-mails on her laptop even though she was supposedly on holiday. "Sexually transmitted diseases never sleep," she said when I reminded her of the holiday concept. Gross.

She used to be a regular doctor, but she kept getting

more and more obscure qualifications and went into community health and health policy, and now she basically runs the Free World from the Sexually Transmitted Infections Clinic in Fitzroy.

If you can think of a more embarrassing place than STIC to visit your mum at work, think again, because there isn't one.

Holly loves it. We went there after school on the last day of term for emergency gelato money so we'd have the necessary energy required to trawl Savers, and this old woman gave us the foulest look when we hit the street. Holly deadpanned her: "At least we're getting it treated."

Beeb was sitting on the comfy sofa, with the beautiful Designers Guild paisley fabric that she bossed Mum into choosing about ten years ago, all the bright colors now softly worn and faded, flipping through some modeling agency "books" online and saying, "Insipid, insipid, dreary, tarty, bland, blah, starved, insipid..." She groaned and stretched out her black-jeans-clad legs. "Where are the interesting gals?"

"They broke the mold after you two," my dad said. Meaning Beeb and Mom. It never works when my dad tries to give a compliment; he's simply not that charming.

"Thanks," I said, thinking *interesting* is after all a modest claim.

I must have sounded way more offended than I felt, because when I glanced up from my screen all eyes were upon me. Upside down, disconcertingly, because of me lying on the floor. When I untangled my legs and sat up, it was as though I'd surrounded myself with flashing lights and arrows. Everyone kept looking at me. Really looking. And I was wishing I'd just shut up, because my mother was probably about to remember that I still hadn't unloaded the dishwasher and if I had time to lie there playing Angry Birds—which is quite a distant rung on her almighty hierarchy of tasks from Reading a Required Text for Next Term—then I certainly had time to unload the dishwasher, and I had to remember the family was a community, and in order for a community to function...

Beeb got up. "Come here, kid," she said, leading me to the window. She was looking at me with a strange frown-and-squint gaze. "What did you do with all those pimples?"

"Roaccutane," I said. "I had dry skin, dry eyeballs, and no spit."

"Till they corrected the dose," said Dr. Mother.

"What about all the hardware in your mouth?" asked Beeb.

"Off last week." I ran my tongue over my teeth. They still felt weirdly slippy.

"Take off your glasses."

I did.

"You are gorgeous. How did I not notice this?" It was a eureka moment, she said later.

"Maybe because you see my visage in my mind," I said, mangling a bit of *Othello*.

"That is true, my sweetie," said Beeb.

"She has a pointy nose exactly like a witch," said Charlotte.

"Her nose is fine," said my father, who never seems to realize *fine* is as good as an insult.

"If you like huge noses, which no one actually does," said Charlotte.

"She's got character," said Beeb. "And that's what I'm looking for."

"You're talking about *her*? My sister? Sibylla Quinn?" said Charlotte, her voice squeaking with growing incredulity. "She's totally fugs. Totally."

"Don't use that word," said my mother, who only recently found out what *fugs* meant, and then only because she used it, so I felt that I had to tell her, and she said, Oh, that's disappointing. I thought it was like a cuddly version of ugly. No surprise this is the same woman who thought *lol* meant "lots of love." It was her all-purpose sign-off for texts till I set her straight a few years ago.

"I don't want pretty little generics; I want different; I want individual!" said Beeb.

"What for?"

"Perfume launch. A billboard and magazine campaign. *Jeune Femme Sauvage*." She was rummaging in her latest designer version of the magic bag that contains her whole office. She pulled out a camera, took some photos of me, and studied the screen. "Perfect. God, you look like your mum."

"Old and tired? Poor girl," said my mother.

We looked at her. She has a high forehead and a bony nose and a big mouth. (In both senses.) She doesn't dye her hair. It's cut straight and parted on one side. It's the same color as mine. Mouse. Only she calls it rat because she's *so* funny. She does have a great smile. And she smiled.

"Take a picture. It'll last longer," she said.

Beeb took a picture of me and Mum together. We're both smiling. And I can see that even though I'm not old and tired, we do look pretty similar.

Mum hugged me and whispered in my ear: *"Dishwasher."*

friday 28 september
    After Fred...

saturday 29 september
    After Fred died...

sunday 30 september
    After Fred died I divided my time between blind disbe-
lief, blank chaos, and therapy.
    The psychiatrist, Esther, said, Write a journal, Lou, how
about writing a journal, would you consider writing a journal, Lou, give it some thought...
    We are in the slowly unwinding transition out of ther-
apy in the lead-up to me going away to school. Who knew:

you can't just walk out of therapy. At least it is not recommended that you just walk out of therapy. No matter
how many times you might keenly wish to just walk out of
therapy.

There will be a formal handover to the school counselor,
whose name I don't know yet. I'll be the new girl, starting in term four. Boarding for a whole term, a whole nine
weeks, in the wilderness.

I've been angry through the whole therapy thing, which
might be a displacement of my guilt/sorrow/depression
at the whole Fred thing. We don't use *depression* in the
usual sense, because truly, if I don't have a reason to feel
depressed, I don't know who...

It is possible that Esther, who is after all a psychiatrist-
with-a-special-interest-in-grieving-and-its-effects-on-
mental-health-in-young-people, is right about writing a
journal.

So I have decided, well, why not write something down?

If you don't want to write about your Feelings, you can
simply write about the Physical World, what you see, what
you hear...facts, things, stuff. Jeez, so it's not compulsory
to eviscerate myself? To slash myself to a slow death with a
million small paper cuts? Thank you kindly.

There are whole nights I do nothing but wait. For what?

You could say I have been spending too much time alone
for too long. Perhaps it is indeed time to start talking to an

exercise book. The internal, external...infernal, diurnal, eternal journal. It is essentially just more talking to myself, but that is okay because my heart is its own fierce country where nobody else is welcome.

Cut him out in little stars. Hard to believe a man even wrote that; it's so fragile.

I completely get that giddy arrogance, the infatuation. The laugh-and-spin embrace of the absent beloved. If you were writing an essay, you'd probably yarp on about the way in which it can be read as prefiguring Romeo's death. A portent.

I love the staccato it-t-t-teration and the soft fading sibilance of *stars.* Imagine the words breathed out, written down fast and hard onto thick, smeared paper, the tarry smell, black sputtery ink. Such potent meaning inside so delicate an image feels risky, implosive, cataclysmic.

But if there's no danger, no risk, it's not love, is it?

I've told Esther exactly nothing of any of this.

Fred and I talked about it like we talked about everything, and decided we were too young to have sex. Then we basically went for it.

Because, sure, head was saying, *Maybe not such a good idea,* but soul was saying, *I know you,* and body was saying, *Come to me.* And that's two against one.

Hey, at least we were older than Romeo and Juliet.

9

Fred did the research. Ever the scientist. The failure rate for condoms mostly relates to misuse, or accidents. We decided we'd go straight to a morning-after pill in the case of an accident. We also decided we wouldn't have accidents, and we didn't. We took it in turns to buy the condoms. Nowhere too near home.

Going on the pill would have meant horrible discussions. My mothers being very responsible and ultimately *understanding* and *tolerant* with about three million warnings and provisos. And the family doctor. Gag. I did not fancy the whole gang metaphorically standing at the bedside. A strange doctor would have been possible, but weird, too. I didn't need the lecture.

Condoms sometimes break because someone is being rough, or the girl isn't ready, which sounds so sad. Sounds more like rape than sex to me. That wasn't us. We were all liquid aching and longing. It was fun being beginners together. You only get that once. It took a little while. We were learning a new language, after all.

If we'd ever asked for a weekend away together, all the parents, including Fred's stepmother, would have been frowning and conferencing and counseling.

But all we asked was to do our homework together a couple of times a week, and hang out a bit on the weekend. So it was easy. And we did homework, our nerdiness as compatible as our lust. We were pretty lucky. You'd have to say.

Next week I am heading off to a jolly outdoorsy camp called Mount Fairweather, where you learn to be jolly and jolly well fend for yourselves and run up a jolly mountain and learn which way's north and how to make a fire and incinerate some jolly marshmallows, no doubt.

Esther says it will be good for me. She says it will do me the world of good. But where is the world of good? I'm pretty sure it's not stuck up a mountain with a bunch of private-school clones.

Dan and Estelle and Janie are all on exchange in Paris. They left last week. More tears. More scattering.

Dan's shrink said it would be good for him. Maybe he said *the world of good*. Perhaps Paris is the world of good.

I do try to live in the moment, but it doesn't work particularly well.

In the wall is the window. On the window is the curtain. Through the window is the moon. You can even write gibberish in the journal if you like; it still connects you to the page, to the idea, at least, of communicating. Apparently.

Sometimes I'll write to you, Fred; sometimes I'll write to me. Sometimes I will just write what I see, because *when I see a fingernail moon in fading sky*... I see it for you, too.

3

It took a whole lot of persuading—mostly of Mum—to get me from the living room floor up onto that billboard. Beeb knew her so well. The four things that clinched the okay were:

- I'll be there the whole time supervising.
- No one will recognize her.
- The vibe is "fairy tale," not "sexy."
- She can put the money in her travel account.

The first three were for Mum and Dad, the fourth was really for me. My parents are notoriously unmotivated by money. Not me. I can't get enough of it. And the fee was huge—it's a global campaign. (I'd have to babysit the current clients into old age to earn that much at twelve dollars an hour.)

My travel account has been going forever. Years ago I negotiated that in the summer break between school and university, instead of going to Byron Bay for senior week, I get to house-sit Beeb's apartment in New York (Upper West Side, two blocks from Zabar's, so I won't starve) while she is here in Melbourne. But so far with babysitting and working during school breaks and having taken out certain essential amounts, I've only ever got about three hundred dollars, which is a fraction of the airfare.

Even when Mum had said okay, she wasn't exactly in love with the whole billboard plan.

When I came home with my hair dyed—and it looked great, by the way—she nearly had a conniption.

Beeb joked her out of it by talking in headlines:

"New Study Reveals Hair Dye Does Not Chemically Neutralize Political Awareness."

"Feminist Survives Professional Eyebrow Wax."

"Makeup—It Washes Off!"

"These things were serious crimes back in the day," Beeb said to me by way of explanation. As though I haven't heard every feminist rant under the sun and am not a proud feminist ranter myself, when warranted, and when I can be bothered.

"And PS, Mother, I am the only person in my grade who doesn't have dyed hair," I said.

"Not anymore, you're not," she said, eyebrows up.

There was a big preproduction meeting at the photographer's studio where Beeb "consulted" the art director, who "consulted" the makeup artist, who had a colorist on "standby." To hear them, you would think my hair was of global significance. But whatever they did, it sure did not look like any other hair I'd ever seen.

They talked about "layering" the color, and "textural" color, and "variegated" color. And the amazing thing was that even though it had about ten different colors in it—all individually painted and put in foils—it still looked like my hair, but as though it was walking along with its own set of glamour spotlights.

Getting it done was outlandishly boring. It took a whole day to do hair and the makeup "tests." But I would have put up with it ten times over to see Charlotte turning green when I got home.

"You don't even look like yourself," was the best she could come up with as she huffed off to sulk in her room.

After pretending like it was no big deal, I went upstairs and locked myself in the bathroom. I actually could not stop staring at myself in the mirror. I looked awesome. It was mesmerizing. And Charlotte was right for once in her scurvy little life: I looked nothing at all like myself. It was me with a work of art stuck right onto my face.

I kept blinking at my reflection. One minute I could see myself, the next, just the beautiful mask. Which looked five years older than me. If I were in a scary movie, this would be the perfect moment to first experience psychosis. Maybe the mask would talk to me. As my now-crazy older self. From the future. I shuddered. I was freaking myself out. I stuffed my hair into a ponytail and turned on the taps.

The shoot was right before the end of third term, and the billboard was up on the last day of the holidays before we left the city for our fourth term, boarding at Mount Fairweather, which is Crowthorne Grammar's outdoor education campus.

"Deadline tighter than a fish's arsehole," as Beeb said.

She swears like a mad thing. She says it comes from spending too much time with crews.

As soon as the billboard went up, it was all over Facebook. Holly was posting it before the paste was dry. In one keystroke I went from being a year-ten "nobody" to a year-ten "unknown quantity."

Once it hit Facebook, Holly applied some pressure, and I got the event invite to Laura Jenkins's party, which was on that very night. Holly had told me about the party a couple of weeks ago. She understands that I prefer to know when I'm being socially outcast. I pressed Attend (what the hell—I didn't have anything else on) and shut my laptop as Mum walked in to check that I was packed, which I more or less was.

"Sibbie, what is this?" She was looking at my supersize, multi-gadget, bloodred Swiss Army knife. "You're taking a weapon?" She frowned, no doubt running a mental checklist of some of the miscreants in my grade.

"It's optional. But, yeah, I'm going totally gangsta."

She laughed.

"I feel like I'm sending you back to the Stone Age."

"You might as well be." I gave my cell phone a hammy kiss. "Farewell, my heart, my life."

"No texting for nine weeks! Your thumbs might drop off."

"They'll get axing exercise."

"Known as 'chopping' in some circles, I believe."

"Yeah, that."

"Promise you'll write lots of letters?"

"It's compulsory. But I would anyway. And everyone says the Letter Home is all that stops you going crazy on the solo overnight hike."

She cast a doubtful eye over my bags and the surrounding mess. "You don't want some help?"

"I'm supposed to be self-sufficient for the whole term or your money back, so I think I'll be okay."

"Have you packed undies?"

"Mum!"

She laughed as she went out the door. "Just saying."

There have been certain trips on which I've forgotten certain essential items. But no big deal, right? You can always supplement when you get there. Anyway, this time there was a list.

Leonie came over to me—he always gets anxious when there's luggage out—it usually means the nice man from the doggy kennel is about to pick him up. I gave him a reassuring back scratch, feeling a bit guilty to be offering last-minute affection. I take him for granted these days, i.e., ignore him heaps.

He wagged his stumpy tail agreeably. Dogs are lovely—they don't even know the meaning of *grudge*. Twelve years ago, Leonie was the most beautiful name I could imagine. A mixture of my friend *Leah* and *pony*. Mom asked if I knew it was usually a girl's name and our puppy was a boy. I pretended I knew, to maintain my four-year-old dignity. I was pretty sure Leonie wouldn't care either way. In the spirit of male solidarity, my dad has always called him Leo.

Before burying my phone in a pair of thick socks to pack it—conveniently not thinking about the contract signed in good faith pledging not to bring phones to camp—I texted Michael: *Skype?*

Michael, my oldest friend, my strangest friend. He prefers Skype to phone because he says the role of voice in conversation accounts for fifty percent or less of communicating. He also counts Skype as a social outing, which means he's off the hook for organizing an actual social outing. He was there by the time I got to my desk.

"Are you jet-lagged?" I asked.

"A little."

"How was Rome?"

"Ancient."

"What did you watch on the plane?" I give Michael pop-culture viewing suggestions for long flights.

"*Friday Night Lights.* You were right."

"So, the billboard went up."

"I saw it."

"Large, isn't it?"

"Extra extra large. *Livin' large.*"

"*Livin' large.* At least it'll be down by the time we get back."

"They've captured an authentic Sibylla look, though."

"It's the unfocused gaze, because I'm wishing to be somewhere else."

"Which obviously translates nicely into..." He was casting about for the desired message of the ad.

"*I smell good,* I guess."

"You nailed it. Will you do any more of this 'work'?"

"I was only allowed to do this because it was Beeb. You can imagine the lecture—my mother is still fifty percent horrified. And speaking of horror—I've said I'll go to Laura's party tonight."

"Celebrity life begins. Don't you want to go?"

"Yes/no."

"Because it will be good/bad?"

"Pretty much."

He nodded.

"What are you reading?"

He smiled apologetically and held up *Walden* by Henry David Thoreau. Of course he's reading Thoreau as we head into the wilderness: he's Michael.

"Michael, you rock."

His eyes shine. "Sibylla, you—tall tree."

"I can't ask you what I should wear, so I guess I'm just here sharing some nervousness."

"I hope it turns out to be more good/bad than bad/good. Here, have some Thoreau." He found a page in the book and read to me, " '*I went to the woods because I wished to live deliberately, to front only the essential facts of life, and see if I could not learn what it had to teach, and not, when I came to die, discover that I had not lived.*' "

"Hmmm, so if I substitute *party* for *woods* . . . I'm already feeling less ambivalent about it."

He smiled, said good-bye, and left, so it was just me on the screen holding up my good-bye hand and contemplating the most immediate essential fact of life: what to wear.

I finished packing and had time to try on five or six variations of "very casual" for the party. A last-minute invitee can't look like she's tried too hard.

That party is how I came to kiss Ben Capaldi, the most popular boy in our grade, someone I never thought even had me on his map. What am I talking about? I know I was never on his map. I was never in the same *room* as his map.

Maps were on my brain because I'd been worrying about getting lost, aware that I have no sense of direction and was about to be in the zero-landmark, everything-looks-the-same-to-a-city-girl, no-buildings, no-signposts, map-dependent…wilderness.

4

sunday 7 october

All packed. Every item ticked.

Ask sadness, How about staying here, sadness?

I know. Dumb question.

Sadness packed.

Bags zipped.

Compose reassuring demeanor for last dinner at home before camp.

Small smile.

Parties are uncomfortable events for me. I do want to get invited. If I'm not invited, I feel sad, and it is horrible hearing befores and afters you've had nothing to do with. Smiling and pretending dog-eared experience is enough. But when I am invited to a party, I straightaway start dreading it.

As soon as I'm confronted with shrieking, giggling, drinking, loud music, random hookups, uninhibited dancing—I feel glum. I don't have fun. I'm not "fun." I'm serious. I'm responsible. I worry about my friends getting drunk, getting their drinks spiked, getting hurt, getting messy, getting used, getting pregnant, getting sexually transmitted diseases, and drowning in their own vomit.

On top of that I *never* know what to wear.

And I don't like drinking, but I have to pretend to drink, so I at least appear to be "fun," and to be having "fun."

I used to like dancing until a boy—Billy Gardiner—told me I looked like a spastic tarantula. So now I can only dance if it's crowded enough and dark enough that nobody can see me.

So a typical party for me usually involves trying unsuccessfully to talk to people who are drunk, hanging around the food, speaking to the parents, visiting the bathroom, hoping that by the time I come out more people I know have arrived, not dancing, finding a kitchen or garden through-road position to prop so I get passing traffic conversation, and later on patrolling to check that my friends are okay to get home. Holly says I'm more like a party monitor than a guest.

But post-billboard, the script for this party ran differently. For starters, some people looked at me rather than around me when I arrived.

After Holly's "hiiiiiiieee mwah mwah," she pulled me into a huddle with Gab and Ava, and started making a big deal out of the billboard thing. Usually it would make me uncomfortable being the center of attention, but because I'd told Holly everything and she'd had three cranberry vodkas, it was more like she was the center of attention, which suited us both just fine.

Hours later when Ben Capaldi, apparently off his face, staggered into focal range and said (to me!), "Your pulchritude defies belief," I was—speechless. I may have lifted one sober eyebrow. I've perfected the one-eyebrow lift in the mirror, never in a million years thinking I'd get to use it in a social situation. I smiled and turned away. I could not think of one thing to say. But as my heart flipped like a hooked fish, I was wondering if a girl like me had *ever* turned away from a boy like Ben.

Was it wrong to feel a little thrill when I caught his look of surprise? This handsome boy? This boy the whole world loves? It might have looked like muscle-flexing on my part, turning away like that, but it was unadorned panic. A when-in-doubt-stick-your-head-in-the-sand move. Nice work.

And he thought I didn't know what *pulchritude* meant? Naturally. It's not like he would have noticed me in the Same Latin Class for the Last Three Years. Dud compliment anyway. It's such an ugly word for *beauty*. Besides which, he's the pulchritudinous one. He is the walking definition of boy beauty.

And I have now kissed that definition.

There is no hope of sleeping tonight. My wakey-dial is stuck up on super alert. I'm freaked out about going to camp in the morning, and I've got the kiss footage on a loop. I hate this. I want a more obedient brain. I want the brain that says okay when I say it's bedtime. Now, brain, sit! Roll over! Play dead. My brain says, get stuffed, I'm having fun. Tonight it is like one of those lab rats that can't stop going back for cocaine even though it needs the food.

Hmmm, food. An excursion into the parental worst-kept-secret dark chocolate stash, in the fridge, is definitely warranted. With a freezing-cold glass of milk.

1:47 AM. Brain still disobeying owner. It happened. It can't have been a dream: I haven't been to sleep. How did it happen? A yelp of disbelief makes its way up from my solar plexus to the pillow I jam against my face.

Holly almost certainly had something to do with it. She is the keen social engineer who has been trying to persuade me since year eight that I need a man in my life. (Defense strategy: eye roll, say no, thank you, no way, never, not even interested, before you get scorned, rejected, ignored, not asked.)

No more than an hour after turning away, of ignoring him, of accidentally appearing to be unimpressed, I was kissing him.

Sibylla Quinn and Benjamin Capaldi?

You have got to be kidding.

Sib and Ben?

Surely not.

Heads turned. He tasted of beer and smiles and popularity, smelled of freshly danced sweat, and didn't seem to realize it was the first time I'd kissed anyone. At least, he didn't mention it.

So the earth must be spinning off its axis by now, plummeting headlong toward a new universe, oceans sloshing

25

and spilling, ice caps sliding, trees uprooted, because some-how I've stepped over the line to stand with the popular girls. Only I haven't. The line must have moved without me realizing. It's disconcerting. And so was the way people looked at me post–kissing Ben. The look said *you?* Then it reassessed me. Shuffled the deck. And it was as though a different backing track started playing. I walked into the party with something like a *la-di-da*, but by the time I left it was more of a *ba-boom-chucka-boom-chucka*.

A text erupts from my phone, which is packed inside a boot. Holly. Unless it's—it couldn't be—Ben? I dig it out, heart jerking, and remember: Ben doesn't even have my number. Of course it's Holly: *biaaatch, are you in bed with him?*

Me: *you are a freak.*

Holly: *as if you don't love him.*

Me: *don't.*

Holly: *then you're crazier than I thought, and that is lots crazy.*

Me: *go to sleep.*

Holly: *perchance to . . .*

Me: *perchance to shut up.*

monday 8 october, 4 am

No news is not good news.

I know it.

Anything might have happened, and the only true fact of life is death.

It is brief. But it is nonetheless a third journal entry.

The end.

7

Sex education used to be called the Facts of Life. It's kind of appropriate, the stern, newscaster tone, the headline vibe. It does loom large; it is some kind of major event on the horizon.

If you read the statistics—our house is full of them—heaps of kids have sex super early, like early high school, but in my little middle-class world there are plenty of kids, a lot more than half, who haven't done the deed at sixteen, or even seventeen. I know that for an anecdotal fact. (I'm obviously one of them.)

Despite that, at sixteen, whether you have, or have not, had sex can sometimes feel like the Great Divide. It's not like friends who used to be close are gone, it's just that they've migrated to another country.

No matter how much you tell yourself that nothing's changed, it has. You worry that all your dumb old secrets are about to be whispered on someone else's pillow, or to be superseded by somebody else's better secrets.

Just as wide as the gulf between "have had sex" and "haven't had sex" is the gulf between my fantasy life and my real life, fantasy boys and real boys.

Until last night, when I kissed my fantasy boy. That was a particularly disturbing, worlds-colliding event.

It's very frustrating, and seems illogical, that you can know everything there is to know about sex of all persuasions, variations, and deviations, in theory, and yet still know zero if you haven't done it. It. IT.

Being a virgin makes me feel inexperienced, childish, gauche, uncool.

It is honest to god like I'm sitting at the little kids' table on Christmas Day, while other girls my age are over there sipping from champagne flutes and using the good cutlery.

Add to that the pressure to act like it's cool...no big deal...my choice...

And that's *me*, and I'm not even a very peer-group person.

My virginity does not feel like some wondrous thing I will one day bestow on a lucky boy; it's more in the realm of something I need to get rid of, like my braces were, before real life can begin.

But annoyingly enough, while I am dead keen to cross "sex" off my to-do list, I don't feel at all ready to remove anything other than a top-layer garment in front of a boy. That is the reason why, before I'm even properly awake, the challenge, and probable impossibility, of fully clothed sex with Ben Capaldi is occupying my thoughts.

What is it going to be like seeing him today? My lips still tender, chin scratched. It had to be a casual hookup, right? A party thing? Please, party-fling fairy, oh, please visit and tell me what face to put on this morning. Friendly but distant? Casual hello hug? Ignore him before he ignores me?

What was I *thinking*? We're going to be in the wilderness together for nine weeks.

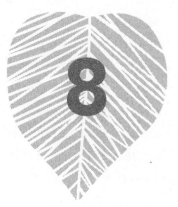

8

monday 8 october, 5 am

If you don't want to write about feelings, you can write about facts, Lou.

I met Fred last year.

Our mutual friend Dan Cereill introduced us.

We saw a movie, ate boysenberry ice-cream cones, kissed, arranged to meet again.

I invited him to our year nine social at the end of term three.

It was a surprise.

I was not looking for a boyfriend.

We had five perfect months together.

He died in a cycling accident. He was dead at the scene,

could not be resuscitated, is believed to have died instantly of head injuries.

There was a funeral.

There was scattering of ash.

I did not go back to school when the school year started. I was a basket case. Everything shut down.

This term I was to be part of a wonderful new French exchange program for government schools.

My three friends, Dan, Estelle, and Janie, are part of a wonderful new French exchange program.

When it came down to it, I couldn't leave Fred.

I decided to stay in the same country as Fred.

I did not put it that way to anyone else but Dan.

It might have sounded a bit crazy, but it was what I needed to do.

Dan couldn't wait to leave the city that killed Fred.

We understood perfectly well that each other's positions sprang from the same place. The place where the floor falls out from under you and nothing can ever be the same.

I have seen a psychiatrist called Esther, who specializes in teenagers and grief, twice a week since Fred died.

I don't sleep well.

I don't wake well.

I have done distance education from home for the first three terms this year. My results have been excellent.

Today I am starting at a new school, in fourth term.

I don't have to tell people about Fred unless I choose to do so.

This school is a private school called Crowthorne Grammar that sends its students away for a whole term in year ten. They/we go to an outdoor education campus called Mount Fairweather *for a whole term* to discover the real meaning of, *to experience*, independence and leadership.

It is a campus in the mountains.

This cushy campus promises to provide an authentic, rugged outdoors experience...resilience...core values...practical skills for...cocurricular...living...blah...educational adventure...foster...blah...connect...blah...challenge.

A quarter of the year ten class is at Mount Fairweather at any given time. I am part of the quarter who will be enjoying the camp experience during fourth term.

There will be lots of wonderful activities in which I will participate, including but not limited to hiking, cross-country running, group and solo camping, rappelling, canoeing, horseback riding, and environmental studies in situ.

Classes will run in a five-day week from Thursday to Monday. Inclusive. Tuesdays and Wednesdays will be our *weekends*, so we can have the run of the wilderness without us bothering weekend hikers/campers, or weekend hikers/campers bothering us.

It will be good for me. That's an order.

Good to make a new start.

Good to get out of the house.

Good to meet new people.

Good to breathe some new air.

Good to be getting fit.

Good to have access to a fine counselor.

So good I cannot fucking believe my luck.

9

Parents were encouraged to say their farewells at home. Schools correctly believe hysteria to be contagious. So I get to have a whispered catch-up with Holly while everyone mills around looking excited or depressed or hungover and the sporty teachers help load the buses.

Ben is in the distance laughing with some of his jock friends, guys I really don't like. Rowing and football star Billy Gardiner with his look-at-me tan, protein-supplement muscles, and blond hair is one of them. But I guess when you're friends with basically everyone, you're going to have some quality-control issues.

"It was nothing, no big deal." I'm trying to mean it.

"You were practically having sex, so it's not nothing."

"We weren't. It was just a kiss. Can we move on?"

"Last time Ben Capaldi did that—well, the time before—it was Laura, and they went out—for a while."

"Forget it. He's not even my type." I bite a shaggy cuticle. I've always wanted to say that—though in this context, it's a big fat lie, and Holly knows it.

"Your *type*? Your type is nerd meets doofus, hun, and you don't want to go there."

"Thanks."

"What? I'm being honest," says Holly. I consider the mixed blessing of having such an honest friend, but there is stuff I'm clueless about, and she's a good interpreter.

"No, you're right—which means Ben Capaldi is definitely not the boy for me."

"Don't you get it? This is not about who you are. It's about who you want to be. You get to decide. Because of the billboard. No one *knows* who you are anymore. The whole class is confused."

"The billboard isn't me."

"You haven't tried on enough 'me's to even know."

"I'm Daria. I've even got the pain-in-the-arse little sister."

"You *were* Daria. Now you can be Hannah Montana."

"She's not even a cartoon."

We both reflect on the shortage of good female cartoon role models in mainstream media. Or at least that's what I'm doing.

"Sibbie, you can go from drab to fab. You can be a

babe—not everyone gets to do that." Holly sometimes speaks as though she's rehearsing for her planned career in the world of fashion journalism.

"Even that word—*babe*—I hate it. I don't want to be patronized, or infantilized..."

Holly sighs, trying to keep her cool. "Think of it as a *visit* to babe-land. If you don't like it, don't stay."

"I won't like it."

"You don't know that because you've never been there. And Ben Capaldi is everybody's type. If everybody wants brainy, funny, fit, handsome."

"If that's true, then I've really got no hope."

"You've got a secret weapon that no other girl has."

"What?" If she means the stupid billboard, I can hardly lug that with me everywhere I go.

She's smiling. "Your best friend is me."

10

Blink

   Emollient

   Blink

   Architect

   Blink

   Refulgent

   Blink

   Overnight

   Blink

   Permeable

   Blink

   Dandelion

   Blink

   Immutable

Nine-letter words.

It's a puzzle in the newspaper every day: how many words can you make from nine jumbled letters in a three-by-three grid, and what is the word that uses all nine letters? And that's how long it ever takes Michael to see the nine-letter word: exactly one blink.

The only time I saw him pause was over *jugulated* (two blinks) and he said, It's the only thing it can be, but I've never seen it used. And come on, I mean, whoa, Neddy! Because what gets me is that *this* surprised him: that he hadn't seen it. I would've been surprised if I *had* ever seen it. I will be surprised if I *do* ever see it used. I don't expect I *will* ever see it. Except in a word puzzle.

He says it's all about how quickly you read, because we skate and slide over letters all the time and read many words, whole matrices of letters, in a blink. But I think it's also about how much you read, and what sort of vocabulary you have in the first place, because, honestly, how many people in the entire world do you know who will ever need to use the word *jugulated* in their entire lives? Not many. Fewer than ten is my guess.

Nine, *maybe*.

And I'm trying not to worry that he's sitting alone on the bus, down in front, right near the teachers.

monday 8 october

Bus did not crash.

Sat with quiet girl called don't remember don't care. Drove past a vast lake in which trees were drowning, not waving.

Camp. Looks just like brochure.

The sign says CROWTHORNE GRAMMAR, MT. FAIRWEATHER CAMPUS, REPORT TO RECEPTION.

Architect-designed faux-utilitarian; probably truly utilitarian as well. What I mean is: functional, but also concerned with appearing to be functional, or in other words, show-off functional.

Smells like heartbreak. Lemon-scented gum trees and eucalyptus.

Food in mouth chomp chomp chomp. No recollection of what I ate. Food warmer du jour.

Colder, much colder here than in the city.

When I see the blues of further mountains... I see it for you, too, Fred.

When I see a girl look with secret longing at the handsome boy...

There is some sort of buzzbuzzbuzz around the tall girl, Sibylla. Is she famous for something? Do I care?

There is so much too much written about grief.

Grief counseling is a thriving industry as well as a personal little hell to get through. It is probably immune from global financial vicissitudes. Like the food industry, maybe.

Grief settles comfortably into any host; it is an ever-mutating, vigorous organism with an ever-renewing customer base. It generates a never-ending hunger, a never-ending ache, an unassuageable pain to new hearts, brains, guts every minute, every day, every year.

It is the razor-edge of a loose tooth shrieking to be pressed again and again into the soft pink sore gum.

It's a one-way tunnel with no proof of another exit.

It is something to be got through. Got over. It is something to hide behind. So wide I can't...so low I can't get...so high I can't...so...it is something to squeeze the lungs, to fill the tear ducts, and feed the dark hours that used to be for sleeping. Must not drown in it. Be crushed by its dark weight. Must not swamp me. Must not overcome me. Must work through it, face up to it, must pummel it like putty into something with which the wound can be dressed, spit and chew and press, the heart can be healed, a shield, a salve. It is a place to hide, to howl, to touch private memories like shy birds, like flicking shadows that must not *must not* disappear.

So where does my big bad sad fit here? Where to put it, in this sunny designer room with six bunks and five strange girls, plus me, of course, oh, the strangest of them all. Must find a place for it, a deeper, darker private little corner.

Must try to appear to engage socially and so avoid excess probing by camp counselor, who is *en garde*! Alert to my special needs! Ready whenever I need her! No matter what time of night or day! Don't hesitate. Don't.

If you had not died, if you had kept your wits about you—yes, I'm still angry with you—I would not need to have spent time with a woman called Esther who wears bad shoes and directs her gaze delicately to one side as I burn to cry but hold it in, control it with breathing and long pauses, because crying there with well-meaning Esther would have been too hideous. And whatever happened, she must not, no never ever be given cause to nudge that large clinical-issue unpatterned box of tissues in my direction across the dust-free-even-in-sunlight teak coffee table. I was not a good subject, Fred.

But I excel at grief privately.

If only you hadn't... then I would not need to be preparing my cat-and-mouse game with the camp counselor. Her name is... Jesus, can't remember, not Esther. Working out the right face for the jolly camp counselor... plausibly grim, of course, after what I've been through, am going through, and yet slowly unfolding, slowly opening up to new experiences. Interacting with others. Gradually healing. Yeah. I know the drill. I can pull it off. Can I pull it off?

But in reality, I'm stuck, Fred. Stuck at stage-three grief, or is it four? Hating myself, and angry with you. Maybe there's also a bit of five, or is it six, in the mix? Depression. But no sign yet of six, or is it seven? Realization. Testing New Reality. No.

Just missing you.

Psychiatrists don't really subscribe to neat stages of grief. I found them myself, printed them out, lost them. The idea of defined hurdles is comforting. Despite not being able to get over any of them.

Greatest pain in the world: the moment after waking. Remembering again as consciousness slaps my face in the morning's first sigh. Nips fresh the not-healed wound.

Should I tell someone about the tangled dreams the sometimes-sleeping pills drag into the not-enough hours?

12

We are summoned to the dining hall as soon as we arrive for our pep-talk greeting from the principal, Dr. Kwong. Kim Kwong. She's tiny, brainy, and elegant, so of course she's known as King Kong. No one is listening—everyone is fizzing with overexcitement, like when *MythBusters* put all those Alka-Seltzers in a confined space, added water, and blew the door out. But there are the usual words like *opportunity, responsibility, leadership, challenge,* and on and on it goes.

House selection happens next. This is what everybody's waiting for. It's just like *Harry Potter,* but with brighter lighting and no hat.

When my name is read out for Bennett House, after

Holly and Eliza, I say, *yes*, and the girl next to me, Sophie Watkins, says, all sneery, that's not a good house.

Six people per house, and even our exact bunks are allocated—each one has a number. No arguments, no swapping.

I'm lucky getting a bottom wall bunk. It's what I wanted. I'm student number thirty-five.

You are supposed to yell out your number while assembled on the oval in case of an emergency. Would it really make the slightest difference in a bushfire or bomb blast? Imagine everyone screaming out numbers at the same time, or forgetting their number. Crazy number soup. As if you wouldn't have something better to do than yell out a number.

It is one of those systems that this place seems to love. If we open our door after everyone's security cards have been slotted for the night into the panel next to the door, it triggers a (silent) alarm. They'd implant microchips if they thought the parents would sign up for it.

I see Michael on the way out.

"What's your number, Sibylla?" he asks.

"Thirty-five. You?"

"Forty-nine. I was hoping for a prime number, but you can't really ask."

His grimace makes it clear that he knows this is a dodgy thing to say, and that he's relieved he can say it to me.

Only Michael could be disappointed at not getting a

prime number. He has whole books about prime numbers. If I ever see Michael with a dreamyvague smile on his face and ask him what he's thinking about, the answer is likely to be prime numbers. When I have that look on my face, I am almost certainly thinking about food. Or Ben Capaldi, after last night. Better knock that one on the head.

If Michael has a worried look on his face, he is likely to be thinking about the complexities of the two-state solution or the nature of existence. If I look worried, it's usually because I've got an awful feeling that I've forgotten something very important, or I've lost my cell phone or keys or glasses (again), or I'm hungry and not sure when my next food intake is happening.

When Michael looks relaxed, it might be because he has just completed a long and grueling run, or cracked a long and demanding mathematical equation, or mastered a long and complex piano piece. Me looking relaxed will often follow a nap in yoga, a good dreamy read inside a nineteenth-century novel, or the discovery of my cell phone or keys or glasses.

As we step out into the alarmingly fresh air, I feel an unexpected heart-tug to home. We've spent weeks planning, preparing, buying strange gear, wondering who our housemates will be—now the nightmare begins.

13

monday 8 october (later)

Upon arrival, while everyone else was basically squealing with unfettered excitement, I had to try hard not to run screaming down the driveway after the bus, don't leave me here, please, I made a mistake.

I tried to ignore the *who's the new girl?* looks, and instead concentrated on my breathing, and took a calming inventory.

I couldn't have caught the bus if I tried.

Twelve dormitory buildings. Outside, wide, shady verandas; inside, one sleeping area: three bunk beds; one kitchen area: bench, sink, small fridge, big table, six chairs; one bathroom: two sinks, two toilets, two showers, one utility sink; one large walk-in drying cupboard.

A handful of bigger buildings. One for the teachers who live on campus; one classroom building, includes a library and art room/multimedia studio; one assembly hall/dining hall/students' common room building, includes music practice carrels; one office admin building, sick bay, teachers' common room/staff room, counselor's office, marked with an *X* on my map. There's one utility building with boiler, laundry, drying room, food and linen supplies storage, and vehicle bays at the side, and a second utility building for gardening stuff, sports gear storage, canoes, bikes, etc. The principal's house is the only older building, an original cottage, which has of course been restored.

A long path snakes from the main assembly/dining building to an enormous, established vegetable and fruit tree garden, the so-called kitchen garden. It's hedged, so you couldn't see it from where they unloaded us. One oval, well manicured.

It is a huge compound on acres and acres of land, and right around the outer perimeter is a large cleared ring road, for fire safety.

The buildings themselves are nestled artfully in well-designed native plantings, strategically placed shady trees, scented shrubs, and winding paths, and all are oriented toward a large central garden area with plenty of outdoor tables and seating and a few attractive stands of trees. We can study and have lunch there when the weather is fine.

Everything is built in timber stained and sealed a silvery gray and, in a sprightly touch, doors are crimson to coordinate with the bottlebrush and flowering gum trees.

Now all I have to do is blend in, zone out, and start crossing off the days on my cell wall.

14

Of all the things I thought I'd hate about being up here—too much sporty stuff, crap food, the great outdoors—one thing I hadn't properly considered was privacy. Like try having a poo when there's no one around. Or squeezing a pimple. Everything is way too open.

I'm used to my whole-world double bed, spreading out and keeping my mess where I want it—laptop, books, magazines, plates, clean laundry that I really will put away one day...I *hate* this single bed. It's like a prison bed (I imagine). I keep waking up when I turn over and hit the wall. There is one crappy little cupboard for your clothes and a big shared gear cupboard for boots and packs.

The built-in shelves behind the bed are the only territory that's really mine. My shelf has three pieces of beach glass.

Three shells. My iPod. Books. A photo of the family. The photo of me and Mum that Beeb took. Some flowers— Mum's idea to pack the little vase. I thought it was stupid, but it's cool. And I brought a Taylor Kitsch poster so I can say good night to him every night.

After everyone has freaked out about it for months, house allocation was actually okay. We are Bennett House. We got the new girl, Lou. So far she doesn't talk, or show the slightest interest in anyone. Her facial expression ranges from generalized boredom to specific boredom. She is fiddling with her camera. She puts it down and starts rolling up balls of Blu Tack, with great concentration. Definitely antisocial. Possible fruit loop.

Holly is doing her nails, iPod in, listening to Sia, emitting an occasional out-of-tune drone-along.

Pippa is reading about ten pounds' worth of French *Vogue*, and calling it homework, *bien sûr*.

Annie, who has no concept of an "inside" voice, is in the bathroom insisting on rescuing a spider that Eliza is urging her to kill. Eliza is saying, "They've got friends, you fool. They'll breed, they'll come back, and drop on us from the ceiling. It's okay for you, but I've got a top bunk."

Pippa moves from *Vogue* to a Sun Signs book, saying, "Omigod, it's so true... it's scary... you won't believe this... it is so accurate... it's like looking into a mirror of my soul... oops, wrong sign... here's me... omigod, that is even more accurate!"

Annie, who would be a large Labrador if she were a dog,

comes out of the bathroom and asks Pippa to read out Sagittarius, but doesn't stop to listen, too busy complaining about having a bottom middle bunk, warning all of us not to treat it as a communal sofa, warning Eliza (miniature whippet, star long-distance runner) not to step on it on her way up to her more fortunately positioned, prestigious, upper-level accommodation.

There's a big emphasis on fitness and outdoor life here. I've got nothing against fresh air, but surely it's overrated? Just a tiny bit? I ran the first compulsory three-mile circuit yesterday. Afterward my face was exactly the same shade as beetroot-meets-tomato, which Holly was very amused to point out to everyone. We do two of these runs, minimum, per week, for the whole term. Today every muscle tendon sinew is howling in complaint. My entire self is aching.

Holly told me today she's had laser hair removal in preparation for coming here. She kept that six-treatment (!) regime pretty quiet. I thought we were going to be wild women up here. Apparently that's just me now. She could have told me earlier.

It is freezing in the mornings. Our (terrazzo-tiled) bathroom floor feels like ice. Each house has an open fireplace. We have to cart our own wood but not chop it anymore after an accident at the end of last term—some idiot chopped his own foot.

Bennett House is on Slushy for the first week. Then we

rotate to some other foul task. The others are Grounds (weeding), Vego (kitchen-garden duty), Community (going to do community service work in Hartsfield), and Maintenance (checking firewood supplies, painting, fence mending, cleaning the chicken coop). House is ongoing—an everyday list of tasks related to keeping our own spaces tidy, laundry done, kitchen clean, beds made, etc. Our house gets inspected for "cleanliness" and "tidiness" every morning after breakfast, which is the one meal we can have either in our house or in the dining hall.

Slushy is disgusting and possibly a health hazard. First you have to set up all the tables—that's the okay bit. But at the end of the meal, you have to scrape the plates—bleugh, which is a total biotoxic pile of spitty food mess—and as you do it, you divide off the vegetable scraps to compost and the meat scraps to rubbish. Holly just scraped everything anywhere and sulked when I told her not to.

Guys and girls are not allowed to touch each other—it's a written rule—and we are fully forbidden to have any "after dark" mingle time. We have classes and meals together, but houses and hiking groups are segregated, which oddly ignores the whole gay and lesbian question.

Outside classes, I've seen Ben at close range only once. He gave me what I would call a distant or reserved smile. So, looks like it was a random hookup. Which is fine—exactly what I expected. Not a big deal. Holly said he was staring after me when I walked past. I find that hard to believe. She's just trying to make me feel better.

I'm too tired and a bit too sad to write home just yet. I miss them, even Charlotte. Who'd have thunk? I don't think I fully appreciated how relaxing it is having someone I can be really mean to. It's going to be so hard being nice all the time.

The one facility they don't have here is a well-padded cell where we can go and scream.

Maybe that is what the bush is for. As well as generating oxygen and providing wildlife habitat.

thursday 11 october

Get me out of here. Even the earbuds don't keep it out.

Who got a good house, who got a crap house.

Miss mary mack mack mack all dressed in black black black with silver buttons buttons buttons all down her back back back. She asked her mother mother mother...

How many buttons will she have?

Love Glee *so much/hate* Glee *so much.*

Twelve buttons down the back of her black dress. Twelve silver discs.

Who has been fingered/bestowed hand jobs/where, when: claims and counterclaims, idle gossip relating to others.

If miss mary mack mack mack stood with her back back back to you against a twilight sky, it would, in just the right light, look as though she had twelve clean holes going straight through her.

She would look two-dimensional.

She would look incorporeal.

Who is hot/not hot. Who is in love with whom: accusations and denials.

A figment, a dream, a specter, a nightmare, a ghost.

...for fifty cents cents cents to see an elephant elephant elephant jump over a fence fence fence.

So we're a house of virgins/what about her?/you're joking, right?

Miss mary mack mack mack all dressed in black black black...

Get me out of here.

16

No one is supposed to go off alone. But if I don't take a walk and escape from everyone else's chatter and clutter and smell and laughing and complaining, and Lou's silence, I will lose it. I need some untangle time. And this is the closest, so "safest," isolated spot I know. It is cold, but I'm well-rugged. Layers. Down jacket. Everyone has the same clothes, from the same outdoor supplies place; name tags are the only way of telling which are whose.

The sun is almost down. It is prep time, but I've created a headache and am officially lying down in the house. Headaches usually work, particularly with male teachers. They're scared of saying no, in case "headache" is actually "period" and they have to deal with the trauma of some gory hemorrhage in the classroom. The light falls from the sky like a sigh, deepening it from blue to lavender spiked with stars. The air is so cold and clean and eucalyptus-loaded it feels like a health treatment. And just when I can breathe easy and feel that I am finally alone, a tall, angular figure comes crashing into view.

"Do you know what smells really good up here, Sibylla?" Michael always starts a conversation as though it simply continues on from the last time we've spoken. Which it does, in a way, our own twelve-year-long conversation. "The dirt; the dirt smells—rich. Ripe. Fecund."

"Very D. H. Lawrence."

"Yes, he overuses it. But, have you noticed?"

"I have not yet smelled the dirt." I roll and sniff. Not bad. Actually beautiful. Rich, rotty, mushroomy, deep. "It smells dark brown."

"Exactly." Michael is delighted. It's mostly nice knowing that I am Michael's safe person—it is like being my clearest self without even having to try.

"What would you say is a good word for it?"

Another deep sniff. "Dirty," I say, laughing. "Dirtastic. Dirtelicious. How's your house? All okay?" I ask.

"Yes. Yours? You're with Holly?"

"Uh-huh."

We are still getting to know where everyone is. There have been only a handful of desperate pleas to change, only a few deadly enemies put together. People know they have to put up with it.

"And you've got Hamish—and Ben Capaldi?" I gulp on

59

his name, hoping Michael doesn't hear the wavering pitch straining to be casual.

"You're not actually going out with him, are you?" Michael asks.

"No. Are you kidding me? Definitely not."

"But it is true...?"

"Yes." I am dying to ask whether Ben has mentioned me, or whether Michael, for the first time in his life, has tuned into any random chitchat, but I bite it.

"It is strange timing." He's knocking one heel against the same bit of dirt, making a half-moon.

"You think he kissed me because of the billboard?"

He shrugs. "There was no kissing before the billboard."

"It was just a—dumb—party thing. It meant nothing."

Michael looks at me, into me. He knows very well that I'm saying a line I have agreed with myself is the lowest-risk-of-public-humiliation line. Just as well it is getting darker by the second.

"Because he is not smart enough for you."

"He's smart."

"I don't agree."

"Michael, he's got the whole grade eating out of his hand. It's hard to know whether the girls or the boys love him more."

"It is a nauseating portrayal of 'head boy in the making.' He's too keen to be popular."

"That doesn't make him dumb. That makes him pragmatic."

"The decision to act dumb to be popular is dumb; therefore the guy is dumb."

"It's not acting dumb; it's more like not offending anyone."

"That stance offends me."

"He gets along with everyone—even the people in advanced math."

"He's courting the Asian-nerd vote—his tactics are crudely obvious."

"Only to you. To me it looks more like he knows how to make people relax. He doesn't threaten people."

"That's weak."

"I'd call it flexible."

"We will see."

"That sounds ominous."

"No—I mean literally: we will see him at close quarters for the whole term."

"True."

"You know, Holly looks at him a lot."

"She looks at everyone. She looks at you."

"But not for long. I look back. I outstare her."

It's true: *Your weird friend*, Holly says, *why does your weird friend stare?* Maybe he likes you. *Shut up. Isn't he—mentally ill or something?* Just a super brain. *Super weird.* Stop saying it. And admit—he's good-looking. *Maybe.*

"I'm still recovering from the sight of you at the junction."

"So am I. At least up here I don't have to see it."

"Was it in any way enjoyable?"

Good question. It was a swirl of people, darlings, makeup, heat, waiting, everyone saying *fuck* a lot—as noun, verb, adjective—in a casual, friendly way, and the only calm focus was Beeb, but even she spent most of the time glued to various iThings. It was the strangest day of my life, hands down—I was the center of attention, but it was also as though I weren't there. As though I could have peeled my skin off, walked away to the side, and looked on, and no one would have noticed.

"It was wonderful, if you enjoy being pushed, pulled, poked at, brushed, sprayed, powdered, and then kept sitting while people fiddled and adjusted the lights for about a million years. It was basically a boredom/embarrassment playoff."

Was it only this morning I told Holly (*again*, she can't hear about it often enough) and Pippa and Tiff Simpson how glamorous it was? How the makeup artist kept her stuff in a huge three-tiered metal toolbox. How she had every single tint of Bobbi Brown foundation and mixed the colors on the back of her hand. How they had a caterer bring in delicious sushi and baby passion-fruit curd tarts and mini roast beef bagels for lunch, how the dress I had to wear was clipped and gaffer-taped behind me to make it fit better, how the fan under my hair, hand held by an assistant lying on the floor, made me stretch and stand up taller, how the hair stylist had invited me out for a ciggie break, and the makeup artist said, *You're not moving*, but then took pity and told me what the best nights were at

Frenzy and Catalina, as though I'd be allowed out clubbing, and wasn't just a loser halfway through year ten.

Both versions are disconcertingly kind of one hundred percent true.

"It's left you with dark eyelashes."

"It's a tint. Do you have to notice everything?"

We are heading back in the now quickly fading light.

"Beeb—you know, godmother—said I wasn't allowed to go into the great outdoors without getting my eyelashes tinted."

"Curious."

"Holly had her legs lasered. And armpits. And bikini line."

"Curiouser." Michael is quietly astounded by the whole girl contortion around clothes, makeup, appearance. He is sane enough not to get it at all.

"What did you do?"

"I've been running a fair bit. I thought it wouldn't hurt to come up here in a fairly fit state."

"More useful than hair removal. I'm starving. Is there enough stuff that looks like itself for you?"

"Yes. But nothing appetizingly so."

He has always preferred food that looks like itself. For example, roast potato: yes, mashed potato: no; chicken leg: yes, chicken curry: no.

I've been stomping along next to Michael like this for so long. Usually enjoying his company. Sometimes feeling a bit smothered by the intensity. Always with the background worry niggles. Is he okay? Is he taking his meds? Is he coping without meds? Is he talking to people? Do I need to "include" him? Has he been invited? Is he going too far in class? Does he need a reminder: hold something in reserve, don't leave everyone behind?

In kindergarten, he always said hello by holding my hand. It gave me a spurt of important grown-up feeling to be the one giving comfort. He trusted me completely, wholeheartedly. And I understood that was how it would be with us. He was someone to look after. I held his trust carefully, a little egg to protect.

No holding hands anymore. He's one of the biggest guys here. And fit. He needs to be, strange as he is, super brainiac that he is—he would otherwise be the ideal bully target. And he hasn't helped things by refusing to join any sports teams. He does the bare minimum compulsory stuff, and he runs long-distance. He's also quite content spending time alone in the gym, but he loathes the whole elite private school sports ethos, and particularly the notion of sport scholarships—that is, buying kids to win stuff that looks impressive in the school's promotional material.

Me? I don't give sport a moral second thought. I don't like it, and it doesn't like me, either, so we leave each other alone and I do the fitness programs, the sort that don't require speed or ball sense or a competitive spirit. Up here we get to do yoga as an option, and that is exactly my speed. Meditation usually equals sleep for me.

He's looking at me, having some internal struggle about whether he should say something.

"Spill."

"Things will change for you now."

"Because of the billboard?"

He nods, worried. "The consequences of the billboard."

I remember asking my mum if there was anything wrong with Michael when we started school, because by then I had registered him as being different from the other kids. She said he was very clever and a bit of a worrier. I've modified that diagnosis over the years to full-on genius and pathologically, sometimes cripplingly, anxious. But it's always seemed only reasonable that someone who understands so much might worry in proportion to that understanding. Maybe that's simplistic, but it's how things look to me.

sunday 14 october

I have survived Camp Craptacular for almost a week.

I'm supposed to start reengaging.

With people.

So, the people in *my* house. Oh, yes, because I feel such a warm community camaraderie.

Sibylla. I like the name. My first Sibylla. She's called Sib, mostly. She seems okay. She smiles. Maybe I'll smile back one day. The buzzy buzz I detected is because her photo is on a giant billboard. I saw it. It's for a perfume and either the hair and makeup artistry or some kind of CGI makes it look as though she is entangled in ivy. Her skin is very white in the photo, and in reality. And she has a dreamy, out-of-the-world look in the photo that is also pretty similar to the way she looks much of the time.

My guess is that she is someone who likes her alone time, and there's not much of that to be had up here.

She is not a model as such, apparently. It was a once-er.

She is very tall and willowy. And I honestly can't work out if she's beautiful or ugly. Maybe both? Certainly very interesting-looking; perhaps she's a fine example of the French *jolie laide*, a cool concept if ever there was one.

Holly, also in the house, seems to be Sibylla's bestie.

She is bossy, loud, and has an opinion about what everyone should be doing, and how they should look, and in Sibylla's case, she seems to be promoting an early-days relationship with someone called Ben. Why? Not sure which one he is.

To me, the new girl, Holly is all bristly attitude, waiting for me to make a wrong move (that won't take long) and very *prove I should like you*. She is waiting for me to want her approval, to feel some fear, to long for acceptance, to crave her friendship, none of which will be happening. If she knew exactly how uninterested I am in fitting in, she'd conserve her energy.

She is always offering her *honest* opinion. Brutally honest. Who'll tell you if I don't? Someone should point out to her that not everything needs to be said. On some topics, she could just shut up.

If I were at all interested in engaging with this lot, I

would have told her yesterday. She stopped a girl, not sure who, outside the classroom building, completely careless of who might hear, and asked her if she thought it was time for some depilatory action? De-what? this girl responded.

Holly laughed. She made as though to walk away, but turned back and said in a loud voice, You've got a freaking mustache. Have a good look at yourself in the daylight, for god's sake.

To another girl, unfortunate enough to be sitting where Holly thought she might want to sit, she said, Shove over, what's-your-name, Van? Truck? Car?... She was speaking to Van Uoc, the smartest girl in my math group. Ten times as smart as Holly, but so quiet and shy. Needless to say she just moved over.

Annie looks like a big strong country lass. Only she's not. She's from the city, south of the river, like everyone else here, except me. She seems to like bugs. She looks and sounds a bit thick. She is always telling us to eat her chocolate/use her shampoo, or whatever. Needy. Or am I too cynical? Friendly, perhaps.

Eliza seems okay. She's some kind of nutty fitness fiend, though. Always coming back from an extra run. And she chews gum, which may compel me to drive a stake through her heart at some stage.

Pippa is the ultimate spoiled brat based on her worldly goods, but she also seems genuinely sweet. She might be Cartier watch and cashmere socks, super-coiffed locks and French phrases, worshipping at the memorial shrine of Alexander McQueen, but she's a contented soul, and I suspect it has nothing much to do with the little cloud of luxury she floats on. She is the third sister in her family to come up here, and she knows the drill.

Holly watches her extremely closely, jealous of the loot. Pippa is oblivious.

18

We need a gossip away from other ears, so Holly and I make our forbidden way to the laundry/drying room. Bennett House is the closest dorm building to this utility building, and we've worked out that we can latch the drying-room door open late in the afternoon and escape the house via an easily unscrewed ventilation panel behind the hot-water tank in our own little Bennett House airing room. My pocket knife has already earned its keep. Our spy-movie exit plan includes getting the others to cover for us by pretending we are asleep if a teacher comes snooping, checking for teachers once outside, breathless dash to drying-room door, and suppressing explosive laughter once we get inside. It's worth the risk of dire punishments just for the blissful absence of other people.

While I unwrap our contraband and only slightly soggy stash—tomato and cheese sandwiches from lunchtime—Holly is straight on to her favorite topic: Ben. "You have to get him alone."

"I don't think so. I can't think of anything more embarrassing."

"Well, unless you completely screwed it up, he'll probably want to kiss you again."

"He doesn't even seem to recognize me." I wasn't kidding. I seemed as invisible as ever to him in class. And chances are I did screw the kissing up.

"That's crap. He's been staring. I've seen him staring three times at least."

I can't help smiling. Because Michael was right about Holly having Ben under surveillance. And because if there weren't any drama on offer, Holly could cook it up out of nothing. I mean, three stares? That's it?

I lift the sandwich-squasher lid and put the sandwiches in. Our friend Maddie who was here last term left the squasher hidden for us.

"I could not eat that carbonara tonight," says Holly with a significant eye roll.

"Why not?"

"Why do you think?" An in-the-know look.

"I don't know."

"The sauce—it was so slimy—like snot or . . . worse—that's the gossip, anyway: Brian."

"As if. That's gross. And stupid. And whoever said it is twisted."

"Well, I'm never going near it again."

"Why would you—who would even think that?"

Holly gives me the *how naive can you be?* look. "My auntie in Queensland had a holiday job once, working at a pineapple-juice factory? Guys used to piss into that."

"Into the juice? Are you sure?"

"Yep. I've never had that again, not since I heard."

"But isn't food production regulated these days? Isn't it?"

Holly looks dubious. The sandwiches are turning themselves into a sizzling cheesy heaven. "Enjoy," she says, with a dark nod, as I slide them out. "We might end up living off these."

Holly has decided that the cook, Priscilla, a former prison cook (true), though she referred to it as "a state-of-the-art remand facility for white-collar criminals," and her boyfriend, Brian, are raking it in—catering for us with poor-quality ingredients and keeping the change. Brian drives our minibus and is a former prisoner (probably not true, but he looks the part).

We refer to them as Cilly and Brain. We speculate about their sex life. This is how conversation degenerates in the absence of TV and Facebook. We've been giving Brain a hard time from the get-go, clapping and shouting out songs all the way into Hartsfield yesterday when he wouldn't put the radio on Triple J. When we called him Brain, he yelled, it's BrIan. BRIAN. We pretended to settle until someone said, Sorry, Brain.

"Do you think Ben regrets it? Or just doesn't remember?" I say.

"He remembers. You just need to get him alone."

Holly strolls up to Ben's table after dinner the next night for a long chat. She carries a dishcloth, which is her token and total Slushy contribution for the night. I'm looking at them, trying not to make it obvious, and wondering whether paper napkins are supposed to be composted. Someone had said something about it.

Michael brings his plate over and follows my eye line.

"She's talking to him about me," I say, taking his plate.

"I never hear her talk about anyone except herself."

"You're cynical for one so young."

Back in the house, Holly reports back: Ben likes me. She is static with excitement. I'm still skeptical.

"What did you tell him to get him to say that?"

"Just that you liked him."

"But that's virtually forcing him to say what he said."

"Don't you notice anything? Force? Ben Capaldi? You're kidding, right?"

"And I didn't say you could. And I don't even know if I do." I'm brushing my teeth, and in my indignation, froth dribbles down the top of my pj's.

"'Course you do." Holly looks satisfied, until she catches Lou looking at us.

"What are you staring at?"

"You."

"I'm not available."

"Neither am I," Lou says. She looks bored, not intimidated, not embarrassed.

"Ignore her," I say to Lou. "She's just like that." Holly treats anyone new with a presumption of dislike. They have to prove themselves likeable. Jump through some invisible hoops.

"I noticed," says Lou. She looks down again, unperturbed, and keeps writing.

"What's everyone doing for the myth essay?" asks Annie.

"Dunno," says Holly.

"Icarus," I say.

"Persephone," says Lou.

"I was going to go Minotaur, but now I'm thinking Dinosaur, only I can't decide which one," says Annie, nibbling the green rubber fingergrip on her pencil.

There is a small hush. Holly looks around, gathering the collective disbelief with a smirk.

"Only, they're not myths," Lou says.

"Okay, mythological," says Annie, as if Lou is being difficult or splitting hairs. "Same thing."

"She means they were real, retard," says Holly.

"Very funny," says Annie.

"Don't you remember—evolution?" I ask.

"That's monkeys, you doofus," says Annie.

"What about trips to the museum, all those bones?" says Eliza. "Seriously, think back."

"That's a re-creation of a *mythological creature*," says Annie with exaggerated patience. "What do you idiots think? That *Jurassic Park* was for real? Wake up and smell the fucking daisies."

She is so indignant, everyone cracks up. We howl. Even Lou smiles, a very small smile.

Annie keeps saying, "What! What is so funny? No one's supposed to go mental until week four. What?" Then she starts laughing, too. "What? Was I away that week?"

Every time we stop laughing, it bubbles up again, and we're off.

Nothing like a good laugh to take the spotlight off the Ben speculation.

monday 15 october

My first mail, letters from Dan and Estelle and Janie. Precious. I've promised Janie I will make a film up here that will make her laugh. Was I crazy? But I've already decided what it will be. My subject is chosen. I will kill two birds with one stone. May take forever; should start soon.

Holly noticed the French stamps on my letters, and I could see her sticky beak curiosity whetted. But she can rot before I volunteer any information.

Dan sounds okay from his own letter. And Estelle is watching him like a hawk for me (and for herself) and is very happy to report that Dan's French family has not only Henri, his same-age counterpart, but also three younger sibs, so Dan is surrounded by busy family activity, which is a good thing. The mother is impressed that he knows about food and can cook a bit. And Henri runs, like Dan. I am relieved and reassured.

He asks me what a typical day looks like, and I write back:

Dear Dan,

A day in the life of a disgruntled inmate:

7 AM Wake, groan, shower, dress.

7:30 AM Breakfast.

8:30 AM House inspection. The indignity. Notices/reminders/warnings.

9 AM First class. To reflect the fact that this is a unique term in the life of the school (and there can't be that many teachers up here), there are specially constructed amalgamated subjects, like Myth, Language, Perspectives—which is sort of historydramaenglish. They call them ISMs: Integrated Study Modules.

11 AM Elevensies. Cakes and pastries and fruit are served. For real. (Imaginative name. Along the same lines is "Sevens," which is a form of punishment, an extra job to be undertaken at, you guessed it: 7 AM.)

11:15 AM Second class.

12:30 PM Lunch.

1:45 PM Third class.

3 PM Fourth class.

4:15 PM Runs/jobs.

6 PM Dinner.

7 PM Supervised homework (prep).

8:15 PM Back to houses. Lockdown—this is when our electronic cards have to be safely inserted into the right slot next to the right front door. Squabble, snack, listen to music, sing, complain, finish homework, read.

9:30 PM Lights out. No more talking.

Our weekends—Tuesdays and Wednesdays—are for our outdoor program, as well as group overnight hikes, solo hikes, longer runs, special working bees—more slave labor, and (not much) time for art and music.

Miss you guys like crazy.

Love, Lou

20

Even though we are not supposed to be alone together, it is completely possible to arrange, and the easiest time to manage it is when you're officially out running after classes and before dinner. You can run in twos, but you have to hike in threes. Because hiking means being farther away from the campus, worst-case-scenario logic is—one person gets injured, one person stays with them, one person goes for help. Which you'd only need to do in the other worst-case scenario of losing or breaking your sat phone.

For time alone you just need partners who are prepared to disappear for a while. I have Holly, with her hand firmly planted between my shoulder blades. She is like a relationship stage mother. Determined is an understatement, and she wants all the details afterward.

Holly arranged the time and the place, and here he is, waiting for me.

I feel shy and stupid walking toward him, still wearing my so-called pretty self like a shirt that doesn't fit. No, more like doesn't exist. Exactly: so it feels like being naked, unprotected. And we've been up here for a whole week, and he hasn't exactly rushed to see me alone. But he is the most relaxed person you can imagine. He holds out his hand and kisses me right away, on the cheek. An unequivocal sign of what—affection—possession—intimacy?

"I don't know what Holly said..."

"She said lots," he says. "But I just remembered the important stuff—time and place."

"Because—I hope you realize—I did not want her to arrange this." I'm finding it hard to remember what I wanted to say, despite having prepared it so carefully. I sound so wrong, as pompous as a little old lady, or a teacher. Who says *I hope you realize...?*

"But—here you are," says Ben, smiling. He's got me there. "Is it just to say you don't like me?"

"No," I say.

"You do like me?"

"I don't really know you that well..." This is a white lie whose objective is to make me appear more socially normal and not as stalkerish as I am, because I actually know him as well as it's possible to know someone without their participation.

He shrugs. "I know you—at least from class. I've heard your opinions about...stuff."

"I guess." I bet you couldn't tell me a single one, though.

"And you've heard mine." Whereas I could quote him back to himself pretty much verbatim. That's only about half as Ben-obsessed as it sounds—I do just remember what people say.

But knowing what he thought about *Romeo and Juliet* last year, or climate change, or how creative his excuses were for being late to first period after rowing practice doesn't really constitute "knowing" him.

"And I know you're off the planet at least half the time," he says. It seems a bit early on in the (not even) relationship for insults—surely that could wait until day two.

"No, I'm not."

"I've seen you reading—sometimes you open a book, and you're just...gone," he says. "Even with your friends— it's like you disappear." Maybe, okay, certainly true, but the thought of being observed by Ben, or anyone, when I'm not aware of them makes me squirmy.

And now I have no idea of my line. But I'm pretty sure it isn't what I am thinking, which is, unaccountably, *stare stare like a bear*...not only what he had just confessed to doing, but also what I am doing right now. I look away, hoping I appear thoughtful, or sensitively observant of our surroundings, not simply moronic. This boy/girl one-on-one stuff is super strange. I am casting about for something to say—something light and witty—and drawing blanks.

I picture Holly, careless and relaxed, always ready with a one-liner or smart retort. Why can't I be like that? Why am I stuck here with no idea of what comes next? Maybe I could ask Ben if he's smelled the dirt? Or maybe not.

"Why me?" I blurt.

At least he doesn't pretend not to know what I mean.

"Versus...a party girl?" We both know that's who he should be going out with—one of the out-there girls, the officially hot girls. The Blondes. Girls with labels and high-heel-walking skills. Girls like Pippa and Laura and Tiff and Gabi and—Holly, for that matter.

"Yeah."

"Because..."

"Tell me it's nothing to do with the stupid billboard."

"Nothing." His face is as open as the sky, and I believe him. He shrugs. "Maybe it's because you're not like them. Maybe it's because when you zone out—I dunno—I'm kind of curious to know where you are." He bends down to look at my face properly. "Do you want some more reasons?" He's within kissing range. I try to keep breathing, shake my head. "So, when Holly said I should meet you here..." he continues.

"I did not say that I wanted to..."

"Yep. We covered that already. I figured that you might not follow things up—from the way you've totally ignored me since we got up here. But why don't we do a little risk/

benefit analysis?" He picks up my hand. The giddiness is colliding somewhat with the...accountancy terminology? Okay, not so promising. Breathing easier. "So—is it worth it—while we're up here? We're in major shit if anyone catches us. And there's nowhere to actually 'go out.'"

What is he talking about? Everywhere is "out" up here. It's more like there's nowhere to be "in." Or am I being "obtusely literal," as my father sometimes says in an impatient moment? Is this a boy code I need to interpret—a rhetorical negative, perhaps—my cue to say no? Let him off the hook, no hard feelings? Formally call quits to something that has not really even started?

His look has a disconcerting hint of mockery in it. "So, do we play by the rules, or have some fun?"

Did he really just claim that he knew me, even a little bit? What I don't like is being the one to decide. I'm a go-with-the-flow girl. A girl who prefers not to rock the boat, unless absolutely necessary. Definitely not a rule-breaker. Not much of a fun-haver. Or a risk-taker. Too careful. More like a killjoy, if we're getting technical. A bit of an approval-seeker. And a massive scaredy-cat, as well.

I look at my feet. What am I hoping—that my toes will fly me a semaphore answer? Who am I again? The billboard model; the gangly, pimple-faced uggie-pie buried in my books; the would-be feminist who is always in trouble with her best friend; the nerd; the sulky but affectionate daughter; the girl who wants to kiss the boy? Can it really be like Holly said: now I get to choose...? It can't possibly be that easy. I must seem like a selective mute by now, which at least forces him to continue.

"Anyway," he says. "The benefits are obvious, to me..." Is he too smooth to be true, or naturally this charming? "So what do you think?"

"What do *you* think?" Ha—when in doubt: deflect. He just looks at me. "I mean—aren't you like super boy, everyone's pick for prefect next year, head boy the year after, captain of rowing, the world is your oyster, et cetera?"

He smiles his big smile.

Oops, I've kind of just handed to him on a plate the extent to which I have been keeping track of his school career trajectory. I pull out a businesslike summary to throw a bit of cold water on that impression: "What I mean is—it seems that you'd be the one risking something. So logically, therefore, perhaps you should decide first."

"Let's go for it." His smile shines with the pleasure—the power—of defiance.

"Okay, then." Okay—so that's who I am? I'm a pushover.

"Okay," he says. "You know when you smile, you look like someone else?"

Oh, right: that must be the girl who wants to kiss the boy. "I got my braces off in the holidays."

"That is not what I mean."

"I guess I am someone else," I say, leaning back against a tree. "I haven't really been me since we got here."

He leans in and kisses me. I get a little flash of old-time news footage, girls getting hysterical about the Beatles.

My mind is screaming *aaaaaaaagh* as Ben Capaldi's lips move from my mouth to the intersection of my earlobe, jaw, and neck, making me shudder.

"Cold?" He looks at me as though he really notices, and cares. His eyes are hazel with very white whites. His skin is olive; his hair dark, as long as he can get away with at school, it hangs in loose curls that he tucks behind his ears. He is ridiculously good-looking. Maybe he thinks I can get him modeling work? No, he's not that superficial. Hey, check me multitasking: I'm kissing, prosecuting, and defending—and truly I've had him under covert surveillance for long enough to know he is not self-conscious about the way he looks.

"No, just—no, not too cold." Just terrified. Because you (Ben Capaldi!) are kissing me, and it feels like I've given you the keys to my body before even checking that you have a license. Although on this, our second outing, it's clear to me that your learner's permit must be a distant memory, whereas I only just got mine. And for the record, I'm the very opposite of cold: burning, melting.

"Maybe we don't tell people about this," he says, now kissing the inside of my wrist. I'm seriously relying on the tree for support now, and hoping there aren't ants or sap oozes.

Because my mother is Dr. Sexpert, I have seen more than my fair share of material about all manner of things sexual in sometimes grossly graphic textbooks, in dull reports, and in lots of work stuff that hangs around our house. But I have never seen a chart that shows direct links between the neck or the wrist and the clitoris, with a flow-on effect causing a dissolving feeling just above the knees, and severe breathlessness. But I am living proof that these links and flow-on effects exist. I am raw human biology data. I am an experiment in train.

"Except Holly? She already knows," I remind him, trying to regulate my breathing.

"Yeah, except Holly."

We're not telling anyone? Secrecy. He doesn't want anyone to know? Shame? Denial? I'm not good enough to be the official girlfriend? Halt! Don't get paranoid. We've already canvassed the fact that this will be a covert operation, in light of the school rules about boy/girl activity up here.

Breathe in. Breathe out. And again.

21

In another of the combo ISMs they teach up here, Ms. Ladislaw takes a mash-up of physical education, orienteering, first aid, biology, and geography classes that they call: The Physical World, Theory and Interaction. She is pretty nice, but suffers from a severe nose-gub tic. She is always, but always, checking around her nose. Sniff, pinch, quick swipe with the back of her hand, numerous excavations with tissues, followed by more swipes and pinches and knuckle checks. I tried counting once, but got lost after fifty-two in about ten minutes. Blow, wipe, sniff, wipe, pinch, back of hand, knuckle can happen in a matter of seconds.

She knows her stuff, though. She's smart and scary-fit,

and has been teaching up here for about ten years, so benefits from older-sibling respect before she even gives her first class. And she is notorious for handing out painful physical-exercise punishments if anyone steps out of line. Because of this, and because people depend on the information she imparts if they plan on staying alive, everyone is basically okay for her.

So we know how to read a map, point a compass in the right direction (north), light our portable stove (the trusty Trangia), and pack our giant packs with appropriate amounts of food for the number of nights away. We even know how to look at the night sky and the sun's position for information. Even if there's no sun out, and we've crushed or lost our compass, we can use our naked eye to deduce direction, based on the side of the rock or trunk on which lichen is growing most vigorously, i.e., the shady side, i.e., south. Once you know south, you have north, etc.

Unfortunately, the maps don't go anywhere useful. Where, for instance, is my map to last year, or a map to some part of my heart, or my head, that doesn't hurt? Just round and round the mountains.

22

"We'll be hiking along this actual line in about an hour," I say, poking what I hope is the right part of the map spread out on the table. "Or that line? I'm not sure."

"Can't we choose which line as we go?" asks Holly. "The easy line."

"We need to choose now, so we can tell them our route, so they know which ledge we've fallen off when we don't come back," I say.

"After you tell me what Ben *said*."

"I told you everything last night."

"But try to remember his exact words. Did he use the word *girlfriend* or *boyfriend*?

"No."

"I'd take that as a plus," says Lou. "Now can we please get back to the map?"

"I don't remember asking for your opinion," Holly says to Lou.

"I give it freely when it suits me," says Lou. "Never feel you have to ask."

I'm warming to Lou. Not quite sure why phlegmatic is appealing, but I like the way she seems impervious to Holly's spikes. Even I'm susceptible to them—and I'm her best friend.

"We seem to be 'going out.' I'm almost sure we're going out. That's enough, isn't it?"

"Absolutely," says Holly. "Are you going to use yesterday or the first-kiss date as your anniversary?"

Lou looks at Holly. "Are you kidding?"

"Anniversaries are important," says Holly.

"Have you hired her as your relationship manager?" Lou asks.

"She's doing it pro bono," I say. It's hard to see if Lou is more unimpressed by me or by Holly.

"Is Ben hiking this weekend?" asks Holly.

"I don't know."

Holly sighs deeply. "You have to get into the habit of synchronizing schedules if this is going to have any hope of working."

Lou sighs deeply, too. "Can we make a decision about the route?"

We stare at the map again for a full ten seconds.

"Which way is up?" says Holly. "I mean, we're here, but..." She is rotating the map slowly, frowning. "How does this relate to that?" She nods at the window: the actual world.

"Didn't you go to the survival sessions?" asks Lou.

"Yes," says Holly.

"Ladislaw kind of went through it then," I say. "Last week's intensive? How to stay alive? Compasses, et cetera."

"Whatever. Did you two listen?" Lou and I nod. "Good enough," says Holly.

"I sure hope you can cook," says Lou.

Holly pulls a mean face out of Lou's eye line.

"I saw that," says Lou. She is madam of the even keel. No anger. No smiling.

Collecting rations from the dining hall is the next thing on the hiking to-do list. Holly and Lou and I head to the dining hall, where they dole them out.

Michael is there with Hamish and Doug, also heading off for a two-day hike in the morning. So Ben won't be out on the mountain. Only one group per house is allowed out at a time.

"Anything decent?" I ask Michael.

He's not happy. "It's mostly canned, vac-sealed, or dried, and nothing looks like itself."

"There's fresh fruit, and bacon, steak, and cheese for day one," Ms. Ladislaw is saying. "And mountain bread.

Please do not forget to puncture holes in any tinned food before you heat it on the fire, or it will explode. What will it do?" She puts one hand behind her ear, and is vigorously wiggling the back of her other hand against her nose—hay fever maybe?

"It will explode," we repeat back to her, like well-behaved zombies.

"All the pasta packs are one-serve, just add water, and heat on the Trangia. If pack-weight is an issue, I recommend you focus on these and dried fruit for your two-days. Gather what you need, and come back to check supplies out with me. Count up your meal numbers and snacks, add one meal in case you're delayed by weather or injury. You'll be burning lots of fuel on your hikes, so remember carbs and trail mix," she finishes. "And don't forget some cutlery."

"How many emergency chocolate bars are we allowed?" asks Hamish.

"One per customer," says Ms. Ladislaw. "And the cocoa is premixed with dried milk and sugar, so you don't need to add any. I recommend you include it; nights on the mountain are freezing, and it's a scientifically proven fact that cocoa and toasted marshmallows make the conditions more bearable."

Lou is talking to Michael as she gathers her supplies in one of the baskets provided; they do advanced math together.

"Nerd girl meets brain boy," says Holly.

How would I feel if Michael decided he'd go out with someone? It has never seemed remotely likely. But those two have already made a connection. Lou is smart, intense, and extremely private and quiet, but that wouldn't put Michael off. Even though I don't think of Michael romantically, I'm used to the fact of him liking me in a way he likes no one else. It's part of my landscape.

Holly comes back over with her food basket. "Did you see the open samples? It all looks like dried spew."

"But at least it's not heavy," I say.

Back in the house, we three look at our enormous, bulging packs in disbelief.

"Thanks for going first," says Pippa. "We can really use the extra room around here."

"Yeah, only we plan on coming back," says Holly.

"Don't count on it," says Pippa. "All I heard from people who went last week is snakes, perilous rock ledges, and possible starvation due to foulness of food."

"And yet they all returned," says Lou.

"Or did they?" says Annie. "Perhaps they were 'taken' and we now have substitutes among us, just waiting for their chance..."

"When have you put down, Pippa?" I ask.

"Haven't. I'm using the principle of going to the back of the line when it's time to jump the vaulting horse in gym. It's a strategy that's always worked pretty well for me."

"They'll catch up with you, for sure," says Eliza.

"Maybe, but by then I will have avoided a couple of hideous excursions into the wild." Pippa pulls a Husk herbal tea bag out of her mug, drops it in the sink for someone else to resentfully bin later, and with a serene smile turns her attention back to yet another phone-book-size glossy magazine.

23

We were supposed to have broken in the hiking boots
by the time we got here. It was on our "Two Months
Out" preparation and activity sheet. Looks like Lou has.
Holly hasn't. Who had time to clump around in these great
heavy things during the holidays? It was bad enough drag-
ging them on once or twice. Our little bits of lambswool
from the supplies cupboard are supposed to provide a
lanolin-soft buffer for any potential blistery spots. We'll
see.

It is amazing how quickly the whole campus has adopted
hike-speak. You'll get to the Bluff in four hours. Avoid the
Sawtooth Spur if the wind is southerly. Don't forget your
shit shovel. Yuck.

The packs weigh a ton—tents, sleeping bags, sleeping

mats, food, water, utensils. It's like walking with an eight-year-old kid on your back. Roll on, first meal stop, so we can eat some of the weight. The rain starts pretty much as soon as we leave the school's boundary. Despite waterproof everything, a steady trickle of rain tickles down my neck and blends with the sweat on my back. My feet hurt, and the pack straps are already digging in.

"When should we stop and rest?" Holly asks.

Lou turns and looks at her with derision.

"We probably need to try for the foot of Mount Paradiso," I say.

Holly groans. "This is boring as shit, and it hurts."

"Bitching about it should make it better," says Lou.

"And why all the happy names—Paradiso, Fairweather, Merrivale?"

"Maybe they were being ironic. Or optimistic," I say.

"Or just unimaginative," says Lou.

Holly stomps on ahead in silence.

We clomp on. It becomes hypnotic. The rain, the pain, the one heavy foot after the other, the shoulder straps, the rain, the pain...A bird calls out with a sound that whips around on itself. A bellbird? How do birds stay dry in the rain with no lids on their nests? Are they waterproof? The sky is massive, even cloud-filled as it is—so vast without buildings eating up all the edges. I feel much smaller here than I do in the city.

After possibly the two most uncomfortable hours of my life, we stop for a breather, water, and a map check, and agree that we seem to be on course. I eat a handful of trail mix and dig out an apple.

Holly looks at me, snorting with a suppressed laugh.

"What's funny?" I ask.

"You. I was just thinking about the billboard."

"What about it?" Surely we have exhausted this topic a thousand times over.

"How you're so photogenic."

"Thanks."

"Yeah—because it actually doesn't look like you at all. I mean, look at you now. You've got the whole beetroot face happening."

"Prize-winning backhand compliment," says Lou.

"No one asked you," says Holly.

I'm not offended. "She's right. No one would recognize me."

"I did," says Lou.

"Well, you're a suck-up," says Holly. "It looks nothing like her. Why don't you want to do some more? Like, get an agent and everything?"

"I just don't," I say, embarrassed.

"You're tall enough. But you'd need to lose some weight—make the move from thin to skinny."

"That's stupid," says Lou.

"Not if she wants to model."

"Which I don't!"

"Never say never. Hey, did you hear Falkner House is doing bulimia for fun?" says Holly.

"No." I haven't heard it, and I can't believe it.

"I know. But they think it's the only way they can survive a term of Elevensies. It's just a dare," says Holly.

"They can't hike and run if they're not eating properly," says Lou.

"They're doing coffee shots to keep the energy levels up," says Holly. "They're going for ten pounds in five weeks."

"Idiots," says Lou.

"I don't think you know them well enough to judge," says Holly.

"They're treating a condition that makes people *die* as some sort of *Biggest Loser* joke. So, I know enough," says Lou. "We need to pick up the pace a bit."

Is she touchy because *she* is bulimic? Wouldn't I know, seeing as we're sharing a bathroom? Also, she seems so sensible. Maybe she's got a friend suffering from an eating disorder. Have the others got this burning pain around the ankles? The hot, fat feeling of blisters establishing themselves? Why didn't I walk my boots in properly?

What am I even *doing* here? Me, a city girl. Ninety percent of my life happens on one highly resourced page of the street directory. I should have been maneuvering my way out of this school long ago, seeing this on the horizon.

It always seemed to be so far off in the future—until now. Now it's got me in its zealously healthy stranglehold.

This will take forever to get used to. By then it will be time to turn around and go back home. So, classic time-waster. My giant boots plonk along like mud-clogged hoofs, every step a challenge to balance already made precarious by the pack and the slidey, muddy trail. My hair is plastered to my forehead with sweat and rain.

All this time it is as though I've been in a tight urban hug without properly realizing it, and now it's like someone's let me go. Everything here feels too big, too open. Like a series of safety bonds are breaking—*ping, ping, ping*—releasing me into this quietness. I'm falling. Filling my lungs with the air of another planet. It's severely unnatural.

After too long, and nonstop complaints from Holly, we reach the base of Mount Paradiso and decide to keep going, hiking up to the first grassy saddle. We argue about where to put the tent. We're not supposed to pitch under trees, because they fall over sometimes, especially after wet weather, and we've had a record wet winter. But we all feel a little insecure about choosing a spot in the open. So we compromise and put the back of the tents close to a rocky outcrop that gives us at least the illusion of protection.

I cannot imagine being okay out here by myself. It feels weird enough, and ominously enough like the beginning of a horror movie, with two other humans; it is unthinkable that I could be here alone. I refuse to be here alone. I assert my rights as a pack animal.

My simple plan to ensure that I don't have to do the solo hike is as follows: log name in the solo hike schedule for the final week (done), at which time I will pull a sickie. And that will be the end of it. The alternative is possible fear-induced insanity or heart failure. If any of my friends want to torture me, they all know they only have to tell me the plot of any horror movie they choose. I have always refused to actually watch one. My imagination, along with accidentally glimpsed trailers here and there, has given me enough terrifying horror fodder for life.

We find a ring of rocks that campers past have used as a fireplace, so that saves a bit of work. Finding dry wood is a challenge, after the rain all day, but we scrabble together enough. We combine our three packs of pasta for dinner—pesto. We tip the dried stuff into a pan, add water, and simmer.

We try it, looking at one another with disbelief as it hits the taste buds. "It's pesto, Jim, but not as we know it," I say.

"Fascinating," says Lou, unsmilingly humoring my *Star Trek* reference, while wincing at the foul food. (And what made me say that? Is there such a thing as a dad-joke vacuum that needs to be filled, even in the wild?)

Lou stares into the fire, eating on autopilot. She has dark hair cut in a bob, with long bangs. She trims it herself. Her glasses frames are heavy and black, hardcore nerd. Her nose has a little dip in the middle, too cute really for her anti-pretty style. She is the sort of girl who would wear heavy boots if she ever put on a pretty frock, just to show she was calling the shots.

"I've never tasted shittier food," says Holly. "And it's probably solid carbs."

"That's the idea." Lou prods and reshapes the fire with the big stick, our poker. It crackles up and throws a comforting heat. "So we have the energy to hike."

I share a discovery. "If you don't breathe through your nose, you can't taste it as much."

Lou and I finish our pasta despite its bizarre flavor and texture (salty, chemically, spongy, and slimy), and Holly eventually eats about half of her portion.

The sparks shoot upward, quick red threads, little help messages to the universe: Get me out of here. Let me back, civilization. Give me some real food.

"What about some nice fireside stories," Holly suggests, her evil smile shining red.

"No! Lou, I'm a scary-story wimp. I'm sorry."

"I'm not interested, either. I think I'll call it a night."

"Wait up," says Holly. "Isn't someone going to make cocoa?"

Because it is so cold, we boil some dried fruit as a hot "dessert," as well as making cocoa and toasting some marshmallows.

"So, Lou, what's your story?" asks Holly.

"I really don't have one."

"You've come here from a public school?"

"Yes."

"Well, how come? Is this like finishing school for you, or something? Last two-and-a-bit years at private school better than none?"

"Holly! Lou, ignore her—she doesn't realize how rude that is," I say.

"It's not rude—what's rude is someone who sits like a lump and never contributes anything to the conversation," says Holly. "Come on—make an effort. Are you going out with anyone? Do you play a sport? Where do you live in Melbourne? Why have you chosen our school?"

Lou gives her a long look. Is she thinking of taking her on? Please don't, Lou; she bites. And I don't want to be the one in the middle.

"I'm off to bed. Night," says Lou.

She stops.

"I'm not going out with anyone. I live in Fitzroy. I've left a school I like just fine to come here because this was my mum's school, and my grandfather also came here. Not that it's any of your business."

Holly and I go down to the stream to get washing-up water, which we should have done when it was light. We're not supposed to leave any food traces overnight because it attracts—*gah!*—hideous creatures like bush rats and possums. I cling to Holly's arm, slender protection—but better than none—from the lurking teen-stalking axe-wielding psychomurderers, drunken gun-toting hunters, and sundry angry undead from various eras past waiting at the inky edges of the flashlight puddle.

Holly is honestly not scared. My mother used to tell me that not being scared was a sign of a small imagination, when I got teased for being the party pooper on sleepovers who couldn't hack the prospect of scary movies. But that was just to make me feel better. I'm sure Holly can imagine. But it doesn't cross her mind that *it might be about to happen to her.*

We fill the (foldable) washbowl and head back.

"Why do you have to be such a bitch to Lou?" I'm only talking in an attempt to make myself settle down.

"She's not even trying to fit in," Holly says, in her ringing *Going on a Bear Hunt* voice. The dark makes me want to whisper, *in case someone's listening,* but Holly could not care less. "She's lucky to even be here. It's really hard to get a place just to come for camp year. My friend Penny from St. Cath's couldn't get a place, and her dad came here. And Lou *is* going out with someone. Her bookmark is a photostrip of her and some dud-looking guy with matching glasses. And she stares at it like a lot."

"It's really not our business."

"It really is if she's living in our house."

The flashlight hits a pair of bright eyes, and I scream. Which makes Holly scream. We run back up the rest of the path and spill most of the water. By now we are both laughing, me, not so much with amusement as with terror-induced hysteria.

"You are a massive wimp, Sib."

We keep setting each other off again, as we have countless times in the past, laughing till we cry.

"Shut up," Lou yells from her tent.

Even though there is probably nothing more than sleepy birds, small marsupials, large possums, and the odd wallaby nearby, the fire still seems like essential wild-beast protection, and I am only able to let it burn down to a smolder with a pang.

Burrowing into the down-filled sleeping bag, everything that involves muscle or tendon is aching, and my nose is freezing. I can't remember ever feeling that I needed to stretch out and sleep more than I do right now. But used as I am to the sounds of helicopters, traffic, breaking glass, the bass pulse of a party a couple of blocks away, car doors, drunken arguments, and loud farewells, I can't settle into this new repertoire of going-to-sleep sounds. Twig snaps, wind shaking leaves and branches, trees creaking together, rock rumbles, the war cry of the possums, nocturnal hunting stampedes, owls screeching. Oh, it is hideous.

24

wednesday 17 october

I trudged back thinking, one down, two to go, one down, two to go. Overnight hikes. And promising myself I would never get stuck with Holly again.

I can't decide if Sibylla is just so used to Holly's needling that she can ignore it, or if Holly's superpower is couching meanness in just enough humor that she gets away with it.

Stomping along for hours, one foot after another, puts you into a rhythm. A physical rhythm seems to call for a thought rhythm, and my brain chose one of its favorite, well-worn tracks.

If we hadn't been speaking about *pain au chocolat* with

Dan and Estelle, Fred would not have been juggling two Les Bons Matins paper bags on his handlebars.

If he hadn't had an extra clarinet lesson after school because his exam was coming up and he needed to rehearse with his accompanist, he would not have been running late.

If we hadn't agreed to meet at my place.

If he hadn't taken Brunswick Street.

If the truck driver hadn't pulled in for a coffee right there at that moment.

If the impact had been to forehead, not temple.

If his helmet strap had been tighter.

If the parking meter hadn't been in that position on the sidewalk.

If Dan had never come to my school.

If I had not liked Fred the first time I met him.

If he had not liked me.

If I had never met Fred.

If he had never met me.

If we had never...

Esther called this unproductive thinking. My mind, for reasons of its own, has chosen to ignore this sound observation. (It has to be what Fred's mother and father and stepmother think, too: if he hadn't been riding to Lou's at that time on that day...)

If you take thinking like this to its logical conclusion you'd never get out of bed, according to Esther.

That would be fine with me.

For a while being dead felt like it would be fine with me, too, but...

But, as Dan said, we are the only ones who have certain memories of Fred.

The keepers.

25

When we get back, there's talk of pranking in the air. A couple of small-scale forays have happened in our absence.

Pranking is a sign that people are settling into the new life. Warming to it. Over the years it must have come to symbolize some sort of "ownership" of the camp experience, because the teachers seem to expect it—and almost tolerate it.

We lead the house-on-house attack. Stupid target, as it turns out. Illawarra House has the biggest percentage of misfits and grudge-holders up here, but proximity is everything, and they happen to be our next-door neighbors.

We decide on a classic attack. The covert flour bomb. Elegant, simple, effective.

We get them on Thursday morning when the jobs roster

rotates and it's their turn to wipe the swill and sluice the decks and risk contracting Slushy-induced hepatitis A–Z.

Eliza, Holly, and I go in armed with flour.

Annie keeps watch. Pippa stays in. Lou opts out. "I could not be less interested," she says. It's a shame. I thought she had warmed up just slightly on our hike. Apparently not. She seems glummer than ever.

As soon as they leave to set up breakfast, we are in. Pippa might not be actively participating, but it is thanks to her—to her older sisters, anyway—that we have the know-how.

Holly positions the three-step ladder we have borrowed from the drying room directly under the kitchen-area ceiling fan. She climbs up. I hand her the flour, which we've managed to stockpile during our week on Slushy, stealing a couple of handfuls a day in small freezer bags. She carefully spoons heaps of flour along the length of each fan blade and climbs down.

Ten minutes' work on our part—surely at least two hours' cleaning up required, if things go according to plan.

We have to wait until after classes this afternoon for our payoff. Fortunately the day has been warm, and shortly after they troop inside, someone switches on the fan.

We can't see them, but we know they've done it from the screaming that ensues.

We should possibly play it cooler, but it is hard to resist the temptation to document what's happening.

Holly and I sit outside, counting down their exit. Five from the first shriek.

Four.

Three.

Two.

One.

"Smile!" Holly says, as she takes photos of them bursting out of their front door, sneezy, shouting, flour-coated. Very angry. Which makes for some pretty good photos.

They do not smile.

26

thursday 18 october

When I see the girl still looking at the handsome boy with such buried longing...

When I read Othello...

Thinking how few of Shakespeare's plays you got to know, and how much you loved the ones you'd studied and read and seen performed, is just one of the things that makes me bite the inside of my cheek hard. The little pain to stop the big pain. Doesn't work. At least we got to see that fantastic production of *Hamlet* together, remember? (Duh, of course you don't. You are no longer in a fit state of consciousness to remember things. Sane me reminds myself that this is a one-way conversation.)

But if you could just see these jackanapes, Fred, the

cream-faced loons that *Othello* is wasted on. I don't even love this play. Things do not end well for Desdemona. And she has done nothing wrong. Nothing to deserve it. Nothing to motivate it. Nothing to precipitate it. Another pointless death. So I do relate to that extent. But she does not die at the hands of a soon-to-be-shattered truck driver. She dies at the hands of an irrationally jealous husband.

I mean, hats off to Shakespeare, he certainly lays it on the line, talk about life lessons in the odd, unhappy ending. It felt so theoretical with *Romeo and Juliet*, though, didn't it? And a bit silly. Kind of avoidable. Too coincidental. So much swings on shitty timing.

But, silly us, so much does swing on shitty timing.

If you'd left a bit earlier.

If you'd left a bit later.

Stop it. Bite down. Stop biting.

They are not all stupid.

Sibylla, for instance, is smart, but she is being pulled right out of shape up here. It's because of the billboard.

Holly put a big photo of the old Sibylla up in our house bathroom. On the mirror. It is very unflattering. In it, Sibylla is pimply, and her skin is dry and red, perhaps symptoms of the pimple treatment, and she looks to have her mouth full. It's nasty. Sibylla laughed, of course. It's important to be a good sport, not to show if your feelings are hurt. What is the alternative? Especially if it's your best friend having the laugh.

So just before class today some of the hoonish, boorish boys...shall we call them jocks? That is what they are, I suppose. Anyway, these boys started singing the theme song to *Australia's Next Top Model* to, or at, Sibylla. At first she didn't notice. But when she did, she looked, I thought, in appeal to Ben, the brand-new going-out person, as if to say, your jock friends, can you get them to shut up? But Ben is Mr. Easygoing, Mr. Hailfellowwellmet, Mr. Friendofthewholeworld, so he seemed not to notice, or maybe he chose carelessly, or coldly, not to notice. The teacher had not yet arrived and the boys got louder and more insistent. And so Sibylla with very pink cheeks, and not looking at all happy, dropped them an awkward curtsy, which I am pretty sure she intended as ironic. But it wasn't received that way. At least it shut them up. They had been baying for attention, and she satisfied that hunger. Or maybe what shut them up was the teacher coming in and saying, *right, good morning, okay now, have we all read and enjoyed* Othello? The round of groans that elicited was depressing.

Sibylla, sitting behind a tight smile, took a while to settle down, surrounded by such unwelcome attention. Holly basks in any reflected kudos. She does not mind Sibylla's discomfort at all. The odd wolf whistle and snicker was still filtering out.

Michael, from my math group, was watching Sibylla carefully; he was anxious, not sure what he could or should do.

The limelight was soon taken off Sibylla when the teacher, Ms. McInerney, asked for our first impressions, overview comments. Michael threw her a curveball. He speculated that Iago was impotent in his relationship with Emilia and had sublimated homoerotic feelings for Othello. Surely, he said, only such extreme passion could motivate Iago to manipulate Othello to the point where he actually murders Desdemona.

This caused an uproar. Ms. McInerney, who doesn't know any of us yet, wasn't sure whether to take the comment seriously, or consider it to be an intentional distraction. She's young and new, and was nodding her neat blond bob up and down with the surprised look of someone who thought she was going paddling but found herself in the squad lanes. Annie yelled out, Thanks for nothing, why should I read it now that I know she dies!

The more loathsome jocks were in ecstasies of gay put-downs: You faggot, Cassidy, only a gay like you would think Iago is gay, etc. Sibylla looked concerned for Michael, but I was starting to think he had concocted this just to take the heat off her. Michael defended his position by citing specifics from the text, which increased the jeers hurled in his direction. Ms. McInerney was staying afloat, trying to shush everyone and put Michael off without putting him down.

She ended up threatening all of us with withdrawal of the week's house Milo rations. This created an instant silence; Milo is like gold around here, a tradable commodity. Once everyone had simmered down, she told Michael we would be going through a more orthodox reading of characters and text in the first instance. Iago is bitter because he is overlooked for promotion to lieutenant in favor of Cassio, and so decides to trick and trap, to punish his general, Othello.

She adds that she would be more than happy to explore further themes or interpretations in which any one of us was interested as we progress with our study of the play.

Noted: Michael checking on Sibylla. It was a deliberate distraction.

Noted: Ben's failure to stand up for Sibylla.

Noted: Holly's constant, preening need for attention.

Yes, I am smally interested in spite of myself. Is this an early symptom of *Testing New Reality*, Fred? I know that wouldn't bother you. But it feels wrong to me. It feels like I'm cheating on you.

27

There is a mystery smell in Bennett House. Like someone's not showering. How can that be? Everyone does
time in the bathroom. So, is someone just running water
and standing next to the shower fully dressed and still
stinky? Or has Illawarra House learned how to bottle
body odor and sprayed it around to get back at us for the
flour-bombing?

Smells are constantly on the agenda up here.

Good smells: lemon-scented gums and peppermint
eucalypts with which the grounds are artfully "natively"
landscaped.

The air in general—out hiking or running—is crystal
clean. It makes me realize how happily complacent I have
been with breathing in toxic city air. I can't wait to get back

to it. I've adapted. It's my natural habitat. But the clean air is certainly a pleasant place to visit. I just wouldn't want to live here.

Foulest smell around is the boy deodorant smell, which is super intensified up here for some reason. Perhaps because of the shorter time between shower and class-room? Wafting stink from boy houses? Why do they put the yuck smell into all the boy products? It's abusive to those who have to wear it, and worse for those who have to sit in class with those who have to wear it.

Misleadingly nice but secretly evil smell is the morning pastry run, Elevensies, which is when the cake shop from Hartsfield brings fresh cakes and slices each day for us to fall upon (at eleven o'clock) as though we haven't eaten huge breakfasts a few short hours ago. It smells cakey fresh, but makes you feel all sugared and larded up and sleepy.

Very ferment-y smell—the compost heap. This smell contains a secret ingredient: fear of seeing rats, mice, snakes.

Sharp unpleasant smell—when they put fee-fi-fo-fum blood and bone on the vegetable garden, we all want to escape and barf.

Oddly pleasant but sort of poo-y smell—the chicken cages. We have our own free-range eggs. Fancy schmancy. But the chookies sleep overnight in big cages because of possible fox attacks.

Girl perfumes. You can have too much of a good thing.

All the perfumes of Arabia come together in our house. Along with the mystery BO. I used to love Dior J'Adore, but Pippa squirts it around with such abandon that I can't stand it anymore.

We'll need to have a house meeting about smells soon.

The laundry/drying room smell—delicious: clean, dry sheets and towels. And toasties.

"So, what are you doing back?" Holly asks me as we lift out our grilled Swiss cheese and ham.

And expanding—in response to my blank look: "He put flowers on your pillow!" Ben did somehow get into Bennett House, and put a handful of banksia roses on my pillow; they had a few ants in them, not that I want to nitpick.

"Nothing?"

"Are you crazy? Has it even registered that you—*you*—have the best-looking boyfriend for ten thousand square miles? Don't you want to shower him with affection? And let the whole world see that you care?"

I really would prefer the whole world not to notice, and I had not considered any affection-showering.

"I guess I could make him a thank-you card."

"You're not in kindergarten, Sib."

"Well, I don't know."

Holly produces a bag of Clinkers. "Ta-da! I happen to know they're his favorite sweet thing. Apart from you, I guess."

"They are? And I am not his—"

"Can't you just hop on board the girlfriend train? Ask him some questions. Get to know him."

"Looks like I can just ask you," I say, hoping I don't sound as petty as I feel. Holly hands them over. "Your crazy friend can let you into their house. They're on Maintenance this week. You can go after breakfast tomorrow morning."

"So—you think I should leave these on his pillow?" I'm looking at the plastic packaging—it's not exactly shaping up as a lotsacutefun love token.

"No, you idiot, have some *fun*—hide them in his pillowcase, his boots, his boxers . . . use your imagination!"

"What if he thinks it's stupid?"

"As if."

"I'd better not risk it . . ." I remember with a surge of relief. "We agreed that we'd keep the whole going-out thing on the down low."

Holly looks a little uncomfortable. "You could have made that clearer."

"I told you! Have you told someone?"

"One, maybe two people." She thinks. "Three, four tops."

"So—great—everyone knows."

"You should be pleased. Ride the wave, hun."

"We're not supposed to be 'in a relationship' up here."

"So, deny it if a teacher asks. Jeez, it's really not that hard."

I consider the Clinkers. "What if I accidentally offend

him because he thinks my gesture is just a hollow, unmotivated reaction to his?"

Holly snorts. "Only your fucked-up family thinks shit like that."

What would I do without my teenage-behavior touchstone?

"Do you want another sandwich?"

"No."

"Are you sure?" I want another one. But I don't want to seem too piggy.

"I'm sure. I'll have a larger arse than I want if I keep stuffing these down."

"Isn't that what our sweats are for: easy storage of the larger arse?"

"You know what the Gorgon would say: Don't let yourselves go, girls. This is an opportunity to get fit, not to get fat." We both laugh: it is so exactly what she would say.

"That does it; I'm going again," I say. I slap some more ham and Swiss between two slices of bread.

The Gorgon is Holly's mother. Glamorous, skinny, tan, and mean. Mothers are generally either starvers or feeders; she is definitely a starver: "Would you like some extra lemon juice on your salad leaves, girls?" Whereas my mother is a feeder (thank god): "More gnocchi, girls?"

Maybe that's why they let us go into the wild this year: this is the age at which we have perfectly internalized our parent-messages, and so are considered to be safe alone.

friday 19 october

You'd think it's silly and so do I, but it just occurred to me that we never had a Valentine's Day.

It's not February 14 or anywhere near that date, but why let that worry me. Time is standing still (you) and racing by (me) in the most arbitrary way.

So here is a little arrow from me, heading toward your still heart. Because I still heart you, get it? Too macabre? You'd appreciate it.

Sibylla asked Michael for something, in a private aside. First he looked happy . . . to be confided in? Then he looked sad . . . or no, it was more a resigned grimace.

Oh, and you would have loved seeing Holly trying to smile with a mouth full of bile when Sibylla told her that there is a magazine campaign that goes with the billboard.

XXX

saturday 20 october

Song
Christina Rossetti

When I am dead, my dearest,
Sing no sad songs for me;
Plant thou no roses at my head,
Nor shady cypress tree:
Be the green grass above me
With showers and dewdrops wet;
And if thou wilt, remember,
And if thou wilt, forget.

I shall not see the shadows,
I shall not feel the rain;
I shall not hear the nightingale
Sing on, as if in pain:
And dreaming through the twilight
That doth not rise nor set,
Haply I may remember,
And haply may forget.

This is the closest one I have found to what I guess you might say to me, based on what I would want to say to you.

I would want you to feel that there was a not-quite-consciousness, not-quite-obliteration, a release, peace.

I can't say it feels anything like *Testing New Reality*, but I have read this poem about a thousand times.

30

The trees make a lacy shade canopy overhead. I'm nibbling when a horrible thought strikes me. "This wasn't in your hiking boot, was it?"

"Nah, I ate those first," Ben says.

"Bleugh."

"You're supposed to like every bit of me, aren't you?"

"Not your foot sweat."

"Why not? I like yours."

"You don't know my foot sweat." Big mistake. He grabs my ankle, unties my boot, and pulls it and my sock off before I have a chance to say no. "I would really not do that if I were you..."

I probably couldn't have said anything more encouraging. He smiles and licks the underneath of my foot from heel to toe. It doesn't have a chance to be erotic, which it might be in other circumstances, because it's so ticklish. Unbearably ticklish.

I've got a major case of can't-breathe, laughter-induced powerlessness, but I manage to grab a handful of his hair and he stops with my big toe between his teeth.

"Release!" He lets it go, grinning, delicately removing a bit of sock fluff from his tongue.

"Delicious."

"*Bull*shit."

He assesses the flavor. "Like salted peanuts, but no crunch." He crawls up to kiss me—

"How about you stop for a Clinker before you kiss me with my own foot sweat?" When we're alone he is easily distractible—like a puppy.

"You know I can tell what color a Clinker is just by smelling it?"

"No, you can't."

"Try me."

I hand him a Clinker. He sniffs. "Pink." He bites through the chocolate coating. It's yellow.

"See."

"Yellow is the closest flavor to pink! I call that half right."

"Yeah, only it's a hundred percent wrong."

He takes another one. Sniffs. "Green." It is green. "Ha! I am the Clinker psychic."

"You have a one-in-three chance of getting it right, and

you've got one wrong and one right. That is not proof of being psychic. Maybe you're just the Clinker psycho, a guy with a sniffing delusion."

"Have it your way—but now I get to kiss you, right?"

I lean back with a sigh of bliss. "Right." Yellow, pink, and green kisses are coming my way.

31

sunday 21 october

There is someone more obsessed with running than I appear to be.

I did say *appear*; you know I'm not really obsessed.

I run so I can be by myself. I usually head out with Eliza (queen of fitness) and a book and go to my cave. That is not a metaphor. I have a spot. It's like a half-cave with a gorse bush in the front (right again, I don't know if it's a gorse bush, but they always hid behind and hid stuff behind gorse bushes in Enid Blyton books, so I have christened this shrubby bush thing: gorse). I have a blanket and a pillow there. It is just over a mile run from school, so I am doing some exercise. Eliza loves running with me, because I don't run, so she gets to do her crazy super-training whatevers alone. We have each other's backs if anything goes wrong. I know her routes. She knows my cave address. We ask no questions and tell no lies. She thinks I'm a loner who likes to read a lot, alone. Which is true.

I can have a private howl here, too. What a relief. No crying in the house. That is self-imposed, not coming from them. They would love to feast on my drama/sorrow. I can't tell you how minutely personal things get unpicked and examined in our house.

The school counselor's name is Merill. My mother cut a deal that I have to see Merill twice a week. I've just had session number four, if you count our day-one introduction, and I'm faking it like a trooper. She thinks I'm doing well. And I am doing as well as I expected, which is not great. I miss you. I love you.

Because my cave is hidden, and it's on the main northerly route back to school, I see plenty of comings and goings.

Ben runs like a maniac. A machine. He has a different look to him when he's running. He is unmasked. He is preoccupied, his focus dark, not at all the cool relaxed face he usually presents. Camp gossip has ensured that he and Sibylla are the worst-kept secret around. Odd, odd couple.

But the one who runs the most is Michael. Brain boy. Sibylla's silent protector. He, who always looks either worried or distracted in class and around campus, is free when he runs. He escapes himself somehow. We're only allowed to run in pairs, but people are running alone all the time. I guess like me and Eliza: sign out together, and then head your own way.

I had to, well, chose to, rescue Michael a couple of days ago. He was on his way back. Pouring sweat, really working hard. He stopped not too far from the cave and started heaving his guts out. Not sick-sick, just vomiting from the overexertion. As though he was at the end of the most grueling marathon you can imagine. He did not look good.

And I have certain supplies in the cave: biscuits, water, glucose tablets, Tylenol, tissues. It is a regular little home away from. I'm not sure why I did it. It's not like he was going to die or anything, but I went to him with water and glucose tablets. I was a mixed blessing. First of all because I gave him a fright. And also I suppose he was embarrassed to be caught spewing and spitting like that because the first thing he did was apologize. How disgusting, he said. I am sorry you had to witness that.

I told him not to worry and offered him the stuff. He crunched and drank and asked if I had a field hospital set up. I said, funny you should say that because I am planning to study medicine when I leave school. I'm not the squeamish type. I said, I come up here to read. He had run all the way from Lightning Gorge. That is a ten-mile run. He'd finished his water way back, and he was running too hard for such a long distance. I did not share my expert opinion with him.

Running is a massive big deal up here. The long runs

we call crossies are unlike city cross-country; here, we are actually expected to run across the countryside—up mountain, down dale, through streams. The goal for the term's running is the equivalent distance from here to Melbourne. The serious runners will double that. There is a big chart in the dining/assembly hall foyer where runs are logged, and everyone's progress is marked.

If you can believe it, people even bring up their parents' crossie cards and try to beat the older generation's records. Ha-ha, not too hard. Why is that? Faster running shoes? I have Mum's card from when she was here. She was a slacker. (Like mother, like daughter.) I wouldn't show anyone her card, because I'm not into all of that, but people are getting quite competitive. Also there's a sort of repulsive elitism that comes with being a second- or third-generation person here. And I don't want to be in that club. The equal longest distances clocked are by Ben and Michael. Eliza and I aren't doing too badly, either. I'm not worried about the lying, Fred, because I'm planning to scale down the false claims and make sure I come farther down the girls' list than top ten. I wouldn't want to rain on a serious runner's parade.

Michael told me he likes everything about running other than the fact that it has bashed his toenails into such bad shape (running downhill does it) that he's losing them. Just on the big toes. He showed me. Bruised purple, dead-looking, and lifting. Gross.

He said thank you, and asked me what my name was. I

said, you know my name, we've got two classes together. He said, Your real name. So I told him—Louisa. And he said, Thank you, Louisa.

He's an unusual person, but I think of all the people up here, you'd like him the best.

32

Fire.
My heart's on fire.
I am smoldering.
Burning.
She's hot.
Spark.
Sparks flying.
Smoldering looks.
He's hot.
Rush of blood to the head.
Goes off like a cracker.
My heart is inflamed.
Smokin'.
Sizzlin'.

Heart ablaze.

Flames licking.

Flames leaping.

Burning passion.

All-consuming passion.

Eating up the oxygen.

Fever.

Igniting.

~~Perfect match.~~

My flame.

An old flame.

Great balls of fire.

Some like it hot.

A hunk a hunk of burning love.

Spontaneous combustion.

Well, not the most interesting English class ever. We were not really "firing," as Michael reflected.

In fact, Ms. McInerney looks as though her head is about to drop off as she squeaks her almost-out marker over the whiteboard.

We are supposed to be squeezing out some similes and metaphors using the idea of fire.

The thing no one has mentioned about the fire/passion/love connection is that the end result—the logical conclusion—of fire is annihilation. Fire destroys. It consumes. It reduces everything in its path to ash.

You don't have to go far up here to see how destructive it is.

But it's a classic love/passion image set. I prefer it hands down to the love/romance image set—hearts and flowers and cuteness. With evil kittens inevitably lurking nearby.

You'd imagine the whole fire thing would make you feel a tiny bit wary about jumping in, when you think about what comes after the heat. But, no. I have to regulate how often I look at Ben. It's amazing how five minutes can drag. It's amazing what a shocking cheat I am. From here I can see a long thigh poking out sideways from his chair, his back, and every now and then about a quarter of his face, a straight nose, a glimpse of high cheekbone.

For the entire class, Rob Marshall and Andy Stone have been drawing stick figures having sex in different positions, and laughing with the combined maturity of one twelve-year-old boy. I don't know how teachers can stand it. Selective blindness, maybe.

33

It's 11:11 PM *again*, and I'm thinking about sex all the time.

One annoying aspect of this is that it's something my know-it-all mother has "warned" me about—or alerted me to. Not sex itself. She's not anti-sex by any means. Sex is her bread and butter, after all. No, it's more that sexual attraction is a powerful thing. And, in her book, something ideally to be shared with the right person at the right time. Which, in another chapter in her book, not that she'd ever admit it, is probably the freshly packaged virgin son of one of her friends after he and I have both completed postgraduate education. But forget that—it's all happening now. In my head, anyway. My unruly brain is so overpopulated by a thousand images of Ben—the beauty of Ben the scent of Ben the taste of Ben the touch of Ben—it's like an all-senses photo file keeps reloading in there, and no one's cleaning it up.

I want a break.

Wouldn't mind a break from pranking, either. I am sick to death of it.

Illawarra got us back with a disproportionate prank. They launched the attack when we were busy digging weeds out of the running track—on Grounds. (Why not call it what it is: slave labor, for which your parents pay extortionate fees.)

We got honeyed.

It was disgusting.

Honey smeared over everything. Furniture, floor, every surface, and every glass, piece of cutlery, piece of crockery, and piece of cookware in our kitchen had to be washed. We had to wash shelves. The floors are still sticky after three washes. All our shoes are still sticky. They even managed to get into a couple of the beds before they were disturbed. One of them was Holly's.

We did our best to clean it all up, but it was really hard.

They got into trouble for it, because we had to get help with laundry and an overnight massive ant infestation. Come on, guys, the party's in here. Double yuck.

Holly was so pissed off that she infiltrated Illawarra one more time and mixed dirt into their Milo tin. Each house gets a weekly ration, and it's eaten and drunk in every possible way. On buttered toast, as a dip for bananas, eaten by the spoonful, made up as a hot drink, made up as a cold, crunchy drink. People depend on it, and if anyone ever guessed what Holly had done, she'd probably be dead by nightfall.

Lou made one of her rare comments about it. "You started it," she said, when Holly was fuming and stripping her bed, telling us about the Milo as she ripped off the sticky sheets, her mouth a hard line. "What did you expect? Treat them like shit, and they'd leave it at that?"

"Honey is much worse than a flour bomb."

"So, suck it up. Dirt in Milo could make someone sick."

"Good," said Holly. "They deserve it. They're scum."

I was with Lou on this one. Holly was making me feel uncomfortable. Just like when we were kids, I had the familiar stomach knot: when her "having fun" went too far and I either went along with it, or got cast as the boring killjoy.

But perhaps there was safety in numbers, because instead of lashing out, Holly flashed everyone her brilliant smile. "Come on, guys, let's get rid of them one at a time, like an Agatha Christie novel." She laughed, and it felt like we all had permission to relax.

It reminded me of all the times my mother has talked to me about my friendship with Holly. She often observed that Holly seemed "unhappy." I knew my mother well enough to know that this was health-professional code for "evil." She also encouraged me to have a "wider group" of friends. But all my friends came via Holly. Except Michael, of course. And then there was the semi-regular don't-jump-through-hoops warning: "You don't always have to do what Holly wants to do."

When I said I didn't, I wasn't exactly lying. Because often Holly wanted us to do what I wanted to do. And unhappy was genuinely unhappy on certain occasions, not always simply mean.

If Holly ever shits me—and believe me, she does—I think about her face when she's attempting to dodge the Gorgon in full bitch-flight, and it's pretty easy to forgive her for most things. It is a heartbreaking (to me, anyway, the one who notices) trying-not-to-care face. It is the same face she wore in grade six when all the captain roles were read out and she didn't get one. Even *I* was library captain. And the face she put on in year eight when Tiff Simpson invited a group (*the* group) for a weekend in Sorrento and Holly didn't make the cut. I wasn't even on the long list.

34

monday 22 october

And that's another session with Merill done and dusted. Woo-hoo.

It is quite hard for me not to stand up and scream when she talks about your *passing*.

No simple passing for Fred, I want to yell. He was smart. Smarter than you, Merill. He was a flying-colors, honorable honors student.

Plus he would have hated, did hate, mealy-mouthed euphemisms for anything, but particularly important things, like death.

Call it what it is: he died. He is dead.

It is his death that kills me, not his freaking *passing*.

To be fair, if I told her any of this, she would probably say death. She is probably being gentle. Taking the eggshell approach. It's just that I don't want to talk to her about Fred. Or his death.

So I say small things about camp stuff. Yes, I'm getting to know the girls in my house. The girls are lovely. No, I don't want to tell them anything more about my background. Yes, they are welcoming to an outsider. No! I don't think of myself as an outsider, not really, no, it's just an expression. I should have said, they are welcoming to a *new girl*. Yes, I am enjoying my classes. The teachers are excellent. No, there does not appear to be any problem with regard to work we covered at my old school being compatible with work we are covering in this year's curriculum. And distance education, too, that's right, for the last three terms. At my own pace. Exactly. Got lots done. Yes, absolutely; it was isolating, but the right thing for me at the time. No, I am not really ready to engage in any more extracurricular activities, but I am sure that I will feel able to participate in the end-of-term celebrations. No, I do not need extra telephone time with my parents. I am happy to comply with the usual camp restrictions. Yes, I am writing to my parents. Yes, I have received letters from my friends. Yes, I am still taking the sleeping tablets occasionally. Yes, I am still taking the beta-blockers for my pounding, racing heart. Oh, a very low dose. Yes, the meditation is slowly giving me an alternative means of relaxation.

Given that I'm not actually speaking to her about us, I could give her the lowdown about some shit that is happening here at Camp Horrendous.

Like, let's see, Sibylla and Holly. These *friends* are intriguing. Holly is still riding high on Sibylla going out with Ben, and is getting very friendly with Ben and some of his friends along the way, whereas Sibylla doesn't even seem that interested or even aware of the whole camp sociograph.

She likes Ben. That is clear. How can I tell? Her reluctance to talk about him. Her dreamy distracted air much of the time. The way she tries unsuccessfully not to look at him in class. The occasional disappearances into the wilderness, after which she reemerges looking flushed and dazed. I know that look. It is hard for very fair-skinned people to hide certain emotions sweeping through the heart, or the tracks of hard-chinned stubble scraped across the face and neck.

But she doesn't seem at all interested in claiming Ben when they are in public. Nor does he show any need to do that. I'm guessing Sibylla's motivation may be an almost old-fashioned sense of modesty, but what can Ben's motivation be? He's not reluctant to show off about anything else. Of course, it's always within the well-worn path of good-guy self-deprecation.

He is not stupid, but he is carefully not alienatingly smart, either, at least in class.

I've never seen anyone who is such a natural leader, or more calculating, or better at hiding the calculation. If in doubt, all eyes go to Ben to read what the next move should be, and he, like a chess player, is always thinking a few moves ahead.

Whatever is happening, though, with Ben and Sibylla, it never appears to be quite enough for Holly, who keeps cracking the whip. She is like the girlfriend personal trainer. And she seems to have a whiteboard somewhere, because she is always reminding Sibylla of some critical date, event, preference, or anniversary.

The two-week anniversary caused some friction this morning. Sibylla forgot it.

Exactly fifteen days of my sentence have been served. Confession: I am becoming reluctantly intrigued by my fellow inmates.

35

Sitting with Ben is one hundred percent like sitting with someone famous. Everybody loves you, baby...

I've got scrambled eggs, a fresh batch, and some spinach that looked okay, but is now leaking green water and has lost its appeal. Ben has his first course—a massive bowl of oatmeal and stewed fruit. He'll go back for the full protein cook-up next. And if he's still hungry, he may have a couple more rounds of grainy toast and peanut butter. He'll take apples and hard-boiled eggs out with him, too. He's got to last all the way till Elevensies.

I'm not even pretending that we can have a conversation. Everything gets chopped up into little bits between stuff like, Dude, who's that New York rapper with that one that goes...Man, have you got someone to run with today?...Ben, run later?...'Sup...'Sup...When are you doing your solo?...'Sup...Man, Beeso's got weed, let me know...You hiking this weekend?...Want a run later?...Man, checked out that chart, you have done some serious running, do you even sleep?...

I try not to feel like the groupie girl who sits with the famous one.

I breathe him in. In the mornings he smells like soap. No stinky deodorant for Ben Capaldi. He told me his mother has banned it at their house. He wears a tea tree one, and I get a little hint of that. By the afternoon he smells like himself; I don't know what I'd call it—Essence of Ben? I'm wondering about smells that don't smell like anything else and how, really, you can describe them to someone who has never smelled them, because smell and taste descriptions rely so heavily on similar smell/taste comparisons (why is it, for instance, that absolute taste qualities like sour, sweet, salty feel so much more limited than absolute visual qualities such as angles, textures, colors? I could describe the appearance of a building more easily than the taste of a curry, for example, without having to resort to comparisons with other structures) when Holly slides along the bench and parks herself on the other side of Ben.

She's got her usual filling breakfast of fresh air and fresh fruit. At least she's picked up a tub of yogurt this morning. Her mother has systematically wrecked her ability to eat what her stomach wants. It's like she's put her stomach on permanent hold while she listens to anything but, and genuinely tries to feel "so full" after eating four strawberries.

"Happy anniversary, you two," she says.

"Thanks," says Ben.

I say, "Huh?"

A look and a smile flicks between them. "I told you," he says.

"I know, but I still don't believe it," she says.

"What?" I want to know.

"I bet Ben that you would remember your anniversary, and he bet me you wouldn't."

"Thanks for that," I say to Ben. *What* anniversary?

"I was right," he says.

Fair nuff.

I look at them. Two people who seem to know all they need to know. Why don't I know the stuff I'm supposed to know, e.g., apparently significant dates?

"Is it really two weeks since Laura's party?" I've figured what the anniversary must be, and I'm going for honest disbelief.

"To the day, or actually the day after," says Holly. "Seeing the kiss happened after midnight."

"So, like, super early Monday, soon after midnight, just two short weeks ago?" Here I'm trying for a sincere wish to sort this matter out.

"Yep," they say at the same time.

"Good. I'll remember for next time."

"What?" asks Holly, trying not to smile as I look blankly at her. "What date are you remembering?"

"The date of the day after Laura's party."

"Which is?"

Trick question. Hard to even remember the day of the week up here in the wilderness blur, let alone dates. "Well, it would be the—seventh?" I guess.

Another look between them—they're indulgent parents and I'm the cute but slow kid.

"Eighth, of October."

"Got it."

"Beeso's got weed, and they're camping at Snow Gum Flat if you want to come," says Holly, getting up to leave.

"I heard," says Ben, easy smile.

"You're coming?" Holly asks Ben.

"You're going?" I ask Holly.

"Maybe. How about you two?" But she puts the question to Ben, as though he'd be deciding for me, too, so I get in first.

"Not me. I want to spend some time in the studio."

"Dunno, but either way, I'm running." He gets up. "Need more fuel." His long-legged walk. His smooth walk. His smooth skin. His smooth manner.

"Anniversaries do mean something, you know," Holly says. "Don't ignore him."

"I'm not. But you could've given me a heads-up about the anniversary."

"I didn't want to butt in."

Since when? "Maybe I'm just not cut out for the girl-friend job." I tip my plate sideways. A green puddle pools in its curved edge. "Want some spinach juice?"

Holly looks exasperated and walks off. She always looks so neat and organized. I feel like a big tall conspicuous twist of loose ends.

Ben plonks himself back down. His plate has a mountain of eggs, about eight pieces of bacon, tomatoes, baked beans, two sausages, and two of the giant hash brown triangles.

"Sorry I forgot."

There is the smallest glimpse of coldness before the smile. "Forget it," he says. "Oh, right, you already did that." Maybe this is my cue to do some soothing, some smoothing, apologize some more, but I don't want to be that sort of girlfriend. And I privately think a two-week anniversary is dumb, and not very optimistic—aren't we even planning to make it to a month?

"What do I smell like?" I ask.

"Vanilla beans and peppermint," he says, not stopping to think. "Roses, when you wear that perfume." Vanilla must be a soap, deodorant, moisturizer amalgam; the peppermint is shampoo. "What about me?"

I blush to think how many times (in—can it really only be two weeks?) I've dwelled on this exact question. His smell is complicated, warm and rich, not like any other boy I've been within smelling range of. It's so good it frightens me; it's clearly some biological lure deviously inviting me to breed with him. Thank god people can't read minds. "I don't know. Boy oil? Hey, that's quite hard to say: boy oil. Listen, too fast, and you've got 'boioil.' It sounds exactly like a spring—boi-oi-oi-oil...boi-oi-oi-oi-oil."

He smiles again and gives me the look, the same look he gave as I turned away from him at Laura's party. I've decided it means something like, *you are not like the others.* Or it might simply be, *you are odd.*

I think he has suffered from too much adoration. It's very hard not to join the chorus, but I try to refrain.

"You do know, 'anniversary'—'anni'—that bit means year. It's from 'annus.' What's the point of us all doing Latin if we don't even use it?" I say.

Michael walks past us, concentrating on not letting his hard-boiled eggs roll off his plate. I nod in his direction: "There's a man who'd never use 'anniversary' to describe something that happened two weeks ago."

"There's a man who's not going out with you," Ben says.

In my smile, I can't hide how much I like him, so I let him see it for a second, swallow it, and head out. This is not the way to start a day of concentrating on work. This is the way to start a day of mooching around with Ben. But that ain't happening.

Back in the house, I circle the eighth of November on my calendar. And for good measure write: *first monthiversary.* Or should it be the fifth, which is four weeks to the day, rather than a calendar month? Better check with Holly.

36

In grade one, Holly dared me to take my undies off at school. She stood with our two mainstay friends at the time, Suzie Barton and Suzie Nguyen, and the three of them stared me down. "Told you," said Holly to the others. "You're a chicken," she said to me. She clucked like a chicken.

I knew the outsmart strategy: "I know you are, but what am I?" Before I could blink, she whipped off her Hello Kitty undies, swung them above her head, and whipped them back on, and they were all staring at me again. And all three of them were clucking at me. Suzie Barton was smiling. I knew she was relieved that it was me, not her, getting the Holly treatment, and I could half sympathize with her position even while I squirmed.

"Told you she wouldn't," Holly concluded. "Let's go look for a new friend, someone with guts."

"I've got guts," I said. I slipped my undies down to my knees and pulled them up again.

"That's not even off," said Holly. "That's cheating. You're a cheat. Now you've got to show your bottom as well."

How did she even think up those complex, escalating rules?

"Bottom" really threw me. I knew it was private. I was in charge of my bottom, nobody else could touch my bottom or tell me what to do with it. But I'd also put Holly in my Inner Circle of Trust when we drew our Stranger Danger diagrams just last week. So, were you allowed or not allowed to show a Circle of Trust person your own bottom? I could never remember that stuff.

"Come on," Holly was saying, ready to walk off. "She's a wimp." Keen to retain three friends if possible, I took off my undies, turned around, and lifted my dress quickly.

Holly smiled in triumph, running her own script of challenges, dares, rules, and judgments that I could never keep up with, let alone predict.

She ran into the playground, shouting, "Ms. Menzies, Ms. Menzies, Sibylla Quinn showed her bottom to us three girls behind the peppercorn tree."

And today, to help me in the public humiliation stakes, Holly is walking across the courtyard, swinging a pair of my knickers in the air. They must have fallen out of my laundry bag when I brought it back. These are large-ish undies. Huge, actually. Low of leg and high of waist. I like to wear big mama undies when I have my period, particularly at night, particularly up here, where you do not want to risk a leaking tampon and the special laundry walk of shame. So I use the pad-and-big-undies safety net. But really, it's a kind of private thing. Not something I want flapping around for everyone to see.

Holly has decided differently. She is doing burlesque va-va-voom as she swings them. And she has attracted the attention she was looking for. "What the hell are they?" asks—great—Billy Gardiner.

"Sibylla's full-brief, maximum-comfort, minimum-sizzle cottontails."

I make a grab for them with a lips-only smile. She holds them out of my reach for one last swing, and flips them gently on my head.

"Gee, you could fit a couple of friends into those easy riders," says Billy.

I give a merry trill, try to kill Holly with a death glare, and walk, bereft of dignity, up the steps to Bennett House, swearing to pay more attention to laundry retention in the future.

monday 22 october (late)

In Paris, there is a wide footbridge called the Passerelle des Arts. It spans the River Seine from the Institut de France on the Left Bank to the courtyard of the Musée du Louvre on the Right Bank.

Its wooden boards curve up gently in the middle and slope down again to deliver you to the other side. To keep you from falling in, there are wavy, crisscross wire panels stretched between old gray-green lampposts.

Like metal scales or petals, thousands of padlocks are fixed to those wire diamonds all over the bridge, love locks.

Each one a love story, a promise, a tribute, a memory...

I could only open my letter from France (yay!) once everyone was asleep.

Lou,

I put up a lock for each of us and F. I know you won't mind. I loved him, too. Don't need to tell you that.

I'm getting by, busy with school, struggling with French, and guessing you have plenty to distract you up there in the cold mountains, too, e.g., survival. Everyone knows boarding school is the last wild frontier. When they start daubing their faces with mud, run.

Here are a couple of photos of the lock. You can visit it one of these old days. See how tough it looks? It will outlast us all, Lou. I got it engraved by a little guy, a watchmaker, in the 5th—Henri took me there—who looked exactly like Rumpelstiltskin. I decided it had to be engraved; I didn't want any of that texta or nail polish crap that you can see on some of the other locks. Mine is right next to yours. They can keep each other company as the years click over.

I look at the photos. A medium-size very solid brass padlock, happily nestling in the midst of other locks of myriad variety. The engraving says *fredlovesmlouloves*; it's in lowercase with the letters forming a complete circle, no spaces, so a casual glance won't decode it. I like that a lot. It is private. It is perfect.

Dan's is right next to it. It says *my friend*; Fred's initials, *FBF*—Frederick Brymer Fitzpatrick; and a date—his birth date. His death date is tattooed along Dan's left

154

Achilles tendon. Not many people know that, particularly not Dan's mother. His friend Oliver talked him into waiting six months, and then took him someplace he knew two weeks before Dan left for Paris.

I've enclosed the key to your lock, Lou—I thought you might like to throw it from the top of some mountain, or drop it deep into a crevice or bottomless lake... or maybe just keep it.

I'm thinking of you lots. Estelle and Janie send love and they're writing soon. They came with me to the bridge and Janie took the photos because my hands were shaking too much. She pretended not to notice, and kindly just said I was a shit photographer and you deserve better. Write soon.

Love,

Dan

I hold the key, pressing it hard between the heels of my hands until it's blood temperature and has left two deep impressions. Don't want to let it go.

Thank you, Dan. My friend, too. Fellow keeper.

I look forward to sitting with him when he gets back and I am released. We will sit and not have to talk. Or we may talk. If we do, it won't be to reassure someone who doesn't feel as bad as we feel that everything is okay.

I can't remember exactly when Fred started calling me m'Lou, it was from the nursery rhyme. *Lou, Lou, skip to m'Lou...* I should have written stuff like that down.

Where was the infernal journal when I needed it?

38

Lunchtime with Mr. Popularity is not as easy to negotiate as you would think. I'm not a clingy type to start with. Sure—this fact has been strictly theoretical till now seeing as I haven't had a boyfriend not to be clingy with. I still feel shy about the whole going-out thing. Living up here this term makes it too public. So I'm not automatically going to be sitting with him. But Holly has no such scruples, no hesitation, and she seems to think that now we both automatically sit with Ben's group.

Ben can sit with anyone. He could sit on his own and people would gather as though around a messiah. But he wouldn't care if they didn't. It would never have occurred to him to have a moment's concern about being alone. It's as though he walks around inside a Ben force field that everyone would like to penetrate.

Holly is always getting annoyed with me about forgetting anniversaries and generally not being observant enough of the whole relationship thing. But even I have noticed that some of his friends are not crazy about me being inside the Ben perimeter.

All-access pass to the roped-off zone in Ben World. I've got it. They want it.

His group is large and multilobed. A mighty social network. I would bet my entire travel fund that Ben has never gone out to eat his lunch with the sinking feeling that he might have to walk a lap and then nonchalantly retreat to the library because his few friends are away from school or have sundry lunchtime commitments that he doesn't have. Sports. Drama. Debating. These seemingly innocuous things have often rendered me friendless for lunch. I was also rendered best-friendless once when Holly changed groups without notice, and let me know that it was a one-person group move and I couldn't come, too. But that was to Tiff Simpson's group in year eight, and it all ended in tears, and with Holly sitting back with me and our other second-social-rung cronies.

But now we're all hanging out together. Happy days.

Tiff, for example, will not hesitate to look up, smile, and move over if I approach. My new acceptance status is a Ben/billboard combination—the ratio is about fifty-fifty to the girls, and maybe seventy-thirty to the boys. Ben is their principal deity, after all. Only a month ago, I was invisible to Tiff, except as the recipient of an occasional puzzled *why would someone wear that in public?* look.

The first couple of times these people smiled, or moved over to let me in, I looked over my shoulder, because it couldn't be for *me*. And it's not for me. It's for some imaginary construction they have made of a new Sibylla Quinn, who isn't me at all. They're smiling at the girl on the billboard. Ben's girlfriend. Real me sits there to one side, watching skeptically, remembering all the mean exclusions and casual put-downs, and preening superiority this group represents to the average kid in our year. New me thinks, They're really quite nice when you get to know them. It's fun being on the inside, with them. Real me and new me can't both be right. Can we? Which interpretation survives if we merge and become one?

Holly acts as though it's the natural order emerging. But it's not. It's double bizarre land—some random social mutation caused in part by me having a particular godmother. And it could reverse out as quickly as it nosed in. Wonder why I don't exactly feel relaxed with these people?

It's also one reason I make a point of sitting with Michael some lunchtimes, forcing him to put his book down and play humans with me, although I am guiltily aware that I could do this more often. Not that a library skulk would occur to Michael, either, though he is frequently alone. He always, but always, has a book in whose company he is perfectly happy. And even though he is absolutely aware that his behavior is in the loser, loner, geek terrain, he could not care less. Which actually shifts his category. He is a loner, but no one so self-contained, and so clever, can ever really be a convincing loser.

On this day, this spring lunchtime with air as sharp as an unripe plum, we are drawn to the sun. We float into it like aimless motes, blinking our morning classes away. Attractive teen people sitting in dappled light on sturdy, rustic benches in our casual sporty uniform separates, various enough to allow us to feel like individuals, similar enough to provide—uniformity. A decent smattering of students from other countries: we are proudly multicultural. We look like a freaking public relations exercise for how wonderful this school is. And it is. And it isn't. Just like every other school is, and isn't exactly what it seems to be.

I walk past the gathering Ben fan club—it's three days after our anniversary, so I don't think I'm transgressing any rules of the going-out universe—over to where Michael has found a sunny spot in which to devour his selection of food that looks like itself. Like Ben, and Eliza, too, he puts away a huge amount of fuel. Runners. His lunch is a quarter of a roast chicken. Two hard-boiled eggs. Two whole-grain rolls. An apple. A tangelo. A large bowl of salad. Two pieces of fruitcake. It barely fits on his tray. I've made myself a chicken and salad roll with two types of chutney, and also have an apple and a piece of chocolate cake. A wasp with designs on my chutney is buzzing lazy circles around us.

As I walk past the mob, someone says, "Man, yo' ho—where's she going?" Ben smiles his lazy smile and gives me the backward nod. Even though it's still hard to believe, I know that I could go over and the Red Sea would part and let me into a spot by his side, but I'm already heading Michael's way and not about to detour.

Lou arrives at the same time as me. "Why do they think it's okay to say 'ho' like that?"

Ben smiled? Did he hear *yo*? Did he hear *ho*? He's okay with me—or anyone—being spoken about like that?

I poke all the ingredients inside my roll so I can close it up properly for a bite. "I don't know. Blame rap." I'm trying to make light of it, but I'm annoyed because I hate that whole pimp/ho thing. Particularly when it comes from the mouths of little middle-class white boys.

"No context," says Lou. "Why do they think they can use language like that?"

Michael looks at me. "Why didn't you say something?"

And why didn't Ben say something? "Is it really worth it?" I pick up lettuce and shredded carrot bits migrating from my roll to my lap and transfer them into my mouth, feigning indifference.

Lou sighs. "Trouble is, if you say nothing, you're really saying you're okay with it."

"True," says Michael.

"I've spent years saying stuff. Nothing changes."

"But maybe it would have been even more severely unchanged—if you hadn't said anything," says Lou.

Michael smiles. He likes Lou. I can't remember the last time he added anyone to his "like" list.

Holly comes over with a bustle of importance. "Did you guys fight?"

"Me and Ben?"

"Duh."

"No."

"So what are you doing here?" she asks.

"Eating my lunch."

She looks at Michael and Lou, as though she can't quite figure out what I'm saying. "Well, you missed out on working with Ben on the *Othello* assignment. He said he'll go with me and Tiff."

"I wouldn't want to anyway." But I'm feeling a small gut punch that he didn't try to persuade me, or even ask me.

"Work with us," says Lou.

Michael nods. "We can have three."

"You're not pissed off because I'm partners with Ben, are you?" says Holly.

"It's not 'partnering' if there are three of you," says Lou.

" 'Partner' implies two people," says Michael at exactly the same time. Pedantry compatibility. Not that either of them looks interested to note it.

"Jeez, okay—so long as we're all happy," says Holly, giving me the *your weird friend* look.

So now I feel triply left out. Boyfriend, best friend,

oldest friend are all paired up for an assignment and not one of them asked me first.

I'm shoved off-balance by a rogue wave of homesickness. It is such a petty grievance, the sort of item I would only ever share with my mother in a private after-school whinge session, during which she wouldn't judge me, after which she'd give me a hug and a cup of tea and I'd feel as better as I did when I was little. Or if she wasn't home, I'd have a comfortable sook into my own pillows, a sulky burrow into my own duvet. I'm so sick of acting like every little annoying thing up here is just fine. There's no end of the day to unpack all the shit. The day goes into the night goes into the day. Over and over, and I'm so over it. I'm overstuffed with trivial irritations that build in the absence of home, my decompression zone. Maybe that's why everyone is running through the mountains like maniacs. Getting stuff off chests. Maybe I should run more? Even considering that is a worrying sign.

39

tuesday 23 october

I told someone.

I told Michael.

I was in the cave, and he came to find me. He said, Knock, knock—ha-ha, no door. He said, I was wondering if you'd like to talk about jealousy, manipulation, betrayal, and murder? For our *Othello* class paper.

I said, As luck would have it, jealousy, manipulation, betrayal, and murder happen to be my favorite topics of conversation. Come on in.

My cave is warm and dry, as all good caves should be, but many are not, with plenty of room for visitors.

He said, I love what you've done with the place.

The Lost Estate was sitting next to me, and he saw it. He said, I really enjoyed this. Are you enjoying it?

I've read about half and said, Yes, a friend recommended it, and I like it very much.

The bookmark you made was visible in the book, and he said, shyly, because he is not at all intrusive, This friend?

I nodded. He looked at us in the photos, and he looked at me.

He said, I wondered where this part of you was. I thought it must be in there somewhere. He gave the wry/apologetic smile that shows he's used to people thinking that whatever he says is often the wrong thing to say.

However I looked, his next question was, This person, he's not around anymore?

I shook my head. I couldn't talk. But my eyes were full. Full of you being gone. Full of tears. Full of the still impossibility of saying the words. And my mouth did the uncontrolled wobble that is trying not to cry.

He said, Oh, Louisa. I am sorry. I'm so sorry.

And he did not flinch, Fred. He could take it. He picked up my hand, and he held it between his warm hands. And sat there with me, holding my hand and my hurt. I could feel the sympathy transfusing, and I was thirsty for it. I hadn't realized how much I needed to let someone in.

40

Not even three weeks in, less than a third of the term gone, and we're getting up each other's noses to the point of brain injury.

Annie and Eliza are in a state of escalating open war about killing versus not killing bugs and spiders. Annie has decided we should all be vegetarians, lectures us about all the horrible aspects of meat-eating, and insists on rescuing every insect or spider that finds its way inside. Eliza is a savage bug-killer and an unapologetic meat-eater.

Though she defends and saves ants, Annie has decided that one might crawl into her ear and eat its way into her brain. She can't be persuaded that there's no connection between her ear canal and her brain.

In classic Annie fashion, even when confronted with

diagrammatic proof, she said, "Haven't any of you losers watched *Home Renovation*? Walls can be knocked down. Or chewed through."

Our menstrual cycles are slowly converging. Six starting-to-overlap waves of PMS is a lot to deal with under one roof. God help us all when we've got PMS at the same time. We'll have a genre leap from "coming of age" to "schlock horror." Hide the knives. I can see the crime-scene tape now.

We are all over Pippa doing nothing around the house. Being sweet doesn't cut it when you've left the cutting board out for the thousandth time for someone else to rinse, wipe, and put away. Or when your contribution to any rostered work always sits in the range of zero, token, and decorative.

And someone still smells. It's a constant low-grade waft of body odor. Hard to pinpoint because we all come in reeking and soaking and muddy after various hiking, camping, running activities. But whose smell is lingering? Or is someone stashing dirty laundry? At our last house meeting, Holly burst out at the end of a list that included pull your own hair out of the shower drains, close the screen door, don't leave used tissues and cotton balls around, wipe up your own kitchen mess, and WHOEVER STINKS, CAN YOU PLEASE TAKE A SHOWER AND USE DEODORANT! So, whoever it is, she must have the message after that.

But of all the simmering animosity in the house, the

real hot spot is Holly's growing annoyance with Lou. She hates it when people are impervious to her withholding of approval. She likes them to squirm. And she doesn't like it when people are so private that there's nothing to talk about behind their backs.

She was needling Lou a few days ago and ended up, after getting either silence or one-word responses, saying, "Oh, I get it, you're a zombie."

To which Lou responded in a monotone, "I am, indeed, a zombie. You are insightful and perceptive." That got a laugh from Pippa, which made Holly snarkier.

Holly jumped up and sat down next to Lou at the table. It was deliberately aggressive, right in her grill. "What's this shit?" Holly had picked up one of the fat Blu Tack caterpillars Lou is always fiddling with.

"It's Blu Tack."

"What's it for?"

"It's for a project I'm working on."

"What project?"

"Project Gee, It's None of Your Business." Lou made an effort to keep reading. Holly stayed sitting right next to her.

Lou stopped reading, put her bookmark in, and said, "*What?*"

Holly grabbed the end of Lou's bookmark and pulled it out of the book. "Oh, dear. You've lost your place."

Lou stared at her with a completely blank expression. Holly smiled at her, and flipped through the book. "What have we got here? *The Lost Estate*. It looks like crap."

"Well, it's fantastic. But I don't think you'd like it," said Lou.

Holly stood up, still holding the bookmark. Lou went to grab it back, and Holly sensed a pressure point. She jumped up and danced out of Lou's range. Lou's face was red.

I told her to give it back, but Holly was not about to turn away from the only chink we'd ever seen in Lou's armor. She looked at the bookmark for a long time.

"Well, isn't that sweet?" she said, holding it up so Pippa and I could both see it—a laminated photo-booth strip.

"Cute pics," said Pippa. "Is that your boyfriend?"

"It was," said Lou, not taking her eyes off Holly.

"Aw, what happened? Did he dump you?" Holly pretended to look again, more carefully. "But he's such an ugly gimp, maybe you dumped him."

Lou stared at her, not saying a word.

"What's the story, Lou-Lou? Love gone wrong? But how'd that happen when your glasses and your zits look so damn compatible?"

"No story. Just give it back," said Lou.

"Give it back," said Pippa.

I walked over and took the bookmark from Holly, glancing at it as I handed it back to Lou. I was shocked. Here was a different Lou: someone I'd never seen, eyes full of happiness. The guy looks just like her, and just as happy. Both of them have long dark bangs and geek-chic thick frames, and yes, some pimples. But who cares, when you're making each other laugh like demented drains in a photo-booth?

"He looks nice," I said.

"Are you seeing him on exeat weekend?" Holly asked. "Maybe you can patch things up."

Lou looked at Holly for a few seconds. "You can't possibly think I'm interested in talking to you." She picked up her book and left.

Up till then, I'd just thought Lou was a low-key girl. A private girl. But seeing the way she looked in the photos, compared to how she looks now, makes me think there is a story there. Something has gone way wrong. She sleeps just a couple of feet away from me every night. She could be hemorrhaging from heartbreak. She might be crying silently into her pillow every night. And I don't know a thing about it.

41

I should have known that the minute she heard about Bee-so's "party" at Snow Gum Flat on the river, Holly would find a way to go and make me come, too.

In order to go, we'd have to pretend we were having a legit two-day hike, and talk someone else into making up a three.

The whole idea made me want to puke. Hippy heaven with the jocks? Give me a break—worlds colliding, and not in a good way, but resistance was pointless.

Holly's response to all my objections was: "Well, I'm going anyway."

I gave up. "Fine. Just remember: Don't drink if you're smoking, because it makes you vomit. And stay away from fast streams and cliff edges."

"Why do you have to be so smug?" Holly burst out.

"I'm not. It's good advice. Those guys are tools. You've seen them at parties. What other girls are going?"

"Tiff and Laura and some others."

"And you're really still chasing Tiff?"

"Don't be a bitch."

"I'm trying to keep you out of trouble. Snow Gum Flat is only a few hours' walk away. It's within teacher prowling range."

"Well, I'm going anyway. And Ben's coming," Holly said.

"No, he's not." I hoped.

"Well, maybe you don't have the most up-to-date information about that."

The force of her determination is overwhelming. She will do anything, say anything, to make me do what she wants to do. It is honestly as though she hears *maybe* or *try harder* when I say *no*.

When I was little, Mum used to give me workshop practice in saying no. Concrete examples of what Holly might suggest, and how I might refuse diplomatically.

Holly is such a wanter. It mostly means more to her that we do something than it means to me not to do it.

Which probably makes me a wimpy invertebrate. But I honestly don't care sometimes. I am genuinely easy. Easygoing. Don't mind one way or the other. A pushover.

In this case, I just got tired and gave up. And I figure that it will count as one of our compulsory overnight hikes, providing we don't get caught, so I get to cross a hike off my list without actually having to hike far. A free pass. That's how I'm rationalizing caving in, anyway.

We get permission for our hike and drag Eliza along. She's perfectly happy to get a hike credit, ignore the party shenanigans, and get some extra time for running training.

42

wednesday 24 october

So Michael told me something.

I like the way he works. No *getting to know you*, no graded intimacy or social niceties, no worry about, Does she like me? Are we friends now? More like: 1. trust, 2. full disclosure.

He loves Sibylla. Not in a teen crush way. He loves her in a soul mate/destiny way. She just hasn't cottoned on to the destiny thing yet. That is how he sees it, anyway.

Sibylla does not love Michael. She likes him. She gets him. She even values him, but she doesn't love him. I think he is heading for pain, but he takes the long view. He believes that they will be together one day. He cannot imagine a world in which that won't eventually happen. It is appealing that Mr. Implacable Logic has a blind spot.

He is so lovely. He's not jealous that Sibylla is with Ben. He's worried. Because he doesn't think Ben is sufficient in any way for Sibylla. Not good enough.

Sibylla is besotted with Ben. She also gets him. And that makes her cautious. Caution means she is holding something back. And Ben still finds that intriguing, but there are so many girls here who would hold nothing back that I wonder how long intriguing will hold up.

Michael has known Sibylla since the kindergarten era. He invented Sibylla tablets around this time. One (shiny, magical) strand of Sibylla's hair, twisted and rolled until it is a tiny little nuggety ball, swallowed when one is feeling anxious or unhappy. Will alleviate said feeling.

Crazy, hey? But it worked. He says it has given him complete faith in the placebo effect.

He is worried now because he's aware that he is becoming overly preoccupied with Sibylla. He's been there before.

How lucky is he that I am his new friend? I told him to write it all out in a letter to Sibylla: the letter you never send. All that therapy, ready to be regurgitated at will. I have a catalogue of strategies as long as my arm, longer than my patience.

He's going to give it a shot. His only worry is will one letter suffice? He thinks it might require a few volumes.

43

Holly and Eliza and I arrive a bit later than everyone else, because Holly forgot to bag some grass clippings for Grounds, so we got slammed with Sevens as punishment, an extra house weeding job.

I wish I'd trusted my instincts. I look around. It's the crème de la crème of my least favorite people. Except for Ben, who I can't see.

And they're all in party mode. Holly is immediately on the prowl for weed so she can catch up. Eliza is getting into her running skins and shoes the minute we arrive, itching to dash off.

Unfortunately, Ben "my body is a temple" appears to be as much out of it as everyone else. He lifts a languid arm as

I approach, but I don't really feel like joining the girl queue surrounding him.

The *flat* in Snow Gum Flat refers to the grassy area next to the river.

I decide to play mother and pitch our tent. Holly and I are in a two-person tent, and Eliza has brought a one-person tent, because she will be spending the whole time sprinting around like a maniac. Like me, she won't do any drugs, and she'll be in bed early and up early. She is so self-sufficient. I asked her this morning while we were yanking out weeds if there is any boy she likes. She said, "Boys are idiots. I'm going to wait till they turn into men, and have another look then."

The river here is a swimming hole, quiet and dark. Mountains slip their shadows deep into the water. Farther downstream, the water spreads out over rocks, shallow, loud, and racy. Old gum trees crowd the edge. Maybe, just maybe, at the height of summer, on the tenth consecutive heat-wave day, you'd be tempted to swim. The water temperature would still be melted ice cube.

Smooth pebbles every shade of gray, from nearly white to nearly black, and pink and yellow run their muted rainbow down to the water. When the rock grinds into coarse clean riverbed sand, it is the color of brown sugar. Standing at the edge, looking down, it's hard to see exactly where the water begins.

About sixty feet farther along the river's edge, there's a bloody mess sending swiveling threads of red into the water. A small pile of trout guts someone couldn't be bothered to clean up.

I get my trowel and start digging. I can't see anyone else here bothering, and the job isn't going to smell any better in the morning.

Holly comes over with the smallest joint I've ever seen, acting like she's stoned and offering me a spitty end—which I don't take.

"Can't you ever take a day off from goody land?" she asks, but doesn't really want to know.

"Just think of me as the designated driver."

"Why aren't you over there?" she asks, nodding in the direction of the boyfriend.

"He seems to be occupied." I really don't like the way Laura and Georgie are reclining on Ben, but it is his body.

"You need to hustle yo' bustle, hun."

"That doesn't even mean anything," I say. "Don't just copy them all the time."

"Jeez, kidding."

I start a new installment of my ongoing rap language rave—how I hate the sexist language, the sexist clips, how I think Lupe had it half right with "Bitch Bad."

But Holly has glazed over. She wonders why I care and is looking much more interested in Ben's friends Vincent and Hugo, who have wandered within range, just as I am realizing I'm going to have to move farther away from the water. The pebbles are just sliding back when I dig them.

"What's this? Not Sibylla, the *model*, complaining about

sexism?" says Hugo. They are barking with laughter. It's not taking much to amuse them in their current state. They're wearing headbands they've made from blue-checked kitchen towels. For a nanosecond, I'm actually impressed they even know what sexism is.

"But—trrrragedy has struck," says Vincent, looking at the fish guts. "Her brain has dropped out of her ear hole."

More barking. But maybe I've got traction with guys like this these strange days, and I decide to use it, instead of pretending to be a good sport and let them say any dumb thing they find amusing while I give what I hope is an ironic, or noncommittal, smile.

"Being gross doesn't make you funny."

"And being on a billboard doesn't make you pretty," Vincent says.

I catch the briefest flash of triumph in Holly's eyes.

"Yeee-owzer," snorts Hugo. I guess he wonders if the blow was too savage.

"You *know* the one thing I can't tolerate is being told I'm not funny," says Vincent in defense of the meanness that has made me go red. So much for traction.

Holly opts for popularity-longing over friend-solidarity. "Lighten up, Sib."

She heads back after the boys, and it's just me and the fish guts.

There's a much bigger fire going than we're supposed to have. Our objective up here is "small footprint." These guys interpret that very loosely, i.e., for "small," read "yeti." It worries me. Why me, but no one else? Holly's right: I am a goody-goody. I should lighten up.

Kevin Trung is here. His dad is a famous TV chef, and Kevin actually knows how to cook. There's a small amount of cooking we can do in the houses, and every boy in our grade was hoping he'd get Kevin. He's got a coal pit organized and is doing good things with the trout fillets. I smell lemongrass and ginger.

After dinner, everyone is in a circle around the fire. People start calling out their numbers, a ripped safety drill accompanied by spurts of helpless laughter.

I want to go to bed. I was hoping there might be some alone time with Ben, but he's still surrounded, stoned, and showing no sign of trying to escape. I'm cold, and either he picks up that signal or, more likely, he's getting up anyway and sees me hugging my knees. He unwinds his scarf and wraps it around my neck, to a chorus of *awwww*s from the people nearby who notice.

Music blasts into the night, fracturing the lassitude. I've got so mean about carrying anything extra in my backpack over the last couple of weeks I can't believe that someone bothered to bring iPod speakers. Everyone is up on their feet. It feels primitive dancing next to the fire. The moon is close to full, the fire bright, and in the freeze and burn, I'm soon as uncut as the next person, despite being sober. We warm to hot in a frieze of twisting shadows, and people start throwing off layers of clothes as the beat goes on and the dancing builds an intense life of its own. I shut my eyes, reckless and happy.

We dance till we drop, and Ben pulls me down so we're lying together, right next to the fire. I sit up again and see we are somehow in the middle of a make-out cluster, so I lie back down again. Why not?

The black sky is sprayed bright with stars, an abundance we never see through the city's competing light. We kiss till it gets unseemly—there's no Ben and no me, just a breathless tangle of wanting. And we have to stop, or go somewhere private. We haven't exactly had this conversation yet.

The fireside crowd has thinned, and I didn't even notice. Someone has put on parent music, "Helpless" by Crosby, Stills, Nash & Young, and it pulls me inside out. I have tears in my eyes, and I'm not sure if they're happy or sad or if I'm just overflowing.

"Hey, check it out, you can see the frying pan," says Ben softly, eyes to the heavens.

"You mean the saucepan?"

"No, frying pan—and look, there's the electric kettle." I stare up until the stars start showing me their secret pictures.

"There's a unicorn with three legs," I say.

Ben follows my eye line and tries to see what I see. "Yes—either a unicorn or—a giant *B*."

"A letter *B*? As in *B* for *barramundi*?" I do see some looping script like waves forming a kind of *B*.

"*Bee*, like *bzzz, bzzz, bzzz*—with a stinger." He bites my arm.

"Ow!" I laugh weakly, and I'm cold again, out of his arms, and shivery with wanting. "Bed," I say, regret and desire and tiredness combining to make me feel like crying properly. Why can't we be somewhere warm and alone?

He rolls back on his side, up on his elbow, and gives me a mock sleazeball, "Your place or mine?"

"Good night."

He tries to hold my hand, but I pull away. The other me drags Ben to my tent and tells Holly to Keep Out. That's the me who doesn't think about consequences like pregnancy, i.e., the anti-me.

Actual me remembers the hideous sex ed person who came to school last year to tell us how satisfying "outercourse" could be, and knows that is about as far as I want to take things for now. I wonder how many people jump straight to "inter," purely because you can just do it, no matter how inexpertly, whereas "outer" must involve some potentially embarrassing conversations, explanations, demonstrations, and maybe a pointer, or flow charts.

"Are you okay? You look like something hurts."

"Just—remembering something—sad." It was kind of sad how that one sex educator potentially put a whole grade off the idea just by using the word *outercourse*.

Imagine if I'd answered, "Just remembering the whole 'outercourse' scenario—sounded like fun, don't you think?"

That word! Who would ever be able to say it out loud? Outerloud.

Holly chooses now to come over with a major need for food and a bag of marshmallows from somewhere. I thought they were all eaten long ago. "You going to bed, Sibbie?" she slurs. "Bad luck, but all the more for me and Benjo."

It's half awkward—I've got no reason to change my tiredness or my plan for bed, so I leave them trying to find a long enough stick for toasting their marshmallows.

I look around—some people have dragged their sleeping bags to the side of the fire. Others have disappeared into tents, their own or others'.

It's a miracle with all the dancing and jumping and staggering and laughing that someone hasn't fallen in. I get a stab of anxiety imagining that happening, the pain, the seared, blistering skin, the screaming, the panic, and how hard it would be to get airlifted out of here, or to try to carry someone out through the dark tunnel of the night.

I must look worried, because when Kevin meets my eye, he smiles. "It's okay—I'll be fire warden. I'm not even tired."

So I walk away, climb into the tent, too cold to get undressed. I'm a babushka—thermals, outers, sleeping bag, tent. I am hammered by the tiredness that comes after so much fresh cold air, after a long walk with a heavy pack, after dancing, after desire that builds and builds and has nowhere to go. I get off quickly—the relief of being alone—with a few hungry pushes into my knowing fingers, and hear the voices of dreams pulling me down as I come. I'm asleep before I even register having settled into my bag.

44

wednesday 24 october (night)

A Slumber Did My Spirit Seal
William Wordsworth

A slumber did my spirit seal;
I had no human fears:
She seemed a thing that could not feel
The touch of earthly years.

No motion has she now, no force;
She neither hears nor sees;
Rolled round in earth's diurnal course,
With rocks, and stones, and trees.

Well, wrong gender pronoun, but the last stanza packs its punch. The cyclic certainty of it grinds over me like a wheel. Dear Fred.

Upsetting letter from Dan today. He is getting to know his French family. And he really likes them. He told Henri about you, and Henri's little brother was listening, which they didn't realize, and so he found out, too. And it caused big trouble because Claude is only eight. He was so upset that Dan's friend (you) had died. He thought only old people could die. So there was this big thing in their house about how it is so unusual, and it doesn't happen very often... You can imagine: basically a whole lot of comforting half-lies to make the poor little guy feel okay about the order of the universe again.

And when I read the letter, thank the god I don't believe in, I was in my cave. I cried like a tap, Fred. Because I realized I'd thought only old people could die, too.

Somewhere deep inside my stupid heart, that's exactly what I'd thought.

45

The tent is empty when I wake up, Holly's sleeping bag gone. I'm hot, sweaty, sticky. I'd love a shower; just one of the many awful aspects of hiking is roughing it. Unwinding Ben's scarf from around my neck, I sit up and reach for my boots.

I walk far enough away from camp for a private wee, and go to the water's edge for a wash using the smallest amount of soap possible—we've been drilled to death about trying to minimize polluting the perfect water. It's refreshing to a painful degree, and I'm hyper-awake when I get back to the tent, dig cereal out of my pack, and head for the fire to see if I can scrounge some milk.

Hiding my surprise should put me in line for an acting award when I see Holly and Ben, side by side, asleep by the edge of the still-glowing fire. The blond streaks and the dark curls are touching.

"With friends like her...am I right?" says Hugo, gleeful, as he sees me.

I take his milk, add it to my cereal calmly, hand it back, and stroll toward the sleeping bags, giving Holly a nudge with the toe of my boot to wake her.

"Oh," she says. "Whoa!" She jumps up as if something has bitten her. "This is not what it looks like."

"What does it look like?" I ask.

"We were just talking. We must have fallen asleep."

"That's what it looks like." I'm eating my cereal slowly, trying not to bite the spoon in half. I refuse to get jealous: Holly is just being Holly. "You were very quiet when you came and got your bag. Thanks for not waking me."

Ben groans and turns, wakes, and smiles. He has none of Holly's discomfiture. He is Ben. The prince of entitlement. "Hey, Sibs," he says. "Got some cereal for me?"

"No," I say, carefully not annoyed. I sit down near him, but not near enough for him to grab my cereal.

"I'll get us both some," Holly says. "My head hurts. Did someone give me alcohol?"

"Me," says Vincent, helping her stand up.

"You are evil," she says happily.

Holly only wants this—popularity, with the smallest of bad edges. I could do a diagram of it: daisy-shaped bad girl: enough risks so she's "fun," but not so many that she ever gets called a slut.

We spend the morning dozing, eating, fabricating our hiking notebooks, and planning our staggered reemergence at school. Different times and different directions, so no one will guess that one mixed-gender group of eighteen spent a "weekend" lounging around three hours from school, resting and partying, when six single-gender groups of three were supposed to be conquering new terrains and hiking many miles.

It wasn't worth the stress. And it has left me feeling grumpy, for no real reason, with Holly and with Ben. But, uncharacteristically, Holly has exerted herself and packed up the tent when I get back from a wander downriver with the—yes—still-beautiful boy.

Eliza has had a ball—she's found (another) perfect running course and plans on coming back here soon. She's happy prattling on about twitch fibers and the differing requirements within her training regime for building speed, endurance, and muscle, and how much and what sort of protein she needs to consume before and after exercise. Holly joins in every so often, offering bizarre "facts" from the world of the Gorgon's eating rules book, which includes weird stuff like no carbs after 7 PM, and sundry other tasty and calorie-free tidbits that she's picked up from various celebrity diets.

They are walking a bit ahead; I am half listening and wondering about the hows and whys of being friends with Holly. Since we were first friends, it was understood that she was the more important one. She called the shots, and I went along. I had to put her first, but she could put me second. I had to be available, and ready to be dropped if a better offer came along. I could be, and often was, in trouble with her over various things entirely based on her whims. I, on the other hand, did not have automatic rights to be cross with her. Although even Holly understood that I would occasionally reach a breaking point resulting from active abuse or neglect, and crack. Then she had the option of soothing me and assuring me we were best friends, and I would sooner or later accept the assurances.

I was always vaguely aware that the power balance sat crookedly. But Holly and I were okay with it.

Should I worry that the passive role has never really bugged me? Is it too weird that I don't really mind being pushed away and wooed back from time to time?

I do get it—that I was, maybe still am, mildly masochistic in this relationship. But it's been this way for so long. And I know Holly's fears and disappointments as well as I know her apparent confidence and arrogance. It might not be a perfectly stable structure, but it has its own center of gravity.

I'm the weak one. But I'm also the smarter one. That's okay by Holly, because "smart" is not high on her list of desirable attributes, so I can have it. This has made a difference, too. It is as though being played is okay, so long as you are aware that it's happening.

She is the pretty one. It's understood between the two of

us that she is still the pretty one, even after the billboard. And she still tells me what looks good on me, or doesn't, or how I should wear my hair—all that stuff—and expects me to recognize her authority.

Only, in this odd time of celebrity, I have some glamourglow that I can see people enjoy being around. It's not that they like me any better, just that it is such a desirable coin for no good reason—I'm friends with the model on that billboard, see that girl up there? She's my friend, she goes out with my mate, she's at my school, we hang out. And Holly is okay and not okay with this. She likes being in the benefit rub-off zone. But she doesn't like threats to her automatic superiority.

She is used to having the last word on our relative merits. But now other people have an opinion, and it's not necessarily hers. I'm going to have to look after her. She will need some extra bolstering. Worth doing, because it's when she feels insecure that she lashes out.

So, sure, we have the seesaw *ker-thunk, ker-thunk,* but the moments of equilibrium are fun. She makes me laugh like no one else I know. And she's hauled me over a gazillion social hurdles. Anyway, who says friendship is always logical?

46

friday 26 october

Can't quite tell what's going on.

Things are a leetle tense in Bennett House.

If you can believe it, Holly seems to be pressuring Sibylla to have sex. With Ben. Sibylla started out by being her usual (in my humble opinion, but I'm right) too passive, too good-humored self. But Holly is really persevering with this. Once again, is it any of her business? Once again, no. When is Sibylla going to grow a backbone? It's getting harder and harder for me to remain silent. And why can't Holly get one of these lovely lads on board, and have sex with her very own boyfriend?

Or is she starting to think Ben is her very own, by proxy?

Little hitch, Ben actually likes Sibylla. In his own special, emotionally deficient, unavailable way, he likes her.

He is pretty much a sociopath, I've decided. Or a something-path. Psychopath, maybe. You could definitely see him as a CEO or a prime minister, any job that requires a truly bloodless heart.

I talked it over with Michael, who knows about Ben's home life, and it fits the picture. Ben's father is some major global advertising guru; it's all about the outer appearance. His mum has had health problems, in and out of hospital for depression on a semi-regular basis since Ben was little. He has two younger sibs who think he's a god, basically, so there is pressure from another quarter to be godlike.

And he's living the god life. It's all under control.

The Sibylla attraction: my guess is that she appears to be the very opposite of someone who might slip into the depression zone. She has a profound sense of self-containment.

She is far from confident; far, even, from particularly knowing just who she is, but there is a real aura about her of safety, or comfort, or security, or home. I can't quite name it, but I see it, too.

Michael knows it like a drug.

I'm not convinced that Ben will be true to that safe place; there are so many other places he is being pulled, and he doesn't mind the look of any of them.

If Holly is feeling possessive about Ben by proxy, is she planning to convert the proxy to actual? Surely not up here, with all eyes upon her. And what would make her think she'd be the next name on Ben's list, or even that there is a list?

Groan. Merill time. Again. Unexpected, but I realize I am actually being taken from a state of near contentment. Here, the bed, the ceiling with its faint outline of stick-on stars that were peeled off at the end of last term. Here, the window, the eucalypts, the sky a clear blue, immeasurably deep. Check my locked box (locked), not risking Holly's prying little fingers on my letters.

(later)
 Hello, Lou.
 Hello, Merill.
 Eyes to the side.
 So how have you been feeling since our last encounter—*encounter* said with a subdued but warm twinkle.
 Pretty well.
 Anything you'd like to talk about—feelings/thoughts/incidents...A thoughtful pause. Just in case I have a second-thoughts blurt.
 No, nothing in particular.
 Accepting nod. She's not pushy.
 How is your management of the negative thoughts going?
 Say: they seem to be pretty much under control, I mean of course, from time to time...
 Merill nods, accepting, encouraging.

Don't say: I still think of the moment frequently: impact, shock, pain. I think of the beautiful brain being smashed too hard against the beautiful skull. I think of the mouth and no more smart words, loving words, living words, funny words, no more kisses, soft or hard. No more. Nevermore. Ever. How can that be so?

And what about activities? Are you feeling more engaged?

Say: yes, a little bit at a time, I do feel that this, the present, the new school experience is becoming my focus.

Don't say: my self, that which defines me, the heart of me, is looking at my watch, standing in a street, sitting in a hospital, holding my friends, choking on the salt of tears that stream from me (my friends, who aren't even in this country, waiting on their every letter, thought) and here, this is nothing to me. Nothing. But before, on the bed, looking at the gum tree. There was a moment, a brief moment, when I allowed this world to exist.

And friends, are you getting to know some of the girls in Bennett?

Say: we're all getting to know each other a bit better each week.

Don't say: Sibylla fine, Holly bitch, Eliza useful, Annie stupid, Pippa innocuous.

Now your academic work is going extremely well, I can see there are no problems there, conspiratorial smile.

Say: I am enjoying it, still getting used to my new teachers, but advanced math is fine.

Don't say: it's my Novocain; I'm going through the motions like a zombie. Actually I do like one of my fellow nutcases in advanced math. I like Michael.

Anything you want to share?

Do: close eyes, look thoughtful, in manner of one investigating soul, in all its minor crevices, where the little bits of self-hate and grief get stuck if you don't floss often enough.

Don't: stand up, slap her face, walk out.

Say: I still miss him. (Jeez, you've got to throw her a bone sometimes.)

Don't say: The chasm is endless, or I'm still on that slow spin in the void, or I don't want to come out, and certainly not: I don't deserve to come out.

That's understandable, and you'll probably always miss him, but (with a small brave smile, why is she playing brave?) it will diminish over time. Not Fred's importance to you as a friend, but the prominence in your daily thoughts that his memory might take up.

Say: nothing. A quiet nod should suffice.

Don't say: let me out of here before I strangle you for the crime of irrelevance to my life, and the second crime of daring to say his name, and the third crime of referring to him as my friend.

A pause. Keep looking down. Don't let her see your eyes glowing red.

Lou, tell me how you feel about this, and I will quite understand if you prefer us to keep meeting twice a week, but I believe you're making very good progress, you have great insight into where you're at, and we could reduce our sessions to just once a week. But only if you're comfortable with it...

Say: I think I could manage with one session a week. Very small smile. Keep it small. Small.

Don't say: halle-fucken-lujah or tap-dance to the door.

47

Mr. Oxley is yelling so we can hear him over the water. Who knew water could be this loud? The outdoor experience never disappoints in delivering ghastly new phenomena. They've driven eight of us, and four canoes, to the very loud water.

"Can't you at least give the poor guy a blow job," Holly is yelling in my ear.

"I'm not going to start my first sexual relationship here," I say.

"Will you tune in? I'm not talking about sex—I'm saying a blow job—" She's yelling so loud that Mr. Oxley stops.

"Would you like to share your comments, Holly, as you consider them to be more important than the potentially lifesaving information I am giving you?" Mr. Oxley is a creep, and probably would like nothing better than to hear the real conversation. Holly stares him down, but leaves me to dig us out.

"She was just reminding me of the blowhole at a beach we once visited," I say, frowning at Holly. "It was very loud. Like this."

The crashing water is making me as cranky as the inappropriateness of Holly telling me to blow my boyfriend. I'd like to find the off switch for both of them.

"Anyway, a blow job *is* sex—ask Bill Clinton," I shout, when Oxley is back droning on about canoes.

"Bill who?"

"You really need to do politics," I say.

"So I can bore everyone to death like you do? No thanks."

That's harsh. I was telling the Ben brigade yesterday about why I thought the current Greens campaign was right in its intention but wrong in its strategy. God, there were a few glazed expressions now that I think of it. But not Ben's. I'm pretty sure...

"Tiff gives you two more weeks if you keep banging on about stuff like that without banging him," Holly says with a smirk.

"Since when are you and Tiff discussing my relationship?"

"*My* relationship? It's his, too. And you wouldn't even have it if I hadn't practically forced you together." Of course, she's cast herself in the starring role.

"Typical," I say. Wrong.

"Typical, how?"

"That you put yourself in the middle of something when it's really not your business." Wrong again, but too late. I've done it. I'm feeling reckless and why not? I'm about to break my neck on thundering water smashing its way over a mile of jagged rocks. Well, smooth rocks. But hard rocks.

I see that look arrive on Holly's face. The look that says *now you're in trouble*. I strap on my helmet. Talk about appropriate metaphor timing. Bumpy ride ahead. Next up: placating, apologizing, cajoling, soothing, making it all better. I know the drill. I've been here—we've been here—so many times.

The first time I saw the look was in our first year together. I had no idea what I'd done wrong; Holly wouldn't tell me. I begged her, but she kept saying, *you* work it out. It was horrible. I felt the unfamiliar weight of doom on my puny shoulders. I think it was the first time I worried. Or even knew what worry was.

I was quiet that night at home but told my mother nothing was wrong. And to be fair, I didn't know what was wrong; it was more like *I* was suddenly wrong, the very fact and fabric of me.

The next day, Holly had a little posse of girls in whom she had confided, but she still wouldn't tell me. "You'll work it out," she said, with an exaggerated solicitude that made me feel sick. Not sick because she disgusted me, sick because I was so stupid.

By lunchtime, I was so upset I couldn't eat my lunch. Our teacher, Ms. Yeats—close talker, bad breath—asked me what was the matter. "I don't know," I started howling. "I don't know, Holly won't tell me," thinking, desperately, I'll do anything to make it right if only Holly will tell me.

Holly came up with her best shiny-bangs good-girl teacher look. "I'm not sure what Sibylla means," she said, her little voice as clean as a slap. "Would you like me to take you to the bathroom to wash your face?" she asked. I nodded, too miserable to talk.

Aware that I was red and snotty—I may have blown a snot bubble—and everyone was staring at me, I couldn't look up from the speckled carpeted classroom floor. "Do you need a tissue?" Holly asked. I nodded—I would never disagree with Holly again—and Ms. Yeats smiled when she saw Holly offer me a tissue from the neat plastic pack in her pencil case.

"You go with Holly now. Try to settle down, and we'll see you both back here in two shakes."

"I'll tell you, but only because you're about to tell on me like a big fat baby," Holly said when we hit the red-tiled corridor. "What you did was—you didn't pass around your box of raisins, and a few of us agreed that is pretty bad manners."

I was bewildered. Who would want raisins? They weren't lunch box currency, not like chips or cake. Holly gave me her official smile.

As we reached the bathroom, she said, "So why don't

you wash your face, and if you remember your manners next time, there won't be any more problems."

"I'm sorry," I said.

She handed me a paper towel. "You're forgiven."

But I'm not sorry this time. Sulk all you want, I can't be bothered with the game playing. I've got enough to deal with up here.

Holly intercepts Lou giving me a half-curious, fleeting look of approval, and that sets the steel even harder. Oh, well, it will take some time for the thaw to come. I've lived through this before, and I can do it again.

I can see my mother somewhere in this picture. Really, Sib? Is this what friendship looks like? And me giving the usual answers: you don't understand, it's none of your business, you've never liked Holly—and thinking, sometimes, sometimes this is exactly what friendship looks like.

48

It was raining, so we ate lunch inside. Michael and I ended up sitting right next to Sibylla, Holly, and Ben.

Ben had two hamburgers, two buns, four cheese slices, and a pile of salad.

Michael had hamburger buns but had acquired grilled chicken. He finds it hard to come to terms with pulverized anything.

Holly had one hamburger, no bun, pile of salad. She ate her salad and perhaps a quarter of the hamburger.

Sibylla sat with her burger and her bun and her condiments. She had tomato sauce, tomato relish, peach chutney, hummus, whole seed mustard, regular Dijon mustard, pickled cucumbers, pickled onions, and beetroot dip. And salad. But that is beside the point.

I was staring. Michael was unmoved. He's seen it before.

She layered it all together, lidded up, and started eating.

I couldn't help it; I asked, would you like a burger with your condiments?

Michael: She likes the condiments best.

Ben: Isn't it a bit... disgusting?

We watched the steady leak onto her plate. Sibylla's mouth was overstuffed with the concoction. She couldn't talk.

M: To Sibylla, condiments are to a hamburger as icing is to a cake.

Ben would be incapable of looking annoyed, or unwilling to; it would give too much away. But he has what I have decided is his annoyed equivalent, which is neutral, with a half smile. He doesn't like that Michael has the inside running on Sibylla.

Michael went to take another mouthful, then added: They are the good bits. They make eating the hamburger worthwhile.

B: I got that. Thanks.

M: Sorry, hard to tell, Benjamin. (snap!)

Holly was looking on with great interest. Just as Ben doesn't do annoyed (too exposing), Holly doesn't do eager (too uncool).

But I know her eager; it is an extra shine of bloodlust

in her eyes. She smelled conflict and she had a front-row seat.

B to M: Why do you always say people's full names? He was carefully still not showing his annoyance.

Michael shrugged, not showing his pleasure in annoying Ben: No reason. It is just an idle preference.

In the *actual* wilderness, these two would have come to blows by now.

49

We all spend a lot of time together. They are together a lot. They get along really well, and it's lovely when your best friend and your boyfriend are friends. It can be a big problem if they don't get along. All the magazines say so.

The wooden slats of the shutters slice them up, pieces of a boy, pieces of a girl. Ben, my boyfriend, is laughing. Holly, my best friend, is making him laugh.

I flip the shutters up and they're gone. Open. Slice them up. Flip the shutters down and they're gone.

Open.

Holly leans in. She touches Ben's shoulder. She is emphasizing something. Emphasizing that she'd like to touch his shoulder.

Jealousy.

Shame. It's a shame. I feel shame.

I would say that Charlotte and I hate each other from time to time, but jealousy is not something that happens in my family as far as I can see; my parents trust each other. They like each other's friends.

Though, I guess, what do I know?

I look at them as parents to me, not partners to each other.

But they are big on generosity—I know they enjoy their friends' good fortune.

It's not like that at Holly's. The Gorgon is competitive about everything. And so nosy about what other people have and how it compares to what she has. Is she thinner, richer, prettier? Is her car, personal trainer, hairdresser, beach house, ski trip better? If not, why not?

It's why our parents aren't friends, even though we are. I used to ask my parents if we could have Holly's family to dinner. We had lots of families over for dinner. Why not them? My mum used to fob me off with, We don't know them all that well, which developed over time as I got older to, We don't have all that much in common. By the time I knew what that meant, I'd stopped thinking it was a good idea anyway. A little Gorgon goes a long way.

But Holly and I stayed friends.

I mean, people are not their parents, are they?

sunday 28 october

Annie came in saying, look, for all you doubting Thomas fools: *A significant astrological event*. See, they're even teaching it in school now. We are studying it. It's official. So who's been totally outed as right? Me. Line up and kiss my Sagittarian arse.

She was waving a piece of paper from class; there's a big astronomical event (lunar eclipse? I think) coming up that we get to observe, and she thinks for this fleeting glorious moment that they've put astrology on the year-ten curriculum.

Astronomy is a legit science, bozo. They're not talking about star signs, Holly told her. Of course it would be

Holly, the one who enjoys pricking bubbles more than any-one else.

Oh, right, Annie said, disappointed. But it's still stars, right? Constellations and whatever?

You will discover new depths of dumbness even you have not dreamed of, said Holly, being a horoscope.

Annie laughed, but you could see her little feelers were hurt. Plus, she's genuinely disappointed we're not study-ing horoscopes. Beam me up, Fred, any time you like.

I climbed up for a short read before the dinner gong and realized someone had been into my shelf. My heart skipped a beat. My box was locked. Okay. But my books were in a different order. I picked up *Perfume*, which I've nearly fin-ished. She'd wrecked my bookmark. She. Who else would it be except Holly? Mean little red spots liberally applied to my face and to yours. Marker pen all over our zits.

I climbed down, taking a breath, and walked over to her. Why did you do this? I asked. She didn't even pretend to deny it. Where's your sense of humor? she asked.

I use it for things that are funny, I said. Not for mali-ciousness, or vandalism.

I turned away, horribly afraid I was about to blow my cover and cry, when Sibylla came over to me. She lifted up my hand and took my bookmark.

Why did you do that? Sibylla asked Holly. But she looked fed up, and didn't expect an answer.

Holly shrugged with affected nonchalance.

By now they've all speculated about who the boy on the photostrip is. There's not so much going on that it could be ignored as a major issue for discussion and interpretation. I think the consensus is that I'm still cut up about the breakup with my ex. Good enough.

Pippa came over, too, and looked at Holly's handiwork. Gee, you're a bitch for no good reason sometimes, she said. (Is there ever a good reason to be a bitch?)

Wah, wah, lighten the fuck up, kids, Holly said as she strolled to the door and left as though nothing had happened.

I'm sorry about your bookmark, Sybilla said.

Me, too.

Looking at it, I wonder why I didn't have a thousand copies made and wallpaper a room with them and lock myself in there and refuse to come to the godforsaken wilderness with these tedious people.

Sibylla took the bookmark from me and said, I think I can get rid of the dots.

I sat down. I must have looked as sick as I felt, because Eliza got me a glass of water. I took it and drank reflexively.

Sibylla had a small bottle and a cotton ball. It's my sticky-goo orange oil, she said. We use it to get sticky stuff off...stuff.

I nodded. She dabbed and gently rubbed. It was working. She was chattering to make me feel okay, to put some normal back into the nasty afternoon. And that was working, too.

After making her way over the whole surface of the bookmark, all that is left of Holly's red pen are the ghosts of pink smudges and a smell of orange.

I can live with that.

Sibylla smiled and said, The scanner in the art room is really good; do you want to make some backups?

I was using all available energy to get the breathing and the shaking under control, but I managed to say, why not?

51

It only took the twenty minutes before dinner, and we've got a heap of scans of Lou's photostrip. As much as I'm inclined to like Lou, I can't say I'm getting to know her. She has an arm's-length wall around her so strong, I didn't even ask her about the boy in the photos.

When we come out, there is a commotion of some sort— we don't realize at first because there was no siren, but parked alongside the assembly hall there's an ambulance.

And someone is being stretchered out to it from Falkner House.

"Jesus," says Lou.

We hurry over. Pippa is there with the scoop. Cassie, one of the "bulimia for fun" girls, has pulsed out after doing twenty straight coffee shots, also "for fun."

"They've resuscitated her," says Pippa. "But it was close."

Pippa folds her arms to impart sister-knowledge. "The ambos are under strict instructions not to use the siren—it happened in Steph's year, and caused mass hysteria. They were overwhelmed—couldn't treat all the girls."

Lou looks at me. "And I was worried about the snakes."

We head back to Bennett.

52

sunday (later)

I hate Holly.

I hate Holly.

I hate Holly.

Only fucking therapy insists I am honest, at least to myself.

She doesn't know anything about Fred.

She doesn't know anything about the state of my heart.

I can't have it both ways.

I can't expect respect for my feelings when I haven't shared those feelings.

There is a price to pay for privacy, for having secrets. The price is Holly gets to say whatever the hell she wants and I get to shut up.

I know enough about these girls now to know that if I did/if I had/if I do tell them about Fred, they would stick up for me against Holly.

Sibylla and Pippa stood up for me even not knowing how it felt to have someone messing with a picture of Fred.

I'm not even sure that Holly would be so mean if she knew.

Maybe what I hate is my life since your death. And not Holly at all.

Definitely not Holly.

Not Holly.

Holly is not important enough to hate.

53

Three unusual things happened today. First, I came back after we'd all headed out to the dreaded minibus of horror to find Lou—all packed and ready to go—photographing a big slug of dirty Blu Tack on the back of one of the kitchen chairs.

"Just making my own fun." She smiled a Baby Bear smile, stowed her camera, and came back out with me.

Second thing was after we got back. I saw Holly slipping out of Cleveland, Ben and Michael's house. She had a look on her face not too far removed from Lou's Baby Bear *juuuust right* look this morning, though Holly's was nudging into the terrain of the cat who got the cream. What was she doing there? Risking a Vincent visit? There's something simmering since the Snow Gum Flat party, but she's not sharing, because I'm in trouble.

The third unusual thing: I had a Ben breakthrough. Not an entirely good one. There was a brief clearing in the hormone fog, and I'm now doubting again that it's possible for us to "go out" up here.

After breakfast, and before getting ready for our rappelling—"breaking bones can be fun, kids"—activities, Ben and I managed to disappear for a few minutes in the art room.

Oh, to breathe that boy in, to gaze into his eyes, to hold him, to place my hand against the warm skin tight over muscles carved from hardwood; to feel his fit heart beat slowly, to make his heart beat fast. It is poetic and powerful. But it's also getting so frustrating; there is an element now of picking up where we left off, we go from eye contact at ten paces to raggedy breathing pretty damn quickly these days.

It was time for the talk, but it didn't quite go the way I thought it would. My script would have included something about never having felt like this before, not being able to imagine feeling like this with anyone else, ever. Wanting—longing—to be somewhere that doesn't exist in time or space, where we can do what our bodies are telling us to do. With no one around for a long, long time except us. Maybe a distant servant refilling the cupboards with really good food... but no parents, no teachers, no friends.

Then, ouch! While I was imagining our (tropical)

paradise—the not many clothes, the nonstop sex, the excellent food—Ben was biting my neck in a way that felt ravenous and was bound to leave a mark. I gave him a shove. "You're not auditioning for a vampire movie."

"Isn't it about time?"

"Time for the talk?"

"Talk? I was thinking, like, time to do it," he said, still kissing very persuasively between each word.

"Wow, sweep me off my feet," I said.

"Come on—you feel the same."

"How do you feel?" (He feels *great*.)

"Kinda frustrated—we keep getting to here and stopping."

"I guess." So now I'm not about to bring up the nonexistent paradise—there's turquoise water and a large four-poster bed with gauzy billowing curtains—where we could be alone. Deep breath. Can I even say the word? "There's always outercourse," I said.

He looked at me like I'm a fruitcake, or a pervert. "Or . . . I can get condoms when we do community service stuff in Hartsfield next week."

"We're going straight to condoms?"

"Is it a problem?"

It? Depends what "it" you mean. These tricky small words *it, this . . .* "This would be a bit of a first for me," I began.

"Yeah," he said. Of course he knows. Every single person in our year could accurately draw a chart of the whole grade's dating and sexual history. Things like that become public fast. I'm a straight-up "good" girl. No form. No boyfriends. No party action even. Until Ben.

"Well, maybe this isn't the ideal setting for us to start that sort of relationship."

He rolled his eyes.

"Roll away," I said. "I've got to go rappelling. You can let me know if you want to talk about outercourse." I kind of perversely enjoyed saying it—it sounds so wrong, so unapologetically stupid. I like to imagine it as pronounced by an American sexologist from the 1960s.

"And PS, that doesn't include oral sex. It's strictly hand jobs. Plus there may be something about…feet. Or perhaps elbows?"

"Great," he said. Another eye roll.

Yeah, great. Does everyone else get to that point of breathless hands in pants without talking about it? Just using instinct, and perhaps a few mime skills? Going with the flow? Am I the only person in the whole world abnormally over-influenced by that early instruction, "use your words"?

The great outdoors is constructed of nonstop handy metaphors. As we geared up for the rappelling, I hardly needed the experience. The sheer rock face was inside me, I was already sliding and looking for a foothold, scared of what comes next. Where were my toeholds, the little safe shelves providing some connection between what I was feeling and what Ben was feeling?

"So, did you have the talk?" Holly asked.

"You and I are barely talking—how do you know anything about the talk?" I said, tetchy.

"Oh, come on, he's my friend, too, and it's pretty obvious to everyone here what's going on. Or what's *not* going on."

Right now is an example of when I could use some time in a well-padded screaming cell.

54

For four weeks I have—against the grain, but with unexpected increasing tolerance—rappelled, canoed, mountain biked, and run long distances twice a week. I've had one real and one fake two-day hike. We've been civil to one another most of the time in Bennett House. I've had several breathtaking close encounters with Ben. And one falling-out with Holly.

Talking to Michael and Lou about *Othello* is the best non-Ben fun I've had in a while. And I've been invited to Lou's cave. It's an honor. Are we warming up to be friends?

We are writing about poor Desdemona—classic innocent victim. It seems such a hopeless thesis: the reward for innocence is...death. Another bad deal for a female character, and after a promisingly feisty, father-defying start, too.

How ruthlessly Iago uses Desdemona—imagine creating a character so heartless. "So will I turn her virtue into pitch, and out of her own goodness make the net that shall enmesh them all." But Iago is the best thing about the play. A pure villain. A wonderful manipulator, "he publishes doubt and calls it knowledge."

No matter what you start talking about with *Othello*, it always comes back to Iago. Why is it so oddly satisfying to spend time in the pits of Iago's mad, bad world?

"We love a good bad guy because we're intrigued by our own shadow selves, the wickedness that resides in each of our hearts," Lou thinks, slowly chewing a toffee stick, breathing clouds of raspberry chemicals into the air.

"And life, real life, is so gray and ambiguous and nuanced, so a 'good' versus 'evil' morality play is relaxing, notwithstanding its extremes; like kindergarten, not that I personally found kindergarten to be relaxing—I found it stressful and often dull—but it is generally thought to be a time of innocence and an absence of complication," says Michael.

Shakespeare gave himself carte blanche for crazy-faced turnarounds, and an all-time unhappy ending by creating in Othello "a jealousy so strong that judgment cannot cure"... Any amount of bleak havoc could be wreaked.

And why would we not enjoy wallowing in some unmitigated misery when we're all enmeshed in the public life of relentless school niceness up here. Hi...Hiiiii, how are you? How's it all going?...Great!

Are we all friends? Yes. Are we a community? Yes. Are we getting along? Yes. Could we strangle one another at a moment's notice? Hell, yes. Will we? No, probably not. Hiii. Mwah.

We have more or less figured out what we are going to say in our presentation, fifteen minutes to stimulate the broader class discussion. So we play some *sounds-like, doesn't-sound-like*.

It's not as though there's a punch line for this game, or even that it's a game as such. There's no objective, no winner or loser, although there are heated disagreements from time to time.

"Lucent," for instance, is a bone of contention between Michael and me. For him it's a *sounds-like*—bright, shining, clear; for me it's a *doesn't-sound-like*—I think it suggests soft, dim twilight or moonlight.

It is not about onomatopoeia, although it can be that, too; it's about the vibe.

I go first. "Liminal—because it sounds like it is lapping or shimmering from one state to the next with its repeated soft vowels and humming consonants." Michael is happy. (I love *liminal*; it doesn't just have to be about light, or landscape, or elements, or metaphorical transitions, doorways. Would you care for a glass of Liminal, my salty sweet sour beverage?)

Michael is next. "Temerity—because it bristles—its tail is up; it has attitude."

"Whisper," says Lou. "It's soft. It promises secrets."

I say, "Luscious—totally a big, wet, licky mouthful."

"Betrayal," Michael offers. "Sounds like a noose, or like wind blowing; a rusty rattling through bars."

Before we get to *doesn't-sound-likes*, Lou remembers something. "Ooh, the thing," she says to Michael.

He says, "Of course. Sibylla, Louisa and I have decided we need to break the law. You are welcome to join us."

Michael scrabbles around in his backpack and pulls out a fat Sharpie. Lou clears her throat. "This is kind of a family tradition, I guess. You know my mother was at school here? And she told me that none of the place-name signs use an apostrophe of possession where it would be appropriate to do so. She did a bit of apostrophe adding—but all the signs have been replaced since those days."

"So, we have taken to carrying our weapons of media with us. We intend to deliver the joy of grammar to wanderers in the alpine region."

Lou shows me "before" and "after" photos on her phone—what was Byrons Trail is now Byron's Trail.

"Are you in?" asks Michael, showing me another photo. Dylans Trail is now Dylan's Trail.

"It's an unofficial mountain-life project," says Lou.

"Never leave home without it," says Michael, handing me the Sharpie.

I take it, looking at them, with their together-hatched plans, and feel a pang of exclusion. A ripping away of something with Michael. And a petty wish that Lou had chosen me to like, not Michael. But my better self swallows that and smiles. How could I not want to be part of such a nerdfest activity?

Lou stays to read, and Michael and I head back to camp.

Holly is weeding the path when we get back. "Where have you two been?" she asks with an insinuating tone.

"We have been in the land of reason," says Michael. An answer, in its deliberate obtuseness, guaranteed to annoy Holly.

"You're a wanker, you know that, right?"

Michael looks at her, declines to answer, and goes to put on his running clothes.

tuesday 30 october

Two letters.

One unsent letter missing: potential major problem brewing.

Michael wrote his letter to Sibylla. His loving, I'm-a-bit-obsessed, get-it-off-your-chest letter. Omitted crucial step of destroying it. Cannot find it. He did seal it in an envelope. He thinks.

He lives part-time in cloud-cuckoo-land, so it is possible he has mislaid it. He's also worried there is a chance he has mailed it to his parents. He doesn't like that idea much, but it's marginally less appalling than someone up here finding it and reading it.

It's flipped his switch slightly, and he has reacted by upping the running.

He is already clocking unimaginably high distances and has been reprimanded for running too late in the day, at the *liminal* time, when light is fading or darkness is deepening, and ankles may more easily be broken. He knows he is addicted, but he calls it a safe addiction. He is used to dealing with his obsessions.

The second letter.

You know I'm not particularly a snoop, Fred. I'm just not. But I have some natural curiosity, and when Holly went running obediently out of the unit when Vincent whistled or snapped his fingers, I did just stroll over to where she'd been sitting at the kitchen table and glance down at her (cough) letter.

It was to Dear Ruby, so a friend, not a parent.

You know I'm a fast reader, so it's not even as though I had time to construct the argument for or against. My eyes ripped down that page so quickly they beat my good manners by a mile.

Mostly it was a rave about how Holly couldn't get over the coincidence of Dear Ruby knowing (dear) Ben. Turns out they went to elementary school together, yawn, but my interest grew when I read that Ben is Holly's *best friend*. They *hang together up here all the time*, he is *soooo funny*, in fact she has *never met anyone she gets along with so well*, who *makes her laugh so much*, who is *such a great guy, who really gets her*, etc. etc. Cutesy little heart and (sigh) next to *great guy*. Definitely verging on implying there is a romantic nature to her feelings. No mention of the person who is ostensibly her best friend, Sibylla. And no mention of this same person also hanging with Ben for significant amounts of time. A slightly skewed account.

I turned away. More the thought of the evil one's return than any pricking of my conscience; I know, hardly admirable. Too bad. I was up in my bunk by the time Holly got back.

Sibylla followed closely, holding an apple, which Holly grabbed and bit into, saying, Halvsies?

If you can believe it, this was a token effort on Holly's part to smooth over their recent trials and snitchiness, and Sibylla read it as such, pleasantly accepting the apple grab.

56

Some days pass peacefully enough. Uneventfully enough.

We're on Vego this week, and it is strangely satisfying. Our vegetable garden up here is beautiful. A generation ago, one of the arty mothers decided we should have a kitchen garden like Sunday Reed's at Heide. With the assistance of a pile of money, a fashionable landscape designer of the day, and our full-time professional gardener/groundskeeper, we get to play at well-composted self-sufficiency with our sun hats and sharp clippers. Beneath established fruit trees.

It is fenced and sheltered by a high bougainvillea hedge. The wind sweeps up across the mountains from the south; if unprotected, the trees will all bend in the same direction.

The beds are built up, twelve symmetrical rectangles, a

central path, and at the very middle of the garden is a large oblong pond with water lilies. The beds are spread with flighty pea straw that the currawongs snitch for nests. Right now we have done our pruning of the hedge, our picking of the fresh herbs for Priscilla, a plucking of beans from their tastefully rustic wicker steeples, an eating of sugar snap peas, sun warm, an ill-advised tasting of strawberries only faintly red—that was just Annie—and a wise ignoring of plums and nectarines that are purple and red respectively but hard as rocks.

We have twenty minutes before which it is too early to return, or we'll be pounced on for not doing our tasks thoroughly enough, and so we lie inside the shelter of the hedge, in the afternoon sun, on grass half-shaded by the spreading mulberry tree. We pluck at white-rooted stems of grass, nibble them, find cowslips and bite a machine-gun path up their lemonsour stems; we forage for small plum puddings, the little seed pods of one of the mountain grasses, like a miniature sweet green nut. We make chains from yellow buzzing, black-hearted daisies with their drifts of pollen and milk-sap-sticky stems.

Pippa finishes a circlet and puts it on my head. "Sib, pretty Sibbie, the only one of us likely to be suspended on a billboard for beautifulness, the queen of the Ben fan club, the clever one." Holly's face through half-closed eyes looks unfussed; maybe she's getting used to the silliness. In fact, she seems almost happy these days. The thing with Vincent must be happening.

Bees murmur and stumble among the daisies; I shut my eyes and let them hum me into a dreamy half sleep.

Pippa says, "We are lucky, when you come to think of it."

"Oh, yes," says Holly, "if slaving away in the bush is lucky. If eating at chez Cilly's gourmet prison mess is lucky. If being bossed around by a mini King Kong and living in overcrowded accommodation is lucky, then we are so totally lucky." Everyone laughs.

"No," says Pippa, "lucky we haven't had a ghost visit yet."

Cold slides through my hot dozing peace of mind.

"Tell us about the ghosts," says Holly. I don't need to open my eyes to know that at least part of her pleasure relates to the fact that she knows perfectly well I am ready to run.

"Well," says Pippa, "where should I begin? How shall I count the ways in which girls have been terrorized by certain unwanted visitors?"

Lou pipes up. Very un-Lou. "My mother told me about the charcoal man."

"Welcome to the conversation, Lou." Pippa is pleased to have another member of the church present. "The charcoal man. Ragged clothes, red eyes. He's searching, always searching for his daughter. The one he let burn to a grisly death in a bushfire because he wasn't home."

"Where was he?" asks Annie.

"He was off drinking at the loggers' camp. He used to leave her locked inside so she wouldn't wander into the bush at night. She was trapped when the wind changed and the fire swept up the mountain, didn't stop till it got to Long Reach. What was left of his burned-out hut was still here on this site when school first bought the land in 1910—right about where the assembly hall is."

"The first sign he's coming is the low, rasping breathing," adds Lou.

Gulp.

"What about Maisy?" Lou wants to know. "Is she still around?"

Pippa is very serious. "Maisy is getting stronger and more angry as the years go by. She was only a faint shimmer when my eldest sister came up here, but by the time Helen came through, Maisy was more visible. And very angry. She is about eleven. She wears a pinafore and carries an axe, and she smiles as she walks toward you, but once close, her face changes, ages, and she screams bloody murder and shows you her neck."

"Her neck?" Annie's voice is a whisper.

"Her mother died in childbirth; her father went mad with grief and knew he couldn't cope with little children, so..."

I'm covered in goose bumps. "Stop it!" I open my eyes and sit up too fast, and nearly faint with the sun and the lying down and the scary level that I can't sustain.

Holly laughs. "Come on, guys, remember Sib can't stand to hear things like that."

"But it's fun," says Pippa. "And you need to be ready if

they come for us. Bennett is the house with Maisy's name on one of the beds. She will visit. One of these nights."

"More benefits for people with top bunks," says Annie bitterly.

Pippa looks around the group. "Don't believe it. She levitates."

Annie and I scream.

"Shut up, they'll come and see us doing nothing," says Holly.

"You're not doing nothing," I say. "You're scaring the crap out of me."

"If Maisy comes, you just have to shout back. You say, 'He's not here anymore, Maisy.'"

"If the charcoal man comes, what do you do?" asks Eliza. She is doing calf raises on the edge of the half-pipe terra-cotta guttering that runs along the inside of the hedge.

"Run," says Lou. "And hope there's no fire. When the charcoal man comes through, he jams all the doors and windows."

"I refuse to believe any of this nonsense," I say, my blood still running cold at the thought of nighttime visitations when everyone but me is asleep. "And I hate kid ghosts, they're scarier than anything."

"Ooooh, she's got a doll, too. Maisy has a little doll," says Pippa, enjoying the horrified looks. "Her doll says, *mama, mama,* and sometimes it's the first sign that Maisy is on her way."

"I *hate* dolls in scary stories," I say. "Especially if they smile."

Pippa nods. "You're not alone there," she says grimly. "One girl in my sister Alex's year had to go home because she was totally convinced she heard a soft little *mama, mama* every night when the lights went out. Turns out she did. It was a rotation of people in her house trying to freak her out for fun. It worked. Full crack up. Came back for the last week a changed girl."

Despite feeling freaked out, a small bubble of happy afternoon remains with me. It's Lou. For this little while she seemed almost relaxed, almost as though she was part of the group.

57

wednesday 31 october

Our mission was apostrophes, but we ended up killing something.

We followed the trail least taken from the valley, heading northeast about three miles out when we came to Fitzwilliams Paddock, which might once have been a paddock, but is bushland now, and which we renamed Fitzwilliam's Paddock. There we heard a rasping, panting noise, and a whimpering.

Not a spooky bone in my body, but after the ghost talk it was a disconcerting sound to hear when you think you are somewhere completely uninhabited.

Hello? Michael called out. No response. But there was another whimper.

Anyone there? I added. It came out as a nervous warble.

We looked at each other, and didn't need to have the conversation. We bush-bashed toward the noise.

The smell hit us a beat before we saw the red wallaby. Shit and piss and vomit and the beginning of rotting flesh. The poor creature was still alive.

There were flies swarming a gaping bloody wound in its neck. Its eyes were rolling back in its head. But it was still trying weakly to get up. All it could do was lift its head a few centimeters off the ground. Which it did, over and over. It was unbearable to see that futility, the reflexive insistence upon survival. The rest of its body wasn't moving at all.

All this, we saw at a glance.

It's been shot, I said, and a sob came out on top of the words.

It's paralyzed. Maybe a broken back, said Michael.

Now it had seen us, its panic and distress were more extreme. It rasped out a noise from deep inside its throat.

A rock, said Michael.

We looked about, and quickly found a heavy chunk of granite.

If you stay there, said Michael, I'll approach it from behind and try not to make it any more scared.

He was completely white, the blood drained even from his lips, but we understood this had to be done.

Do you want me to . . . ? I wanted to give him an out if he needed it.

He shook his head. I'd better do it; it'll need some force, so . . .

I nodded.

I stepped in a bit closer but didn't make eye contact with the poor thing. I sang. I didn't know what else to do. I was the distraction.

Michael found his balance and heaved the rock down as hard as he could with a horrified noise of someone who knows he is inflicting a fatal blow. The wallaby screamed a final shrill, pure note of panic. I heard the cracking thud into bone and mush, and Michael's guts convulsing until they were empty.

My face was a hot lather of tears and snot, and still I couldn't look, but I carried the animal's final cry inside me as I pushed back through the scratching scrub, my heart pounding with the fear and pity of it, leaving Michael to cry his tears privately.

58

tuesday 6 november

I've volunteered for an early solo hike for a couple of reasons. One of them is not that I am keen as mustard on wilderness.

Mainly, I want to get away from the collective Bennett House hormones and Holly in particular, and second, I want to endure and survive something. Sounds dramatic. But I need it. Pop outside my bubble. Scarify my flesh. I know, Fred, big on the religious imagery for one who does not believe.

If I were a runner, I'd want to run till I dropped; if I could yell (without risking increased sessions with Merill), I'd yell till I was hoarse. I am looking for some excess, and the solo is pretty much all that's on the menu.

I'm preparing. I'll do it in the purest way.

Some kids freak out at the idea of isolation. They choose the sites closest to the mothership, and make sure they are within shouting distance in case something happens.

To me that evades the challenge completely. Why bother doing it at all?

I'm going as far afield as we are allowed, and I'm staying two nights. You get to skip class if you do a two-nighter, because you're hiking back on morning three. I've asked not to have a teacher food-drop, so I'm carrying everything with me. I know my spot. And I have my central task. I will write to my parents; it's compulsory. And I will write to you. And I will throw the key somewhere deep or far. Into a pool or a crevice.

There are not many opportunities for this type of activity anymore. And historically it is more of a boy thing. Test your strength, fight a bear, survive the wilderness, prove your courage.

So I'm glad to be a candy-arsed little middle-class kid who is getting the experience constructed for her, as though it's the future and I'm in a virtual GeoDome full of authentic old-world simulacra.

Which I sort of am. It is certainly the future. Tick tick. And I have a clearer past/present delineation than most kids, I'm guessing. My past is you.

You, my loss of innocence. We covered the big stuff: sex and death.

So, I've packed the pack. I've packed the tent. Weather

is still too unpredictable to rely on the biv, the little open shelter, though it would add to the wild-girl experience. Ground mat. No clean clothes. Going grotty. Pad, pens, pencils in case I experience arty compulsions when confronted with the inner depths of my own soul.

Food. Luxurious food—the solo hike means extra treats and trimmings. Cookies, granola bars, vac-packed cooked meals, juice. Cereals. Fresh fruit. It's heavy.

We leave in half an hour, at 8 AM. I'm being driven to the Bluff Trail, then I'll hike in up to the spur and along Lizard Ridge, and from there across to Mount Desperation.

(later)

My pack was digging in, my quads burning up. And all I could think was: bring it on.

Two hours walking on a marked trail, and I was almost at the point where the final trail across the ridge and finally up Mount Desperation should start.

No one had been this way for ages. It was about a four-hour hike from here, and I didn't plan on stopping. I had a bag of trail mix in each pocket, and water in a back carrier.

The trail is overgrown with bracken fern in parts, and I was glad I had my walking sticks to bash ahead a bit and let the snakes know to get the hell out of the way. It's reassuring to be wearing heavy boots and gaiters as a backup; I'd have to be the first human some of these slithery critters encountered, so they might not even know to scram.

Finally, after the toughest part of the climb, a last steep

rocky trail through a belt of stumpy snow gums, I got to a grassy clearing not far below the peak, with a view back across to the west side of Mount Fairweather on the far side of the valley. I was as far away as I could get, and I could hear water. There were springs on my map, and with any luck there would be a pond, too.

I dropped my pack and lay down beside it, panting. I have never felt so physically exhausted. My heart was pounding like a mad thing, the blood beating in my ears.

It was quiet but for my puffed breathing and a wheeling spray of parrots, bright against the clear sky. I got up, legs trembling, and started looking around. There was a pond, and it was full of fresh water after all the rain. No grazing allowed here these days, so that means minimal animal poo in the water, which is always a comforting thought, although we still boil or use purifying tablets. I was about to strip off and plunge in when I saw a nice fat tiger snake sunning itself on the rocks. I made a ruckus, and the sensible thing headed off in the other direction. I knew there might be others nearby, but I was boiling and my feet were hot and sore, so I couldn't resist ripping off gaiters, socks, boots, and shirt and walking into the icy water. Heaven to bend over and splash my face and head till water was trickling down my back and front, soaking my singlet and turning it into a cooling system when the breeze hit the wet fabric. Felt delicious. Black sun spots burned into the red of my closed eyelids when I blinked. I filled my hat with water and put it back on.

Pitching a tent is easy now with a couple of trips under my belt. I even know where the best place to pitch is: facing east near a stand of young trees. I found a small overgrown fire pit and flicked some wallaby shit balls out of the way with a stick.

I stretched out on the grass, arms thrown wide open, shoulders saying thank you, looking up into the limitless blue, and realized I was starving. So it's just me and the infernal journal and my very late lunch: a relatively unscathed salad roll, a huge chocolate chip cookie, an apple, and a cracker-and-dip pack.

I collected a good pile of dry wood. Mad homemaker skills. We are meant to be all about MIB (minimum impact bushwalking), and we usually are, but fires are a sometimes-necessary comfort.

I sat and stared into the distance. This is what I've been craving. Complete solitude. Merill even agreed I'm ready for the challenge. After maybe an hour I felt more properly rested than after the longest sleep.

And then I was bored.

I deliberately have not brought a book, because I wanted to Confront Self, rather than Escape From Self, my more usual objective. So I looked for my own entertainment.

I imagined I was a resourceful, now-mature Pebbles Flintstone. I constructed a goal with some fallen branches.

I gathered some balls (rocks), put myself at a challenging distance, and started taking shots at the goal.

I felt a bit silly. How did the average Stone Age kid my age fill her days? Ugh. Unwanted pregnancies, no doubt. But even so, the day is long when you have no classes, no book to hand, and no people to creatively avoid interacting with. I threw a few more ground hoops. It was good healthy pointless fun, like all sports.

I really should have been grinding the wild seeds I'd gathered and dried into a rustic flour and fashioning some unleavened bread from it on a handy flat rock. But of course I hadn't been gathering any damn seeds. Thank god I don't have to make my own flour. Which really is just thanks for the sheer fluke of being born into a first-world community.

I thought of the World Vision kid we sponsor. She maybe has to grind her own flour. I know they have a well, too, so she probably has to carry water. Jesus. Okay, I know, more religious content. But seriously, some days she must feel like she got the short straw. I hope she gets to do nursing like she writes in the information sheet, and manages to get the hell out of there. Oh, you weak freak, Louisa, she might want to stay and help her community.

Rocky goal as a game has its natural limitation, which is that your hands start to get sore.

Soon it will be time to write to Fred, but not yet.

The night.

When the sun set, and the temperature dropped, it was

time to think about food again. I had the special-occasion vac-sealed solo food, ravioli with bolognaise sauce. And a bag of salad and a self-saucing butterscotch pudding for dessert.

Now, I am not afraid of the dark. I'm practical. But there is something a bit different about darkness in which you are totally alone. It is deeper, and both quieter and louder.

All the noises have a rational source. There is no charcoal man. Or not anymore. There is no Maisy. But it is vaguely possible that you could be unlucky enough to encounter a group of hostile campers. Say, some people hunting. Drinking. What would they be hunting? Deer? Kangaroos? Rabbits?

I've got my security-issue sat phone. But my outpost teacher is a five-hour walk away, not a huge amount of help should something go wrong.

So I need to be able to trust that nothing will go wrong. It was a lot easier to live in that default mind-set before the very big thing did go wrong. Fred dying brought every possible worst-case scenario just a little closer. But to counter that, in a strange way, when the worst imaginable thing has already happened, you are somehow free to stop worrying.

So leave me, worries, to the probably benign evening I've walked so far to meet.

The stars.

My self.

Let me survive it. Hey, let me enjoy it.

Too late for letter writing, no light left, and I'm stuffed.

I climbed out of my top layer clothes, every muscle saying ouch, and got into the little tent, and into the soft sleeping bag. I let myself hear the night noises without trying to identify them or be frightened by them, and that was enough. I slept. A truly tired body does that well.

59

The sunlight woke me early.

Is this too basic for words? It feels good that bed happens when it's dark, and I wake up when the sun says it's daytime. But I didn't have to do anything in particular, which was an amazing luxury, and I let myself drift back to sleep.

Starving for breakfast when I woke again. I cooked bacon in a little pan on my Trangia and had it in a gigantic pita bread sandwich, with a sliced tomato and a travel sachet of barbecue sauce squeezed inside.

I took my watch off. I was going to have a day without time, the sun my guide.

I decided to document my area. It is encouraged.

Wildlife: The air was full of little things I don't see in the city. A flying bug with a bright yellow abdomen and black lace wings, black legs and head. Long-bodied black beetles with bright red legs, oh, dear, having sex on my gaiter, I was assuming they don't usually walk around joined at their bottoms like that.

A lacquer-backed beetle, brown with a purple tinge and perfectly glossy, like a tiny manicured fingernail. Bees. Introduced? I guess so. They were hovering around a clump of everlasting daisies. A drift of very small mauve butterflies. Black beetles with spiky backs splashed yellow and red. Pretty. I went back along the trail to where it was shady and nudged away some leaf litter with a stick.

There I found a slater bug, but not gray or brown, or grown, or bray, the usual repertoire of slater colors. This one was vivid fire-engine red. If it stuck its head above the leaf litter, it would be a neon sign to a bird. I picked it up and marveled at its freaky beauty. Here we go, I thought. Fame at an unexpectedly early age. The Lou Bug. Louisa Slater. How would I get a significant scientific discovery documented? Mild excitement.

In my driveling speculation, the first thing (well, second, after personal fame) I thought of was you, Fred. You would love this. You'd love it. Wish you were here. You're such a pain in the heart.

I made a leaf-littery fun park for my red friend in a plastic specimen box. We carry them with us in case we find anything of interest to bring back to the group for Physical World, etc. class.

I got out my sketch pad. Drew and described my buggy finds. I'm sick of you not being here, Fred. So sick of wanting to show you stuff. Sick of restuffing it into my head that you're not around anymore. It is like starving for a food, and remembering that it doesn't exist.

I guess I'll show the slater to Michael. Sure. Why not? He'll like it. But it is no substitute for being able to show you. Can that be quite clear?

Part of this is that I don't want to leave you out, and I love you by remembering you. If I don't think of you every time there's something important, then doesn't that mean you are no longer important to me? And how can I let that happen when you were so very much the important one to me?

Part of it is that you are irreplaceable. That is an immutable fact in my life. No matter how long I live.

Touching base with you is like touching something for luck. Touching the sore spot, the tender bruise that misses you. How can I let go, let you go? Why would I want that to heal?

The key is in my pocket. The key that locks us together somewhere on the other side of the world.

Our, now my, photos lock us somewhere else.

Our, now my, texts lock us again.

But my best lock is memory. And if I don't keep you

always in my mind, won't memory walk away? Or starve thin? Don't memories need maintenance?

The trouble is that keeping it alive, giving it all that energy, will, determination, stops me being alive in the present.

I'm not stupid, I don't need Esthers and Merills to tell me that is not a brilliant way for a sixteen-year-old to live.

I know what you would say.

You'd say, get on with it, Lou, m'Lou.

There's lots more to do than thinking about me.

Don't hang out somewhere that isn't anymore.

Don't haunt the landlost past, you'd say.

Read the Christina Rossetti poem again, *for Chrissake*, you'd say, in homage to Holden Caulfield. No one I know does that now.

I've written you a hundred unsent letters.

Maybe if I keep writing and sealing them, they can sit somewhere safely. Our story as a one-sided correspondence—I know that's oxymoronic—and I can allow that to be it. I can put a lid...I can just go there sometimes...I can know it's there, safely; we are there.

I haven't written in a single letter about the time you told me that you loved me.

You didn't mean to say it. But it brimmed out of you and wouldn't stop.

Remember we decided that we could probably make some fairly superb puddings in the microwave? It was a big thing at the time—everyone was having a microjunkbake after school. Plan B was at work, and the Gazelle was at some conference. We had the run of the pantry. We thought if we put cakey stuff with nice-bits in a cup and nuked it, we'd be in the fast lane to pudding heaven.

So was it eggs, self-rising flour, M&Ms, and Milo? And Nutella? A chopped Snickers bar? Lightly stirred.

We would name it after its inventors: us. It would be Fred & Lou's, like Ben & Jerry's, only warm. We zapped it one instant minute at a time.

Smells like deliciousness, we thought, after four zaps.

I put a spoonful in my mouth.

It was super disgusting and still a bit raw-eggy and flour-gluey. And we'd somehow forgotten sugar, a vital ingredient if you want a cake-pudding thing. We didn't use any butter, either, also probably a desirable ingredient.

And was it just my face as I tasted it? You cracked up. You were looking at me and laughing.

And I said, What? And you said, I love you.

And we were both completely shocked. Because it was a little premature, surely.

And you said it again, as though you were checking the flavor, and it tasted perfectly right. You said it again, softly, I love you; you were looking right into my heart. You said it again, almost shouting. And you were laughing and it was as though you were so happy you couldn't believe that someone had given you this good thing.

And it was partly that, and it was partly because you

were thinking you'd had a premature declaration, whereas guys your age were more generally associated with premature ejaculation. As well as inability to speak girl and commitment problems to anything other than games with buttons.

And the best part was when you said, You love me, too. And all I had to do was nod. Because it was true. Because I could hardly talk, because my mouth was still glued together by the foul and truly monstrous thing we had created in the microwave.

God, when I remember that afternoon every part of me hurts like I've been in a car accident; like I'm bashed to pieces inside and out, and bits of me are missing and other bits are put back the wrong way.

So.

Guys your age, hey? Wouldn't want to be making any generalizations.

But most guys your age get to be older one day.

I love you, too, and I never said it enough.

Lou

XXX

60

The sky-watchers are already getting prepped for the eclipse. There is a whole truckload of mathematical stuff about where and when and how fast things move through the heavens above—endless star-mapping and moon phase calculations for the math brains.

For the rest of us there's the "huge cloudy symbols of a high romance," generalized literary appeal. I guess it will be a new and strange beauty looking at the shadows and textures of planets and stars, but I can't get as properly excited as I should apparently be.

We have a super-excellent high-powered Meade telescope that we can use only under supervision. Mr. Epstein has told us that bumping it—which could strip delicate gears—will earn the punishment of weeding the oval with tweezers.

We've been warned there are hunters in the mountains again. It's illegal, but that doesn't stop some people. There is the odd, unsettling crack of distant gunfire.

Ben and I are plotting and planning an escape, a whole day out together next week during which we will try not to get shot.

Michael is overrunning, doing too much gym, and over-practicing piano, but I am not his freaking mother. Neither is Lou. She told me when she was packing for her solo that he has already run through one pair of sneakers and one set of toenails. They're growing back (nails), and I keep in mind that he's not the only one to have messed up his feet a bit, and hope I shouldn't be getting in touch with his actual mother to say he seems a bit on edge.

Miss having Lou around the house.

61

Tramping back down the mountain felt like flying, gravity on my side. I had eaten most of the weight of my pack;
it probably went from thirty to fifteen pounds, and I really
needed my poles on the slidey paths so I didn't go career-
ing down headfirst in a rock rumble.

A huge stampeding noise was happening at the outer
reaches of my hearing range, and coming closer. Only
sounded like one thing, an animal or a person, but I stayed
still till I could see what it was.

Michael. And it was not an accident. He ran to meet me.

What flavor would you say blue snakes are, he asked.

Fair question, it's puzzled me, too, but the closest I ever
come up with is blue, or perhaps we are supposed to link

the color to a food, in which case blueberry? Or maybe it is linked to the other hard-to-define non-flavor, blue heaven?

But let us be frank, it tastes like chemicals and colors.

He nodded, agreeing, his breathing slowing up, and I realized what a super-fit machine he is turning himself into, because he was pounding, sprinting up the mountain a second ago, pouring with sweat, and it was only a few breaths before he was breathing very easily.

You are a super-fit machine, I told him.

I believe I have run farther than Ben, he said.

But you're not going to put it like that to anyone but me, right? Because you know it makes you seem a bit vulnerable, or Sibylla-focused, I said.

It could simply be a man-to-man competition, he said.

But it's not, and everyone who knows you knows that you don't care about bullshit like that.

There is a night of entertainment when we return, he warned me.

Oh, dear. They spring this random fun on us. We wake up and find invitations slipped under the doors of our house. We are expected to participate from time to time. Sometimes it's house-devised group fun stuff, other nights it is individual fun stuff.

Individual fun, or house fun? I asked.

Individual.

Right. I had better do something, or I will start putting myself in the Merill spotlight, I said.

You are very manipulative of that relationship, said Michael.

Not manipulative, I'm just keeping it at arm's length to as great an extent as possible under the circumstances. I want her to believe that I am making the sort of progress I should be making.

Did you throw away the key?

Not quite, I said. Not quite sure that I ever will be able to, I thought.

What would you propose to do to entertain your new friends? Michael asked.

I think my new friends would enjoy hearing me sing. They will at first hope to ridicule me, and get a laugh out of someone falling on her face, but I will sing something simple, and I sing in tune. I have known this is coming and so I'll just do it, as the sneaker advertisement exhorts us.

You are a pragmatic soul, Louisa.

What else has been happening in the big smoke while I've been hunting the bear?

Michael looks with some concentration into the middle distance. I can't quite tell you. I've been practicing piano and running. Not quite sure what everyone else is up to. Holly appears to be going out with Ben's friends, particularly Vincent, it seems, as much as Sibylla is going out with Ben, he eventually offered.

So she is happy?

Who?

Holly? Happy?

She seems to have what she wants, which is a slight shift in the sociograph with regard to whom she spends most of her time with.

How are she and Sib getting along?

Michael thinks again. Sorry, pass.

How does Sib look? Easy question. His special topic.

She looks as much herself as she can; she is tired from the sharing with other people.

Hey, that is the best thing about the solo; it's such a relief, I recommend.

I imagine.

When are you down to do yours?

Two weeks.

Sorry about how I smell.

It could be a lot worse. It's not too bad.

But you can smell me?

I can smell you.

(later)

New true pleasure.

A shower when you really need it. When you have proper grime, dried sweat and mud, and a thousand little nicks and scratches, a longish hot shower with citrusy soap and shampoo is heaven.

I can sing. But I haven't felt like singing at all since Fred. It helps to be joyful when you sing. Though, conversely, singing can induce joy. I haven't felt like I deserve joy, or want it.

So my voice is as rusty as shit.

After my shower, I took a walk far enough away to warm it up.

Hello, voice! You haven't forsaken me. You're just sounding a little thin.

I went to the kitchen to scrounge a few strawberries from Priscilla. I explained that they help singer's throat, and she handed over half a container. She didn't ask for money, but she has a black-market vibe about her, no doubt.

I've looked over my lyrics. The song is short.

I'm ready. As ready as I will ever be. As ready as I need to be to look like I'm joining in. And, hey, I will be joining in. Fake it till you make it. No big deal, just a song to keep the counselor lulled into thinking I'm doing okay.

I am doing okay, low-end okay. Low-end okay is great, considering.

My song is *Blackbird*.

62

Wow. Lou is bringing down the house. She has an amazing voice. Who knew? She doesn't even sing in the shower.

She started singing "Blackbird," unaccompanied.

People were still buzzy and unsettled for the first little bit, but she just kept singing, really relaxed. Her "relaxed" lives deep in the land of "don't give a shit." Her voice is pure and perfectly tuneful.

By the end of the song, there was dead silence. And a chant started up: Again, again, again, again. So she sang it through from the beginning.

And now we are all screaming it out with her a third time. Not so tunefully.

It's a pretty beautiful song. And it's one of those songs that somehow everyone seems to know.

You could say that for an audience of people who are mostly sixteen it's the perfect money-shot lyric, punching us right in the heart, given that we all feel like we are waiting for the moment to be free. Or for some other moment to arise. Usually the end of a class. Or someone realizing we are the center of their universe, or something.

When she finishes, everyone is up yelping and cheering and whoa-ing and whistling. And Holly (of all people—but then again, it is an opportunity to put herself in the middle of it) gets up and leads another chant: Bennett, Bennett, Bennett. And we Bennetts get up and do our dance. Usually it's an in-house private affair—just for when we manage to get all our jobs done, or someone gets a letter they've been waiting for, or someone gets a contraband food parcel, or we don't have prep, or someone just farted—yes, okay, that is gross, but it is the wilderness. The dance involves some pointing—at each other, at the stars, nodding, gyrating hips, smacking own arse, pulling bits of nothing down from the sky, and doing some arms-out fists-together stirring. Vary and repeat as required to imaginary funky beat.

Michael has gone onstage—thankfully he is doing a piano piece. You never know with Michael, he could have decided to recite a poem or perform a Gregorian chant or do any number of things that would make him a total mockery magnet. Not that he would care, but I would.

He is playing something obscure, very dramatic, with

odd pauses. Rachmaninoff? Hats off, and I'm sure it's perfect. Who'd know? Half the audience is using it as a chat interlude. Not that he notices. But I do. Lou is sitting next to Van Uoc, and giving Michael's performance complete attention and trying to ignore people who are telling her that she's a good singer.

Like she hadn't noticed already. But they're being all make-an-effort nice—which has not happened so far this term, as far as I've seen. She has gone from quiet, invisible new geek girl to indie-singer geek girl, a handle everyone understands. To this point, with rare exceptions, she has maintained her distance, not given any sign that she wants to be friends with anyone, apart from Michael, and maybe me, to a lesser extent, more by friend association. And she manages to show solidarity to anyone Holly is mean to. Mmm, maybe that's why she's nice to me, not the Michael-friend link? Maybe I need to explain that Holly's mean is not really meant to be mean—it's just Holly. And you get used to it. I try to imagine encountering the Holly treatment now, for the first time. I have to admit, it's not something anyone new might want to get used to.

Lou seems to have in common with Michael that thing of not caring at all about other people's approval.

It's a cold night again, and they're too tight to have any heating on in the assembly hall. Ben and Holly are talking. I shush them and get the looks.

Ben whispers to me, "Have you still got my scarf?"

His scarf? I had it at the Beeso party but haven't seen it since. "Sorry, you can have mine."

"No, don't worry."

I remember waking up hot, still wearing it that morning, and taking it off. But since then...?

"Oops, I've got it," says Holly.

I must look blank.

"You left it at Snow Gum Flat, Sib. I packed it and brought it back."

"Thanks, Hol," says Ben.

When Ben kisses me—risky (lights will be turned up, sirens will blare, nets will drop from the ceiling, we'll both be suspended, plus I'm trying to listen to Michael)—I pull away and he says, "Jeez, relax. The whole world is not always watching you, Sib."

"That's not what I think. It's as much for you as for me."

"Well, how about I decide what I want to do?"

Only a few days since our freaking monthiversary, and here we are bickering.

Holly leans in. "Guys, come on, no trouble in paradise, please. You two are my camp parents." She pulls a pathetic face and crosses her eyes.

Ben smiles. So do I. For someone who makes a lot of trouble, Holly also knows how to smooth things over and put people in a good mood—when it suits her. She's had years of practice, living with the moody, hungry, dissatisfied Gorgon.

261

The last act is Hugo and Vincent, who are wearing suits and ties, doing a recitation of the lyrics of "Changes" by David Bowie in urgent newsreader voices, in robotic unison. They do it straight, both quite serious drama students, and it's surprisingly good.

A couple of houses are going through a complete David Bowie craze at the moment. They have "discovered" him. They find his genderflex look to be cool. They love his voice. They love his characters. They love his mismatched eyes. They love his art. They love the movie his kid made, *Moon*. They are madly out-retro-ing one another and also digging into the Smiths, the Ramones, the Go-Betweens. It's such a relief from the metal and the crap rap.

Holly hasn't exactly said it, but it's pretty obvious she and Vincent have something going on, so I expect her to be basking right now, but she looks a bit closed off.

"He's an idiot," says Ben.

Holly shrugs. "He's got to work out what he wants."

I give Ben a *what?* look. He whispers, "Later."

Turns out Vincent has a girlfriend in Melbourne he hasn't exactly decided if he's going to break up with yet, and Holly is understandably cut up about it.

I thought we were back on okay terms, but I must still be getting the partial cold shoulder.

63

saturday 10 november

I did not want to overhear, but I didn't want to say I was there, either.

We were all supposed to be at a fire drill assembly, but I had a headache and was nicely zoned out under my duvet when Holly whipped back into the unit to get her phone. It's amazing that nearly every single kid broke the don't-bring-your-phone rule, but they are all out in the open now, being used as cameras, and there isn't any reception up here anyway, so I don't know why they bother doing the thing of forbidding them. Perhaps they just want to get us away from our button addictions.

That is by the by, but what is not by the by is that I heard what Holly and Tiff were saying. They were talking about Ben. Holly was all very, oh, we've got so close up here, he's my total go-to guy.

He used to be my go-to guy, said Tiff, but then we went out, and you know what they say, you can't go back. What is he doing with Sibylla, though? That I cannot figure. Like sure there was some novelty value for five minutes with the billboard, but come on, that clueless-virgin act is no act, am I right?

I waited for Holly to defend her bestie, to say that Sibylla is a sweet girl, a funny girl, a clever girl, that it's none of Tiff's business whether Sibylla is or isn't, has or hasn't been, sexually active, and why wouldn't Ben (or anyone) want to go out with her, but Holly didn't say any of that.

In fact, she didn't miss a beat, saying instead: I know, right? Where does that come from? No sign she's planning to put out while we're here, that's for sure.

Poor guy. He never signed up for the monastery.

(He did, actually, or at least his parents did. Close to zero sex going on up here from what I can see, no matter how much some people may be thinking about it, or talking about it.)

Yeah, said Holly.

What's wrong with her? I'd jump him in a second, if I hadn't already.

264

So would anyone sane. She has a strange mother, messed-up ideas about sex.

Weird girl. What about you and Ben, Hol? Maybe you should go there.

Don't want to ruin a good friendship, said Holly.

You and Sibylla?

Me and Ben.

Right.

They laugh.

Holly said: Do I seem like a complete bitch? (Yes.) It's just Sibylla drives me mad sometimes.

Don't be crazy! Tiff reassures her. I hate heaps of my friends.

More laughs. (Oh, the fun of it.)

Anyway, Tiff said, your thing with Vincent is totally going to happen. I hear he's breaking up with whatserface on exeat weekend.

We'll see, Holly said.

Sibylla isn't stupid; she knows Holly, but she also believes that she and Holly have a special friendship. She trusts her, in other words.

Holly acts pleasantly enough to Sibylla when they're together. In fact, anyone would think they were still best friends, but it sounds as though she has jumped ship.

Sibylla gave Holly a free ride to Camp Popular on Ben's shirttails, from what I can gather, but since Holly has landed, picked herself up, and dusted off, she seems happy to forget how she got there.

So now I have stuff I do not want. And I'm not sure whether I need to, or should, tell Sibylla, Your friend is every bit as mean as she seems, or let it float to the surface all by itself. Like scum.

64

sunday 11 november

The witching hour.

I'm not scared of ghosts. I long for a ghost.

Sibylla hates anything with even a half-whiff of paranormal to it. Holly is so cynical and skeptical; she'd take a lot of convincing. Eliza is averagely distractible, but not one to dwell in the silly zone. Annie would believe anything. Anytime. And Pippa loves a bit of drama.

So we were primed for something to erupt. We have been away exactly five weeks tomorrow. Everyone is settled. We are learning to rub along together, managing to avoid most fights. People are getting fit.

It was time for a big house-inspection spring cleaning. Kitchen cupboards emptied and scrubbed out, mattresses turned, etc., and unfortunately Annie found the word *Maisy* written on one of the slats of her bed in faded ink, in a very believable-looking copperplate script. She screamed as though she'd seen a cockroach murdered.

We all inspected. It must have been there when we arrived.

I didn't see it, Annie said.

It's the marked bed! said Pippa.

Marked?

Whoever has this bed in Bennett will have a special connection to Maisy.

Annie is freaked: But I don't want a connection. I want to swap, she moaned.

Holly could debunk this by declaiming it as crap at the top of her voice, but I can see her getting in the mood for a little careless evil.

It's not Maisy I mind so much as the thought of her doll, she said.

Don't, said Annie, really upset. How didn't I see it? Why did I get this bunk?

You didn't know the story when we got here, said Holly with fake kindness, you didn't know what your fate was to be: that you were the chosen one.

The weather was wild. Hard, wailing gusts of wind and furious blasts of rain coming in sideways from the south, dumping a lot of water in a matter of seconds. We threw rain jackets on to go to dinner. It was curries, which is one of the least worst, and a berry crumble, so everyone came back afterward in a good mood.

I was writing letters, and other people were mostly doing homework, which we call prep up here, just to remind us that we are somewhere super special. When everyone was in the middle of stuff, the lights went out. We could see across to other houses, they had gone dark, too, so we knew it wasn't just us, it was the whole campus. Once our eyes adjusted, we could see dimly, though the storm was making it darker than usual. Holly took advantage of the blackout, saying, I wonder if it's a sign?

A sign of what? Sibylla asked nervously.

That Maisy is walking tonight, looking for shelter, Holly said, assuming a fake, monotonous, trancelike voice.

Oh, don't, Hol. Not when it's dark, said Sibylla.

It's just the generator, said Eliza, and I'm late with this essay, so let's hope they fix it. She was setting up a flash-light on top of a jam jar and trying to continue.

Pippa said, But it has happened in years gone by, you do get some signs of disruption when Maisy is preparing to visit. It's as though she changes the electrical charge in the atmosphere.

I hate you all, said Annie. Just stop talking about it, or I will literally die of fright.

The wind kept changing direction. Sheets of spiteful rain slapped down hard on the roof. The trees were whipping around loudly with the odd branch cracking and crashing down. The atmosphere was unsettled inside and out.

The lights came back on after about half an hour and stayed on till bedtime, and lights out at 9:30.

Sometime in the middle of the night, in a very loud voice, Annie asked: What's that? Guys! Did you hear that? She was no doubt intending to wake everyone up to lend support if she was about to get a ghost visit.

I could hear a noise; it was a pipe shudder that happens when one of the taps in the bathroom is used.

Did you hear it that time? asked Annie.

Shut up, Pippa moaned, annoyed to have her sleep interrupted.

It's nothing; it's the wind, said Sib, clearly unconvinced by her own words.

By now we were all awake and this time clearly heard a rummaging, then a tap going on and off in the bathroom.

Annie looked around. W-who is it...we're all here. She went to flick her light on. But the generator was down again.

Pippa whispered, Maisy! Even she sounded frightened.

Maybe it came from outside? said Sibylla.

She's in our bathroom, said Holly in an urgent whisper. You go and check, Annie, you're the one she wants!

It's not M-M-M- her in the bathroom?

Who else? said Holly. Everyone else is in bed.

Annie was sitting up, peering around in the dark. Oh, no, she whispered.

Sibylla was hiding under her duvet.

The bathroom door slowly opened in the dark, and Annie screamed as a small figure emerged in the gloom, carrying something in one arm.

Annie was screaming her head off. Sibylla joined in. Eliza shouted, terrified, WHAT? What's going on?

Annie's light flicked back on again.

And there was Eliza standing in the bathroom doorway, clutching a hot-water bottle.

Annie started laughing, seeing Eliza, only she was crying at the same time.

Someone should probably slap her face, said Holly.

I'd like to slap Holly's face.

Sibylla emerged from under the duvet, white and frightened. No sleep for her tonight, I'm guessing. So, no ghost? she said.

By now everyone, except me, was laughing or crying or both.

Nice one, idiot, said Eliza, it's bad enough having the most shitful period cramps without living in this fucking lunatic asylum. Roll on, exeat weekend! Get me out of here. Can everyone please shut up now so I can get some sleep? I need to run tomorrow.

Our outside light flooded on, and Ms. McInerney barged through the front door (perfect bob still perfect in the middle of the night) and gave us all Sevens the next morning for our SelfishImmatureDisruptive behavior.

Don't we realize that other people have work to do and would like to sleep tonight?

Pippa whispered a little, *Mama, mama,* when we'd all settled, and everyone was soon snorting with laughter again, trying to keep it quiet.

I hate you all; I really mean it, wailed Annie.

65

My mother was on some committee developing or approving sex ed (life education) programs when I was thirteen, and as soon as I found out I made her swear that she would neverneevernever come to my school with a fun-facts-for-teenagers presentation, which I knew would include all her hits and classics:

- that oral sex is SEX, kids (featuring ten easily transmissible diseases), and not just a pants-zone kissing activity,
- that girl genitals are as individual-looking as people's faces, and so are boy genitals, that pornography bears (bares, lol) no resemblance to lifeography,

- that people should not get their girl fur blitzed in the Brazilian fad, because (a) why should women be infantilized, (b) you'll feel all bald and breezy when the full bush is back in fashion, and have to buy merkins, look it up, and (c) there are physiological reasons for the hair, but I can't remember what they are—that is me not remembering, not her,

- that it is never a good idea to take or send, or let anyone else take or send, photos of you or your friends or your enemies in any form of undress, or drunk, or drug-affected, or hooked-up,

- that whatever contraception people choose it should always, but always, include a condom, because you only get one chance to look after yourself and your reproductive health and your sexual health, and even though god knows *the last thing you want right now* is a pregnancy, one day you might and you don't want to find your tubes are clagged and scarred because you didn't or you wouldn't or you forgot to use a condom, and you got PIDs left, right, and center,

- that straight is normal, gay is normal, lesbian is normal, bisexual is normal, transgender is normal, but if you're worried about anything, talk to someone, visit these websites, here's a help-line number, etc.

- that if you are a boy you should encourage your parents to get you immunized for HPV, because it's not just for girls,

274

- that no means no, drunk means no, off your face means no, and I don't know/I'm not sure means no,
- that you can also get STIs from the ball sac, human not sporting, so you're never completely safe unless your partner is basically wearing full fishing waders and rubber boots as well as having a condomed penis (if your partner has a penis)...

And—never forget, kids—sex is a joyful, integral expression of being human. It's fun!

Yep, I know it by heart. But, in her defense, I can't imagine she would have okayed the word *outercourse*, or the term *sexual organ*. And she would never, in a million years, condone the use of *pleasure* as a verb.

monday 12 november

Brian is losing it because we want to listen to Triple J and he has the bus radio tuned to a really annoying country music station, as usual.

The bus is an automatic war zone: us versus Brian. Sometimes he loses it because people are singing along too loudly. Sometimes it's because people are late back at the departure point. Other times because kids yell out the window and he thinks he'll be the one who gets into trouble.

When we've pushed him too far (I use *we* loosely; I'm usually sitting there reading) he will inevitably say, I didn't fucken sign up for this. And then everyone (most people) says, ooo-oooh swearing, and he says, I'll deny it, so don't bother, and we all say, what *did* you sign up for? And he says, I said I'd drive the fucken bus. Finito. The things you do for love. Then everyone says, finito, the things you do for love. And he calls us disrespectful. That is not inaccurate, but he misses the point that it is not really personal.

People are just frantic to break out. They'd complain about whatever music was being played, to whoever was driving the bus. They'd demand something different just to flex their muscles. They'd impersonate whatever came out of the mouth of whoever was the unfortunate chosen to take us into and haul us back from the land of faux liberty.

To start with we had ten free minutes. This was notional shopping time. Our chance to spend pocket money buying stuff we mostly didn't need.

Girls buy tampons and sample the three pathetic cosmetic brands at the pharmacy. We flip through the maximum and buy the minimum of magazines at the newsstand. We can buy a small amount of candy, but we are not supposed to bring any back with us.

Today, Ben and Holly headed to the pharmacy with Eliza and Gabi trailing after. Pippa and Sibylla were lingering at the newsstand.

I dragged Michael into the milk bar, where he bought a slab of Kit Kat and some dark chocolate. I needed new supplies of raspberry toffee sticks. I bought and tested one before I committed to a bulk buy. Phew. It snapped. You don't want a bendy toffee stick, they are utterly pointless; you want a snapper.

We sat outside on a bench under a plane tree on the grassy median strip that was like a little park, and I broached the subject of the missing letter to Sibylla. He still hasn't found it. It definitely hasn't turned up at his parents', and he is convinced that he must have left it lying around, and even though it may innocently have disappeared during a general house cleanup, it may equally be in someone's possession. He's got the little tic in the corner of his left eye; I've seen it before when he's tired.

Michael and Sibylla and Pippa and I were on the roster for our second visit to the old people's home. Other people went to the kindergarten to help wrangle kids and poster paints, to the library to mis-shelve books, and to the Historical Appreciation Society to do minutely slow restoration work on crusty old bellows and saddles under the nervy supervision of Mr. Rattle.

No one minds it because wherever you end up at least it's a break from the bucolic-idyll meets gladiator-outdoor-skills-training meets all-your-usual-school-work life.

The old people's home is called the Dorothy and Randal Hayes Retirement Center. The building is a large and spectacularly ugly 1960s cream-brick block with concrete paths, pink geranium flower beds, and white-painted window frames. It was purpose-built; inside everything is wipe-downable, polished linoleum floors, ramps, and laminated tabletops. Such areas that are carpeted are covered with prickly tiles of carpet, easily replaceable in the event of nasty accidents.

Super-spacey residents are propped in a circle of saggy vinyl-covered recliners in front of a television that stopped making sense to them long ago. The whole place smells doddery. Cabbage, urine, and pine air freshener. But if you breathe through your mouth, you can't smell a thing.

Pippa brought makeup this time, making good on a promise to glamorize Dolly. They chattered away like old pals, and Pippa learned the secret of lovely skin at eighty (no sun and Pond's).

Michael's guy, Lindsay, has advanced dementia, and Michael thought reading aloud to him would be the best thing to do. Lindsay would ask Michael every now and then, when's Roy coming? Michael replied politely each time, he'll be in tomorrow, I think, to which Lindsay said, tomorrow, of course, as though remembering, and sat back happily, sucking on his dentures, for a bit more reading.

Sibylla and I were allocated time with Betty and Maureen, two old demons who shamelessly cheat to beat us at carpet bowling. Maureen has lost a few marbles along the way, and gets cranky if she doesn't win, so it was our job to try to make sure she won at least every second round. Last time we visited she had to be escorted back to her room for some time out, and we didn't want to revisit that shame upon her.

They brought food in for us, but we all said we'd just eaten. The food was depressing. It was all cooked, warm, watery, and smelled of instant gravy. Pudding and main course were on the same tray. Today's pudding was a cracked baked custard, sprinkled with nutmeg, that looked like it would bounce. It makes me feel ashamed of all the complaints we make about our prison mess; it is gourmet heaven compared to this.

Lindsay has to be fed, and Michael braved up for the job when the usual caregiver offered. He takes the community service responsibility seriously. Nearly everyone else is happy to do the bare minimum.

Lindsay's skin is stretched tightly across the bones of his face, mottled and blotchy. He opens his mouth like a baby bird, but does not always remember to close, chew, or swallow, so there is a bit of leakage. One of the nurses tied a kitchen towel around his neck, which I guess is marginally better than an actual bib. His eyes stay fixed in a place somewhere between vacant and terrified. Everyone he ever loved is dead, and he isn't far behind, so no wonder.

By the time Michael had fed Lindsay, he was as somber as I'd seen him, and he's never Mr. Smileyface.

As we left, Pippa, who had been the picture of shiny goodwill and smiles during the whole visit said, can one of you guys please shoot me in the head if I ever get that old, I'm not even kidding, and walked back to the bus alone.

Michael gave me a quick squeeze in the elbow region to acknowledge that the casual mention of death might have upset me. But it didn't. What upsets you when death has been on the agenda is when it doesn't get mentioned.

He wanted a magazine (*New Scientist*) at the newsstand before the bus left, and I dropped back and walked with Sibylla.

He does it hard, she said. The rest of us are there thinking the place smells bad, and when are we getting out of here, and trying to remember to be pleasant, but I know Michael would have been sitting there with the weight of mortality bearing down on his shoulders, becoming more and more concerned about the idea of losing his marbles one day. She was right.

Has he ever gone out with anyone? I asked.

No, but he likes you, she said.

I'm not in the market, and let's be real, it's you he likes.

Yes, but only in theory.

And we both know he's a guy who's big on theory.

She had the honesty not to deny it.

Staring out the bus window—watching the trees whip by and sky stay still—might be my favorite pastime in the world, even if we are going back to school. I'm sitting next to Lou, who is reading, as usual. Ben is right in front of me, sitting with Beeso; they're making each other listen to obscure rap tracks.

Lou remains a woman of mystery. Even in the emotion-incubator house setting, where we've all had various meltdowns, even since the singing, even though I see her at close quarters every single day. It's clear she doesn't have a single romantic thought in her head about Michael—but why not? Could it be something to do with the bookmark boy? Are they still going out? Is he the one who sends letters from France?

Since her public performance, she has garnered quite a following of arty-indie admirers. Not that she seems particularly interested, but I know that she is being courted by Miro, the only serious band in our grade.

She spends lots of time reading, and lots of time doing stuff with her camera and Blu Tack and fluff, fibers, and twigs. She may be putting together a "unique" and "idiosyncratic" piece of "new media" for her folio. That's what our art teacher, Ms. Bottrell, tends to call any material that lives in either the conceptual or abstract zone.

When I ask Lou about it, she gives her closest version of a happy face, which is a small, dry smile.

"All will be revealed," she says, enigmatically.

tuesday 13 november

One of the things Michael read at the old people's home was a poem by Wilfred Owen. He figured out that Lindsay is very likely to have been a part of and/or certainly had friends and family who were dragged or went willingly into the Second World War.

He read the poem, *Futility,* about a dead soldier that starts *Move him into the sun— / Gently its touch awoke him once,* and as he read I saw that he didn't really need to read it; he knew the poem by heart.

He had planned this in advance, caring about an old guy with dementia, thinking about what might have meaning to him.

If Sibylla would ever go out with Michael, she'd have

the second-most-thoughtful boyfriend ever to walk the earth.

When we got back he was still worrying about the letter; in fact the worry seemed to have built with the afternoon. He is starting to imagine he sees smirks and looks here and there, as though people know something. Nothing explicit has been said, and he accepts that this could be paranoia on his part.

I can't help asking him more about the Sibylla tablets. Wasn't he worried about getting a fur ball, and having to cough it up like a cat?

No. His intake was moderate, and he spaced them out. No more than one per week. He didn't want to overdose. A little bit went a long way. Because of their special power. He smiled his apologetic smile; if he took too many they might have lost their magical potency.

What made him think of it in the first place? He was just fiddling with a strand of hair until quite by accident it turned into a tiny little pellet. He had read that hair can be used to determine DNA and so he thought he might be transferring some of (what he considered to be) Sibylla's power into his own system. He knew about DNA when he was how old?

Four.

Okay. Completely logical. I could imagine doing the same myself if I'd known stuff like that when I was *four* and wanted medicinal benefits from a friend's powerful DNA.

69

Ben and I hike out from school with our respective groups for a day hike. The weather is perfect, crisp and still. Insects flick and snap through the air, and clouds stretch thin their semitransparent ripples against the morning sky.

We meet at the arranged spot, the three-mile mark of the home trail. As planned, Ben and I split from the groups, and head off on our own. Ben leads the way; he found a place on one of his runs that he wants to show me. We take a path that follows MacMahons Creek in the direction of Dead Horse Gully. I make a mental note to Sharpie in an apostrophe on the way back.

We're both wearing boots, shorts, and gaiters. Ben is wearing a T-shirt; I have on a light long-sleeved shirt and a brimmed hat, with sunscreen on every bit of skin that is unclothed. Always in the prevent-burn mode with my fairer-than-fair skin, so unsuited to the climate.

How different might it be if we had started going out in the usual place? In the city. Not here in the fishbowl. What might we have done by now? We could have hung out at each other's places. Mooched about doing nothing much. Gone to some more parties. He is invited everywhere. Seen a movie or two. Met each other's families?

Holly's massive pep talk is pecking away at me. She thinks this is our big chance to get it on. By which she means get off together. To do it. Why are the words we use about sex so prosaic and unenticing?

When we've walked for well over an hour and I'm starting to wonder if Ben has any idea where we're heading, we come to a clearing. Here, in the middle of nowhere, the remains of a stone wall covered in a tangle of overgrown banksia rose throwing out canes as tall as trees. I walk around. Time has swallowed any other traces of a house or hut, but there are paving stones deeply overgrown with grass leading down to the creek. There's wild feathery fennel, and mint, and, farther up the bank, a gnarled apricot tree. A forgotten, once-upon-a-time garden.

"So, how do you like it?"

"It's beautiful." I pick one of the yellow roses and poke it through a buttonhole in my shirt.

He looks happy. "I knew it was your kind of place."

I drink some water and start unpacking food. "What did you bring?" I ask.

"Forget food," he says, bending down to kiss me. And here we are again, back in the debatable land of want and denial.

I can't see Ben simply as beautiful anymore; it is something more pervasive. I need to pack the swoon back into the wrong end of the telescope before I drown in the distraction of him. He won't stay neatly in one compartment of my brain; he invades; he spills all over my consciousness. Perhaps skipping ahead to the heart of the matter is the only place to go.

Deciding to do it is less momentous and certainly less rational than it should be; I can't even say it is a decision; it's more like a switch has flicked. In one breathless look, we are both taking it as read, a need that this time we will act upon. I think of animation graphics that blast people into hyperspace. I'm in go mode. This is happening. No thought of turning back. I'm just doing it.

And neither of us has mentioned the four-letter word that comes before this three-letter activity in all my schemes and dreams.

Afterward I feel wobbly and slightly shocked, climbing up from under the rubble to check out the new world.

Orgasm, huh, sooo much easier on your own. Who

knew? How do people even coordinate it with all that distracting...sex...going on?

Did we really just do that? I want to hide my face. I want to look into a mirror in private, to check if I'm still me. A stone is pressing into my left glute, and the weight of him is starting to hurt my breast. I move and he lifts his head, kissing my clavicle on the way up and meeting my eye with a new ounce of shyness behind the usual smile.

Who is this boy, with three pimples on his perfect Heathcliff chin? A chin whose whisker shadows don't quite join up yet? Surely this exact moment is my cue to start feeling older, but it isn't working. I have never felt younger. I'm a kid with homework, and hikes, and a single-bed dormitory, and this...affair? Relationship? Mistake? The last couple of minutes just hand my inexperience to me, neatly wrapped.

New sprouts of bracken fern pushing up through the ground look like little alien embryo heads. What Have I Done?

I've had sex before Holly! A surge of satisfaction after so much coming second—not that I'm going to tell anyone about it. I have to trust Ben won't tell anyone, either.

I shiver with the cold and newness as the colors around us deepen, super saturating in this exact moment of fading light as the day becomes overcast. I close my eyes over the picture, and put it in the album of Significant Moments.

We lift ourselves out of the soft muddy leaf meal—my shirt and bra are both still hooked on one arm, so I drop them on a dry-looking patch of ground with our other discarded clothes and walk into the stream. "Don't look," I say.

Ben follows me, laughing. "Don't *look*?" He's right, it's a little late for shyness—but still I walk to the water with my arms wrapped protectively around myself. The day is warm, but the water is beyond freezing. I take a deep breath, dive under, and come up gasping with the cold. Ben cups water in his hands and washes some mud off my shoulder.

"Sorry," he says. "It's supposed to last a bit longer." He picks up my hand and pulls me closer. I shiver at the touch of his hot mouth on my cold breast, my cold neck.

"Are you okay?" he asks.

"Yeah, good."

"Didn't hurt too much?"

"No. Hardly at all. It seems awful that sex should hurt, so..."

Okay, shutting up now; there is no way in the world I know Ben well enough to tell him that a year ago at least, before there was even a remote prospect of sex on the horizon, I put enough fingers into my own vagina, in a nice warm bath, to make sure there wouldn't be a pain and bleeding situation if and when I finally did have sex, of which, at the time there was realistically zero prospect. I believed it quite likely that I would die a virgin. Can't remember exactly why I thought that...no boyfriend. Never had a boyfriend. But in the unlikely event that sex ever *did* happen, I didn't want to associate it with pain or discomfort...and now sex *has* happened, so it was just as well...Hmmm, was it an unnaturally control-freaky thing to do, or good old Girl Scout *be prepared* common sense? Not that I was ever an *actual* Girl Scout.

"Sib—so...?"

"Yeah—so it's really good that it didn't hurt." I put a hand against his face. "You were gentle," I say, kissing cold lips to cold lips. "And it was pretty quick."

"Do you want to try again?"

I want nothing more than to take him somewhere comfortable and have sex until we both die from happiness and exhaustion, but I'm looking at the tightly curled heads of those fern-frond embryos, and thinking of all the microscopic sperm swimming their little tails off. "You think the condom worked okay?"

"Yeah, I guess."

I'm remembering the banana classes. We definitely put it on properly. Did we take it out in time for no leaks? I think so. I hope so.

"Handy that you had it." I don't mean it to come out sounding bitchy, but there wouldn't have been any sex if there hadn't been a condom. It would have made my non-decision to have sex completely different: a decision not to have sex.

"I told you I was going to get some in Hartsfield."

"Tell me you didn't buy them with Holly."

"She was there."

The last thing in the world I can stand is the idea of Holly being happy that Ben and I...and then no doubt claiming it as her idea. "I'm not telling anyone about this. Including her." I stern-look him. "Nobody. I mean it."

"Relax," he says.

"I am relaxed—I just don't want anyone dissecting our private stuff. I don't like it that everyone knows everything. Whose business is it but ours? Nobody's, right? Am I right?"

He kisses me. It's a *stop babbling* kiss if ever there was one. Which is annoying. At the same time as being a truly great kiss. And from deep inside that kiss, I remember there was a crashing noise in the scrub, like an animal, nearby, while we were making our bed again, and lying in it.

Eclipses. A solar eclipse happens when the new moon is aligned between the earth and the sun, blocking the sun's rays and casting its shadow on the earth. A lunar eclipse is when the earth lines up between the sun and the full moon and casts its shadow on the moon.

In the first one, we see the object obscuring the sun.

In the second one, we *are* the object obscuring the sun.

We will observe a lunar eclipse in two weeks' time. We have a few good telescopes, plenty of binoculars, and a sky clear away from the city lights.

It is not exactly a historic once-or-twice-in-a-lifetime-if-you're-lucky event, like, say, a transit of Venus; you can get a few lunar eclipses in a year, but I've never seen one.

Light will dim; but even when in total eclipse, the moon will be softly lit by a red light, by such sunlight as can bend and scatter itself through the edges of the earth's atmosphere.

So we are all moon moon moon in class right now.

I do want to see it, I guess. Just can't feel the hype.

I suppose I must have known and forgotten, but I did enjoy hearing about the way the moon's gravity stretches the earth into a gently oval shape, and the oceans are stretched farther, because they are liquid, creating a tidal bulge on each side of the oval, which we see as high tide, low tide.

The huge silver moon, opening and closing the fragile anemones as water rises and falls.

No wonder time and tide wait for no man, they are busy dancing with the moon.

When I see the moon in eclipse...

Michael came back from his run yesterday as skittish and jumpy as I have ever seen him. He said he's worried about the hunters.

You couldn't pay me to go out there while there are crazy people with guns wandering about.

Well, hello, stranger: automatic and pretty strong impulse to stay alive.

71

Oh, noes. Oh, dear. I decide that my brain's decision not to start a sexual relationship up here on school camp, as opposed to my body's decision to jump on in, was and is the right decision.

Not that I didn't want to—omigod. *Omigod!*—etc.

But the place feels all wrong. And the timing is wrong. I feel as though I have leapfrogged into the sexual bit before the boyfriend bit, or even the friend bit, is right.

It's as though the relationship has a limp. Or as though we ran before we could crawl. Or some other uncoordinated-movement metaphor. Not that Ben seems aware of it. It's all leaps and bounds to him.

And—annoyingly—everyone assumes we've done it. Of course they do. Am I a complete idiot? Going off like that from our hiking groups, together with Holly's helpful news bulletin that Ben had bought condoms, is enough to get the smoke signals up all over camp. But no one should know, except me and Ben.

It's bringing out the straight-backed, tight-laced Jane Austen spirit in me. I believe my hymen is crocheting itself back together in protest at all the improper speculation.

I am so sick of Holly's gleeful interrogations, which start with, "I totally know you guys did it, so just spill. Share. If you keep excluding, I'll report you for bullying..." She's even resorted to begging, *pleeease pleeeeeeease Sibbie-pie, give me the juicies*. And bribing. She got some gherkins from Priscilla to put in our cheese-and-tomato toasties, and tormented me with their tangy, condiment-like appeal. But I'm not blabbing.

I manage to hold out all day Thursday, and on Friday we head home for our exeat weekend and I finally get to escape Holly's cross-examinations.

I walk into the house an unvirgin, and *no one notices*.

My mother tries to X-ray-read the history of the term to date but can only see that I am physically healthy.

Part of me wants to tell her everything, but the sensible part rounds the rest of me up like Aragorn. Sensible Sibylla lifts her sword and gallops up and down before the army of wimpy Sibyllas shouting forcefully: There will be time to tell your mother about your first sexual encounter. There will be a day to confide. There will be a time to ask certain questions like, how would you feel about Ben staying over? But it is not this day!

All we could possibly cover in a long weekend would be interminable talks about contraception and emotional responsibility, when all I want is food, rest, unconditional love, and some TV. That's not too much to ask, is it?

One day away from Holly's insistent presence, and I'm missing her. Go figure. So I text to see if she wants to come over for a *Misfits* marathon, but she doesn't answer. I'd feel hurt if I hadn't been giving her some pretty clear back-off signals for the last few days. We've had a tetchy couple of weeks, and a break is probably exactly what we need.

And, oh, the relief of being home. Home with my doggy, with the nice home smells, the home warmth, my own big bed, my own little bathroom. The privacy. The good food. The people who love me best in all the world, the people I can snap and growl at who will *still* love me best, regardless. I celebrate the return to the womb by rereading *Looking for Alibrandi* and fall asleep after tender, ten-layer lasagna and lemon tart, in a trance of perfect contentment.

72

friday 16 november

Mum came to school, met me at the bus, and took me home. Biff has a long surgery scheduled and won't be home till dinnertime. We're going out to our local Japanese, Japonica, where we go every Friday if we're around and there's nothing else on, and I'm looking forward to it. Gyoza and spicy tuna roll, it's been too long.

So, the counselor's happy...Mum said. Classy communicator, leads with an open-ended observation.

I live to serve.

Not that she can give us any details, of course, she said, slight increase of pressure.

Of course, I said.

Want to talk about it?

I shook my head.

She held my hand and smiled the tired-eyed smile of someone whose kid has had a very hard time.

More time has passed, and more time will pass, she whispered into my hair. It's all I've got, Louie. Not much, but it's the only thing that doesn't feel like a lie or a platitude. I rested my head on her shoulder and breathed in the faint comforting smell of her Chanel Cristalle. Home. My mum. Understanding.

Harriet's pregnant, she said. She looked at me in the assessing way: will it make me any sadder?

Harriet is/was Fred's stepmother, Plan B, and she works in the history department at Melbourne University, right near where Mum works in the fine arts department.

Were she and the Gazelle trying before...?

They've been hoping for a few years, and they were just having the IVF discussion when it happened.

Poor Fred's mum, I said. Because even though it is a happy thing, surely this might make her feel even more alone.

My mum nodded.

She put the kettle on for a cup of tea. She'd made my favorite orange cake, and soon I was in the shadow version of the old zone, making her laugh by telling her about Annie's literallys, making her grimace with recognition over stories of the Sawtooth Spur on a windy day, making her jealous with descriptions of food that is so so so much better than it was in her day, and the work schedule that is so so so much slacker than it was in her day. (They had to chop their own wood for the boilers, or there'd be no hot water. So, quite a lot worse, really.)

You were right, I told her. It was the best thing to do. Different place, different people.

73

Back at school, brooding.

Having completely wimped out of the first "talk," i.e., a full, mature, and unembarrassed discussion with Ben about sex, should we, shouldn't we, pros, cons, when should we, what are the alternatives—?

Without even discussing it properly *with myself*, I went with: okay, I seem to be having sex right now, yes, thanks very much; which means that I'm now in the horrible and perhaps illogical—though it feels right—position of having to have the no-more-sex-for-now-but-would-almost-certainly-like-to-be-heading-back-in-that-direction-again-soon-if-things-work-out-between-us-the-way-I-hope-they-do talk.

Is it just me who gets twisted into these tangles of my own construction?

And it's kind of annoying that I am the one with the talk agenda in mind. Ben doesn't seem to think we need any talking at all. What is it with boys that there's so little hashing-over required?

He thinks it is sufficient that he looks at me with those clear, hungry eyes. And it is distracting and electrifying—which is enough in its own way—but it doesn't get to the core of the discussion, which is—well, good question—but something like, what kind of relationship do we want together?

And I really don't like some of his friends, and does that matter (a) significantly, it's a deal-breaker, (b) sure, a little bit, or (c) relax, not at all?

"Training as soon as we get back, counting the days now," said Billy Gardiner, when we were taking back our lunch trays today.

"Oars before whores, dude," added Beeso.

"Yeah, man, back on the water," said Ben, slotting his tray in, as though he couldn't care less about the language.

I've bitten my tongue about this so many times I was ready to explode.

"That's disgusting," I said.

"It's a joke."

"It's not funny." I might have kind of yelled that.

"It's just a play on 'bros before hos,'" said Ben.

"I can't believe you're saying that as if you think it makes it better."

"Lighten up, Sibs," said Holly, adding to Ben, "Don't worry, it's time for her meds."

Now I was being patronized in stereo?

"I'm not some nutcase. I'm the one being sane here."

Michael heard this as he dumped his tray. "Taking drugs doesn't make you a nutcase."

"I'm sorry," I said. "I don't mean you." So everyone was looking at Michael.

"Thanks for that," he said quietly, and wandered off. He does take medication from time to time. I didn't mean to tell the whole world, but I was too angry with Ben to worry about that just then.

Michael will be fine. He's always fundamentally fine, based on the convenient fact that he doesn't care what people think. Lucky him. I wish I didn't care that I always seem to be shooting myself in the foot in the popularity stakes.

As we reached the door, Ben tried to take my hand, but I pulled it back. "I left something in the house," I lied.

He shrugged and headed off in the direction of the art room with Tiff, head shaking, and Holly, giving me the *bad girlfriend* look.

Holly loves being the conduit between me and Ben, smoothing things over, but I wish I didn't need a mediator.

"Who the hell do you think you are?" Beeso said as he walked off. "You're not even hot."

It's a fair question, minus the gratuitous insult.

I am really sick of the people who need to tell me I'm

unattractive. Somehow they feel duty-bound to put me down because I've been in that stupid advertisement. Surely my neon "self-esteem/appearance" sign is still visibly flickering on "below average." Nothing has changed there.

Q: And who the hell *do* I think I am?

A: I have no idea.

monday 19 november

Hello, infernal one. It was so good being home for a few days, but it felt weirdly right to be returning to the mountains and Camp Endurance for the last three weeks of term.

It is as though only by leaving and returning could I appreciate being here. The oldest travel cliché in the book. They don't get to be clichés for nothing. And I did think about people when I was away from them, which I didn't expect to do.

I wondered how Sibylla would be coping over the weekend; would she see her boy, or would all of Holly's plotting and planning with Tiff mean something was cooked up to keep Sibylla out of the loop?

Would Eliza be able to run enough to satisfy her manic fitness requirements?

What must Annie's family be like that she is who she is, wonderful and strange?

Would Pippa have been able to fit in all her beauty appointments and gourmet low-fat noshing?

And how would my one friend up here, Michael, have spent his three days? Was he able to restock on chess time with a worthy opponent? Restore his nine-letter-word puzzle levels? Was he able not to speak, and not get called up on it? Could he indulge all his fastidious food-that-looks-like-itself inclinations? Could he read at the table, with other family members all happily reading at the table, too?

Lovely long Skype with Dan yesterday, so good to talk to him. Estelle and Janie arrived right at the end. I promised Janie her film was nearly ready, but I have to get going with the edit.

Dan is so much older-looking. How does that happen with boys? It's only a couple of months since our last Skype. And his voice is deeper. He walked me around his host family's house, and I said *bonjour* to Henri and his parents and his little brother.

We talked about Fred and missing him, and no one gave us encouraging reminders about *moving on*.

Dan told me about Paris, and I told him about mountain life. And I feel...happy, it's true, when I think of seeing them in a month.

So, all in all I was feeling as close to okay as I've felt since it happened.

And this morning Michael gave me the most amazing thing. He had spent some of each day of exeat learning *Ode on a Grecian Urn* by Keats, to recite to me.

He learned a poem just for me.

This is the only quite-comforting poem I've read about dying young, he said by way of introducing the recitation. It's not quite analogous, of course, he said apologetically when he finished. But the sentiment, the notion of someone being suspended, remembered at a point in time at which they were perfectly happy... to be able to remember someone at that point, always, might eventually be some kind of comfort. I hope so anyway, Louisa, he said. I am sorry to have made you cry.

He left me to be alone. And truly, it wasn't that I particularly agreed with him about the comfort, because to me it is piteous, sad beyond imagining, that someone is forever suspended at a point in time, even if it was a happy one, and it was.

But the kindness of him doing that... the layered, risky, painful, pleasant thoughtfulness of it quite overwhelmed me.

In fact, the only person in the world I can imagine devising such a complicated kindness is you, Fred.

So when I read Ode on a Grecian Urn...

75

Holly and I slip out of our house for a first-night-back reunion sandwich and catch up in the laundry/drying room. We had a wobbly start today, but I'd like our last three weeks of term to be fun.

I've barely plugged in the squasher and thrown together some Swiss cheese and bread when she starts.

"So—Ben told me all about it."

"All about what?" I know Ben is true to his word. We agreed not to talk, and he wouldn't.

"I used the oldest trick in the book, and he fell for it." She is smiling, eyes shining. "I said you already told me everything, and so it was fine for him to talk—he wasn't telling me anything I didn't already know. Except that you did it twice. I didn't know that."

"You didn't know anything."

"I know how to improvise, though. I knew the sort of thing you would say, if you still trusted our friendship. We used to tell each other everything." She has the gall to get pouty and act as though she's cross with me.

"I've never had that much to tell," I say.

She looks nothing more than mischievous, as though great fun has been had by all.

"So you slept with Ben, and...how was it?"

I get a chill as I recognize the old Meggy MacGregor-doll look from way back: jealousy/hatred versus admiration/envy.

"You really think it's okay to trick him into telling you? Now he thinks I've blabbed."

"Listen, he didn't mind who knew, he was just humoring you because you have such a bug up your arse about people knowing."

"Did he say that?"

"Words to that effect."

"He's my boyfriend. Why do you always need to get involved? It's like you want an equal share of his attention."

"Whoa, don't be so jealous. Guys hate that. Anyway, he's my friend, too. I am allowed to talk to him. God, he needs someone to confide in; you're so neurotic about letting him say anything up here."

"I'm not neurotic. And I'm not jealous." I'm lying. I am jealous. Maybe I am a clueless girlfriend, but I'm not prepared to job-share the role with Holly anymore.

As we make our stealthy way back to Bennett, it occurs to me to ask Holly exactly when this conversation with Ben happened. It was on the exeat weekend. While I was bickering with Charlotte about what dinner *I* wanted for *my* special first night back home, and what DVD *I* wanted us to look at, Holly, Tiff, Ben, Vincent, Hugo, Hamish, and Laura had a big night out. They went to The Duke in St. Kilda to see Vincent's brother's band, Molière and the Bear.

"Did you think of inviting me?" I can't help asking.

"You know you would have been more than welcome," Holly assures me. "But I didn't bother. Your mum never lets you do anything."

"That's not true."

"Except go to lame-arse house parties. Only after she's rung the parents."

I feel as gutted as I would have at being left out of something at primary school. But this is all past tense, so it's like flinching in response to being slapped days ago.

"Why are you doing this?" I hiss as we wiggle our way back through the panel behind the water heater and into Bennett House.

"What?" she wants to know, all innocence.

"Trying to come between me and Ben, trying to make me look bad."

"I'm not—I mean, do you have a fake ID that I don't know about?"

"No. But I can look eighteen."

"Good luck with that one." She rolls her eyes. "Of course, I'm not the sophisticated model."

"Did Ben want me to come?" Gah! I'm so weak! Why am I asking her?

"He didn't say, but I'm sure he would have. You're in the middle of a major, passionate love affair, *n'est-ce pas*? Only you've made such a big deal about keeping it secret, no wonder he feels a little hurt."

"Did he say that?"

"Just guessing. Plus, you're all about being an independent woman, and not being a 'girlfriend.'"

"I am too a girlfriend."

"So maybe you're sending mixed messages." Holly shrugs.

Even though I'm annoyed with her, Ben didn't *have* to go out with them. He was invited to my place any time he wanted to come over on the weekend, only he said he thought he should spend the time catching up with his own family. Or, as it turned out, doing whatever the hell else he wanted, but not bothering to include me, or even *tell* me.

It makes me feel mad at Holly, mad at Ben, mad at myself for caring, and mad at my mother for being so tight about me going to licensed places.

"You're not mad, are you?" Holly knows me well enough to know that I am fuming. "I mean, poor guy—he deserves one night off the leash."

"He's not on a leash."

"No, he didn't act like he was."

76

A disturbingly electric kissing rendezvous with Ben makes me so dizzy in the pants I forget what I need to speak to him about.

Note to self: talking before kissing.

Now we have a small difference in body language—I'm trying to hold him at arm's length, and he is maneuvering us into a horizontal side-by-side thing, which of course reminds me of the most pressing agenda item: backpedaling on the sex.

So as I sit up, why is the first thing that comes out, "How come you didn't tell me you were going to The Duke on exeat?"

Ben sits up, too, with a groan. "Right on cue."

"What does that mean?"

"Holly said you were pissed off. Don't make a big deal out of it, okay? It was a spur-of-the-moment thing."

I'm doubly annoyed. Not only was I not going to mention this at all, and yet have managed to blurt it out accidentally, but it sounds like Ben and Holly have had *another* conversation about me behind my back. And now I'm even *more* annoyed, because why shouldn't they talk? They're friends. And why should that make me cross?

"You know me, I don't like everything all locked down."

"I don't want to lock anything *down*—I'm just saying, if we're going out, tell me if there's something on."

"What do you mean 'if we're going out'? Are you breaking up with me?"

"Did Holly tell you that, too?"

"She said you might find it all a bit too intense." Now I must look as pissed off as I feel, but I manage not to say anything. "The Duke was just crossed wires. I thought Holly was going to tell you, and she thought I would, and when we got there, turns out you couldn't have come anyway, because your mum's so tight or whatever, so we didn't bother calling you."

I try not to scream. "If you bothered coming over to my place you could have met my mother, and she isn't even that tight." Now I'm defending the person I have yelled at till I'm blue in the face for being so tight about the whole fake ID issue?

"Thanks, but I already had my own family stuff—all I wanted was to go out, have a drink, and hear some music."

313

His face closes over, and I realize he's never even told me about his family.

"You sound like you're angry with me—but what for?"

"For making a big deal out of nothing," he says.

"It's not nothing if I felt—" I don't want to say "left out." I feel like such a sad loser. "Look, I don't want to fight. Just next time—ask me if I've got plans, will you?"

"And—you're getting ID?"

"Yes. God."

He moves back within kissing range. "So now we can get on with it?"

"Now all the annoying talking is done?"

He sighs. "Is there something else?" he asks with exaggerated patience.

"Are you expecting us to have sex now—here in the great outdoors?"

"Well—kinda. Aren't you?"

He smiles his irresistible smile, kisses me on one side of my mouth, bends down farther, opens his mouth on my throat, and folds me into all that heat and hardness and muscle. Unfair. Unfair!

"I'm going on my solo tomorrow—you won't see me for two whole days."

I go into autopilot instruction to self, conserving language energy: Must retain cerebral presence. Must not let body take control. Time for the talk.

So I try to explain that even though I am attracted to him in a very, very, very big way, we jumped into—we just

314

skipped right over lots of things I wanted to do before we got into a full-on sleeping-together relationship.

"Such as?" he wants to know.

"Are we really any closer since we first decided to go out? Despite...you know. We haven't actually spent much time together. Or talked that much. I don't even know what your political views are. I don't know if you have a pet, or if you ever broke your arm when you were a kid, or how you get along with your family, what you want to study after school, where your favorite place to spend time alone is, and even though I've seen you put away an awful lot of food up here, we've never even gone out for a single coffee together. I don't even know if you drink coffee. I don't. I mean, an occasional latte, but I'm more an herbal-tea person."

"This is all very boyfriend/girlfriend stuff—I thought that was the zone you weren't that interested in."

"Based on what?"

"I dunno. Like you forgetting anniversaries."

"That's sort of the whole point. I've never had a boy-friend. I want to find out more—to start from scratch, properly, maybe even get to a year and have an actual anniversary, and, I don't know, spend time together, kiss at the movies, read books, talk about stuff, listen to some music...It feels like we've skipped the prologue and we're somewhere in the middle of things too soon."

"I don't get why it can't all happen together. Like while we're gettin' it on, I can sing you a song. Let's not be all linear here." He's trying to make me laugh.

"It'll be a pretty short song."

"Ouch."

"But like even the sex thing. I know it's something that needs a bit of time, bit of practice, but how do we even do that?"

"Jeez, Sib, we can start right here, right now. How does anyone do it? Grab it when you can."

"But I don't want it to be like that. Like people who have sex at parties and stuff. It's too public."

"So you're basically going cold on me."

I wish. I look at him and truly part of me just wants to jump him and skip this conversation, but the romantic me wants to be wooed, to walk together nowhere in particular, watch some bad TV, have a song, confide in and be confided in.

"Tell me, for instance, who is your favorite poet?"

He's trying really hard not to be impatient. Even while I'm pushing him away, I feel half sorry for him. "I haven't given it a lot of thought—maybe William Blake. Now, can we..."

"You can't see how I'd want to do things in a more chronological way?"

"Actually, no. Isn't this like the age of multitasking, three screens, parallel universes...?"

He looks at me, getting glummer as it sinks in that I am talking to him from a different country. "You know, what you're describing, the take it slowly, the talking, and books...that sounds pretty much like what you and

Michael have already got going. So maybe you're nearly at the stage, after what? Ten years?..."

"Twelve."

"... where you want to fuck him."

"Wow, that's mean. What's Michael got to do with this?"

"Yeah—shit, nothing, I guess." He stands up. "Just let me know if you have a change of heart."

Heart? How can he even say the word?

"The door's open," he says. "My body is yours," extending his arms, turning, walking off.

I lie back down, watching the blue sky burn through the light and dark of green leaves as tears slide out sideways, running hot through my hair to the ground.

How do you *feel*, Sibylla? What can I say to make it okay? Of course we can put the sex thing on pause. I will do whatever it takes, seduce you as slowly as you like.

I will court and spark you. I will wait till we can catch up on the other stuff. I will wake you with an enchanted kiss at just the right time. I will sing to you on a starlit night. I will savor you like the first peach of the first summer.

He's walking back. I sniff and wipe my face, but he just comes close enough to say, "Wu-Tang Clan."

He turns away, not noticing—or "not noticing"—the tears. Which is either heartless, or sensitive. And surely you don't sleep with a guy unless you know him well enough to know if he is being sensitive or heartless, right?

As he leaves, he says, "So, music, that's a start, yeah?"

After he's gone I say, "The Lucksmiths, Patsy Cline, the Velvet Underground, Chairlift. This week. Thanks for asking."

I tell myself that people have disagreements when they're going out. I tell myself that the perfect boy exists only in imaginary land. I tell myself how lucky I am that Ben Capaldi chose me. I tell myself to relax, anyone can have a bad day—it's not like we broke up.

Turns out none of these is the off switch for the tears.

friday 23 november

On this black day Holly has surpassed herself.

Dinnertime. Friday. Friday frittata, which is bad enough.

Priscilla chops up all the leftover vegetables she can lay her hands on and constructs an eggy cheesy housing for them, which she brownifies until rubbery and cuts into slabs that we try to digest.

Holly had the letter.

I'm not sure what her plan was; why bring it out right now? It's a couple of weeks since it went missing.

So she was—I still can't believe the nastiness of it—reading bits aloud without saying who had written it, or to whom it was written.

Everyone was enjoying the performance, laughing along as she fed them little morsels of poison.

You are my rock, my center of gravity.

You guide me through planet normal on which I am ever an alien.

There was general scoffing and derision at every line. I was ignoring it, just trying to finish dinner and get out of there, when I looked over and saw Michael. He was white.

He was watching Sibylla laughing with the others. It was his letter.

Who's your mystery lover, Holly? Sibylla asked.

I wind up your strands of magic hair and swallow their innocent power.

Oh, you've got a hair-eater? Sibylla said. That's new. Where did you find him? On the internet?

It was like watching someone about to be hit by a car, but being four lanes too far away to prevent it. Holly was ready for the kill.

You think he sounds strange? Holly asked.

More than strange. Weird. Sibylla laughed.

Not the sort of attention you would want?

Are you kidding? said Sibylla. Would I want someone to eat my hair? No. Thank you.

Well, that's back luck, because it's for you, not me. From your friend. Holly pointed at Michael and handed Sibylla at least ten handwritten pages, saying snidely, Like you said, weird.

All eyes went to Michael.

He looked only at Sibylla.

At that moment she could have saved him. But she hadn't even processed this. Her face was a picture of embarrassment, horror, disgust.

As she held his letter, she denied him.

This is not about me, she said. *Michael* and I...? We've never gone out. That's ridiculous. She was vehement, but also flustered, so that anyone might believe her discomfort was due to being found out.

Michael had insulated himself from the general ridicule and abuse that was flying around the room, and had just been waiting for, was only interested in, Sibylla's verdict. He accepted her position with a look, and left.

That guy is such a freak! said Holly.

Ben, who had been holding Sibylla's hand under the table, looked pissed off. Could he think that Sibylla and Michael have some secret history?

He gave his neutral smile, the one he produces when he's angry. Oh, boy, has that boy had some practice at covering up his feelings.

Sibylla was left holding the letter. She looked at it, still not sure what it was and why she was standing there holding it. Someone snatched it, and she grabbed it back.

Ooh, look, Sibylla doesn't want her secret relationship revealed, someone said.

There is no relationship. He is not my boyfriend.

But you're nice to be so protective of the letter, said

Holly. It's a laugh, truly, I haven't had so much fun since we got up here.

I've never met anyone I dislike as much as Holly.

Sibylla wants to be alone to read, or decide not to read the letter.

She wants to go after Michael.

She wants to be Ben's girlfriend.

She wants to be one of the relaxed and popular girls.

She wants to see if Michael is okay.

She wants to be cool about this, and not to look foolish.

She wants not to drag Ben into her embarrassment.

She wants Ben to know he has nothing to worry about.

She stuffed the letter in her pocket and said, all very funny, but I'm so starving, I could even eat some Priscilla frittata.

Holly looked at Ben, *what did I tell you?* And he shrugged back. Whatever game Holly is playing, it is not a nice one.

Time to say good-bye, internal journal. Time to enter the fray, and speak some sense to Sibylla.

I nab her later, on her way back into the house.

Have you seen him? I ask.

Not yet.

How could you do that to him, Sibylla?

Me? He wrote the letter.

It wasn't supposed to be sent.

How do you know about it?

I suggested he write it.

How come?

You know how he feels about you; it's a way of getting something like that off your chest.

Dumb idea.

It's an okay idea, I say. It's a standard therapy thing. The problem was Holly. She shouldn't have stolen it. I cannot believe she read it out loud, made *fun* of it.

No. Did you speak to him?

I haven't seen him.

I'll talk to him tomorrow.

Will you read the letter?

I don't know, would you?

I...probably, to be honest, I say.

But if it's not meant to be sent...?

It might help you understand him a bit better.

It's kind of annoying, you telling me what I'm doing so wrong with my oldest friend, she says.

No one else is telling you. You sure don't have much time for your *oldest friend*. You seem to care more about Ben's idiot friends. Since when are they more important than Michael?

You've known me for less than a term. You don't get to ask *since when?* What was I supposed to do? What would you have done?

To me it's obvious: I say, I would have acted like it was a joke between us. Like we have a whole history of silly letters we write to make each other laugh. That's it. Nothing to it. And then I would have turned the heat up on Holly. How did she get the letter? What was she doing snooping?

You're quicker on your feet than I am. I have to mull over stuff before I know exactly what to do. I'm still mulling. I'm still on *he eats my hair?* she says.

Can you stop obsessing about yourself, and think of Michael? He must be feeling like shit.

I let him down tonight. Fine. Sure, she says. But it's off the back of picking him up and looking out for him for the last twelve years. Do I never get a day off?

He hasn't got anyone else to rely on, I remind her. From what I can see, it's just you and me. Or is it just me?

A shot rings out in the dark, making us both jump. It is a noise that seems much closer in the dark. Another shot bites blind into the blackness.

Sibylla is giving me a long look: should she trust me, Michael's other friend, the quiet nerd, the person she less than half knows in the next bunk bed along?

She asks, when are you the girl in the photo? Is that just with your friends, like your ex?

I give her the condensed version: the girl in the photo died when the boy in the photo died.

She wants to know more, but I've kept her just out of reach for so long that she won't ask.

I'm sorry, she says.

She looks so lost; I step across the gap.

Sometimes I think I see you, Sibylla, but then you get all blurry about what people think about you, how you should act, what everyone expects of you, who you are pleasing, or not, should you say what you think, or not, is Holly onside, or not, do you really belong, or is it just because of Ben, or because of the billboard... The only person you should be is yourself. You can't control perception. All you can control is how you treat someone else.

I didn't mean to make her cry.

I say, tomorrow, you've got to show all those idiots that you're his friend.

She's still crying; I hope she's more relieved than pissed off to hear someone telling her the truth.

Strangely, I feel relieved, too, to find myself at this tipping point where it's taking more energy to withhold than to give.

So I give her a hug, and feel some hard knots untying themselves in my chest.

78

As much as I want to see Michael and try to make things okay, it's not going to be possible to have any boy house contact until tomorrow.

So I tackle the other conversation.

Back in Bennett, with a stomachful of home truths from Lou, I ask Holly to come with me to the laundry/drying room. We've got ten minutes till lockdown.

It feels like so much longer than seven weeks ago that we had our first toasties here. I didn't know if I'd be going out with Ben. Everyone was all *ooh* and *aah* about the dumb billboard. We were excited about the idea of camp and dreading it in equal measure.

Now I can run. My face still turns into a tomato, but I'm fitter and stronger. I've had sex, and decided to backpedal on that because it feels like the right thing for me. I'm still not one hundred percent sure if I *am* right, but I have to trust my gut, or it'll stop working.

And I've kept believing that Holly would come back to me, that we'd get back to the good place in our friendship. Now I don't even know if we can recover, or even if I want to. Lou was right, I need to grow a backbone.

"How did you get the letter?"

"He left it right on his bed."

"What were you doing there?"

"Visiting Vincent."

"Was the letter in an envelope?"

"Yes."

"Addressed?"

"It had your name and *not to be sent* on it. So naturally I took it. Always got your back, hun."

I look for it out of habit, but my Holly-being-Holly excuse has disappeared. She's dragged me into such cruelty I could not have imagined. I don't even know how I'm going to look Michael in the eye tomorrow.

"How could you do that?"

"How could *I*? Shouldn't you be asking how could he write that weird crap?" She laughs again, shaking her head, remembering it. And then has the effrontery to be indignant. "I thought you'd appreciate it. I had the guts to shine a light on the way that guy thinks about you. Someone needs to show you what's going on. Have you read the rest of the letter?"

"I don't think I should. He didn't mean it to be read."

"Oh, please, don't be such a goody-goody. It starts, *My dearest Sibylla*...It is full-on. You'd think he really loves you."

"Perhaps he does." I know he does. "But only as a friend. That's not a crime."

"The letter doesn't talk about friendship. It talks about *love*."

The letter is still in my pocket.

"Come on, Sib, what are friends for? You're not saying I shouldn't have shown you?"

She's taking such pleasure from the drama. Humiliate Michael? No problem. Embarrass Sibylla? Bring it on. Too easy. Right now, this minute, I hate her.

"You went too far with Michael," I say. Feeble start, when I feel like strangling her. I'm trying to keep Lou's sane words in mind, trying to be myself. Only I'm too upset to construct a sensible sentence.

"He went too far. You should read the letter. He used to eat your hair, for fuck's sake—and you're okay with that? You don't think that deserved a little airing?"

"I'm sure he doesn't do it anymore." Hmmm, no doubt unusual behavior, but I'm not going to be distracted. "How do you think Michael is feeling right now?"

"He should be feeling ashamed of himself. Trying to shoehorn his way in with someone else's girlfriend."

"I don't belong to Ben. You know I hate all that stuff."

"So you thought you'd have a bit on the side with Michael?"

"Don't be stupid," I say.

"Exactly, so what's the problem? Will you at least admit he's weird now, a creep?"

"He's—Michael. He's lovely. He's not a standard-issue boy. He's my oldest friend." I feel a punch of nausea as I try to imagine what he is doing right now. Did he go back to his house? Did he get anything to eat? Who is looking out for him? Will the other guys give him a hard time, or leave him alone?

"Who has creepy thoughts about you," Holly continues.

"Creepiness is in the eye of the beholder. He is not creepy. I still can't believe you did that, Hol. In front of everyone. It was so nasty." Tears come into my eyes.

"Honesty is the best policy."

"I don't much like your way of being honest."

"Does Ben know how defensive you are about Michael? Do you remember who you are actually going out with, where your loyalty lies? Because someone listening to you wouldn't be able to tell. Did it ever occur to you that Ben might be jealous of your friendship with Michael?"

"Alas the day! I never gave him cause."

"What?"

"Nothing."

friday 23 november (late)

Michael's gone.

Run off into the night. It's the worst thing he could have done.

For someone with a sophisticated understanding of the world, he has no real concept of front. He should have faked it. I, Lou, the grand mistress of fakery, could have shown him how, no sweat. Too late now.

They come to Bennett at 11:30 PM.

The interrogation happens in the staff room.

Sibylla and I tell them yes, he was upset, no, he didn't say anything about planning to run off, yes, he *was* upset, some kids were teasing him, can't remember who, no, can't remember about what, yes, he did leave the dining hall seeming a bit agitated, no, he wasn't being systematically picked on, bullied, or intimidated.

There is no point amplifying his distress by blabbing details to the teachers.

We didn't even need to coordinate our stories. The code of kid versus teacher communication is understood. Everything is on a need-to-know basis.

It seems like just half an hour ago the night was clear. Now a huge wind is whipping around the campus, and the rain is starting to bucket down. There's a nearly full moon, which would possibly help Michael, wherever he is, if the rain clears.

Where are you?

80

His face is going through me and through me on a loop. As he looked at me, looked at my reaction to the letter, he was white. He was afraid. He wasn't afraid of public humiliation. He wasn't afraid of Holly's nastiness. He was afraid I cared so little. I betrayed him. He has run away thinking I don't care at all. I care very much. How have I managed to treat him so ill? The cold rain will be nothing to him compared to my coldheartedness. As I sat there surrounded by the laughers and jokers and laughing along, I had lost myself.

Lou is right; why was I trying so hard to be a part of that? Is that the price of going out with Ben: that I don't know how to be myself anymore?

Holly said I get to choose. She was so wrong. Things happen around me, and I react, ad hoc. I haven't stayed strong enough to be myself.

81

(late)

Mum has told me that when kids went AWOL in her day—yes, it happens nearly every year—there's always someone who can't hack the isolation, the pressure, the homesickness, the general *Lord of the Flies*ness of it...the whole school would fan out in formation and start walking the countryside in a search party.

These litigious days they probably wouldn't do that anyway, but even less so with gun-carrying hunters in the mountains.

They have rung the police, and Michael's parents, who are on their way up. Two teachers, Helen Ladislaw and our math teacher, Jerry Epstein, are taking off against the advice of the principal, Dr. Kwong, who tells them that they are under no obligation to risk their own safety, etc.

We'll sign a disclaimer, says Mr. Epstein. I'm not going to face Michael's parents and say we sat here and didn't go and look. Mr. E has kids of his own. His whole family lives up here. I can see he is simply doing what he would want someone to do for one of his kids. Michael is his equal favorite person in class, with Van Uoc, and me, probably.

I give them as much detail as I can on Michael's favorite running routes. The two teachers will take the Paradiso path wearing their boots and reflective jackets, armed with flashlights, sat phones, optimism. The police will go out along the Coldstream trail. An emergency crew will be free in a couple of hours, and they will take the inland trail to Hartsfield, and work their way back toward school.

Sibylla and I ask to help, and are not allowed. Sibylla is crying.

There is good reason to worry. You only have to run fifteen minutes out in any direction to start coming across some really nasty, rocky falls, some cliffs, loose ground, narrow paths. You'd be unlucky to get shot, but you'd have to be lucky to avoid one of those hideous falls in the dark. The rain will make things slippery, but will also slow him down, cool him off. Maybe on balance, it's a good thing. A good omen.

An almighty crack of thunder shakes the windows as they leave.

Seems like hours later—but it's only 1 AM when I

check—someone brings hot chocolate for us. Sibylla is still crying, which is getting annoying, but at the same time, I completely understand.

I imagine Michael falling, broken, alone.

Be safe be safe be safe.

We are allowed to wait up. His parents will be here in two hours.

82

Why did Holly do this?

And why didn't I think to respond as Lou suggested? It would have defused things so quickly. Why do I whirr or stall when I need to be going zip zip? I froze. I go over and over and over my rejection of him. I know the face Michael would have seen: it was my *erk, ee-ew* face. A look of squeamishness, repugnance, revulsion. That is the face I showed my old friend. That face shoved him out of there, white, into the hollow lap of this bleak night.

Fear pours through me. Don't die. Please come back safely.

Let me say sorry. Please let me say sorry.

I hate myself; even now, I am thinking of my comfort. *I* will feel better if I can say sorry. I'm no friend to you,

Michael. But if I am allowed to say sorry, I will mean it from my heart, and never treat you carelessly again.

Tears keep slipping out. Love, self-pity, self-loathing, regret, hope, all leaking from my sorry heart.

I wake up with a jolt on the sofa in Dr. Kwong's office, which has become emergency HQ. Lightning horror-movie-bleaches the view outside.

Lou shakes her head, no news. Thunder thumps through the sky, and I'm wide-awake again.

One of the great things about our art teacher, Ms. Bottrell, is that she's an old-school technician. She might not be completely comfortable with conceptual art, but she's the bomb on color theory. It's way out of fashion, and not con-sidered to be very creative or whatever, but I love knowing that stuff.

There's an exercise she did with us. She held an orange in front of a large piece of white sketch paper and said, "Gaze, gaze. Still gazing. Don't stop gazing." After a cou-ple of minutes she took the orange away. "Continue look-ing at the paper. What do you see?" Those of us who had dutifully gazed saw a burning spot of blue, the absence of orange. The opposite of orange. Anti-orange.

Now that Holly has stepped away, I see the opposite of friend, anti-friend, in the place she has been standing all these years. And I see the childishness of my sometimes-embarrassed feelings about Michael. He is not someone for when there's no one else around, or a basket case who needs the odd bout of babysitting. He isn't just a relic from childhood. He's smart. He knows himself. He knows me. He has always been a friend to me, despite my own flickering and inconstant friendship toward him.

Lou is there, too, in the burning blue space. A friend brave enough to be truthful—very different from Holly's "honesty."

83

(late)

The night brings us nothing, gives nothing away.

It's 3:30 AM, and a car arrives: Michael's parents.

I'm not sure why Sibylla and I are even allowed to be here. Perhaps it has something to do with proving to his parents that Michael was having a fine time here at Camp Disaster: look at these two lovely, concerned friends.

His parents seem nice; they're worried. His mother gives Sibylla a hug, and makes a point of telling me that Michael has told them about what a fine voice I have, and how he enjoys my company in math. I can see that she knows about Fred: she is not talking to a girlfriend.

The police make contact.

They have covered a certain amount of terrain, and they

will backtrack and head north again, but beyond that, there is little point in doing anything else until first light, when they can get a helicopter out, *if* the weather clears a bit.

The wind has dropped to a moan, and it is still pouring. It's actually weather Michael loves running in, but I don't say that; it is unlikely to be received well.

And I hate to guess what state of mind he was in when he ran out into the night.

84

It's something I have to do now, before I think it through—
I pick up the megaphone they use for safety drills and walk
out into the storm, flicking the on switch.

It is dumping down. A waterfall, and I'm wet through in
a matter of seconds.

I announce to the night, to the school, to the warring
elements, to the universe: *Michael, you are my oldest friend,
my best friend. I'm sorry. I am so lucky to have you in my life. I
won't let you down again.*

85

(late)

I'm holding Sibylla's hand. She's sitting with a towel hooded over her wet hair, ignoring the latest in the series of hot drinks.

She is anguished. Maybe she thought the boy who would do anything for her would also come in from the night if she yelled hard enough.

He didn't.

She is even whiter than usual. I can't bear knowing how much worse it's about to get for her if Michael doesn't make it back.

86

I don't deserve it, but I'm the one who sees him first.

A little white light, a hovering dot like a firefly.

He's wearing a head lamp. He didn't run off to end it all; he ran off to run.

Someone screams out, "He's alive." (It's me.)

I grab Lou, and we run outside; the others follow.

I'm shouting his name, and I can't stop. He runs in from the end of the home trail, pulling off the head lamp, and understanding in a glance what is happening. He says something about where he's been. WHO CARES? HE'S BACK.

I grab him and hug him. I cannot let go. I'm crying and laughing.

I'm thanking all the gods of every persuasion ever invented throughout the whole of the history of the world and their squads of angels and Santa's helpers and the universe which has decided tonight to be benevolent.

saturday 24 november

When Michael runs back just before dawn, he is surprised and (one half second later) acutely embarrassed at the kerfuffle. He has been running for six hours.

Made it to Walcott Spur, he says, as he removes his head lamp.

He apologizes to all, didn't think he'd be missed.

Dr. Kwong looks him over, contains her relief, smiles, shakes her head at his parents, and says she'll alert the police and SES.

Sibylla probably needs someone to slap her face really hard, but I know what it is to wait for a friend, so it's not going to be me doing the slapping.

Michael tries to distribute the hugs that are needed; his

mother, controlling herself with every fiber: now her boy is safe, she is not about to do anything to add to his discomfort. She is shaking and she crosses her arms to hide it. His father is contained, and tired. I realize looking at him as he hugs Michael and pats his back that he was at least half confident that Michael had run off in a planned way. Michael is just like him.

Sibylla's volume of happiness has woken a few people; Ben and Hamish filter out from Michael's house, Cleveland.

I made it to Walcott, says Michael, already almost recovered.

I hand him some water. He smiles his thanks, and I get a hug, too. This unaccountably makes me release a large sob I didn't even know I was holding.

He is boiling hot, soaking with rain and sweat, and alive. He bends down to my eye level. I'm so sorry to worry you, he says quietly. I really needed to run.

More people are coming outside and realizing what has happened. Ben is one of the first people to congratulate Michael; back-slapping and handshakes are added to hugs.

That's so awesome, man, I'm never going to make up that distance. I hand it to you. He is formally conceding the distance-running trophy/record for our term to Michael.

Ben looks a little uncomfortable at Sibylla's extravagant happiness but knows that now is not the time for quibbling.

Sibylla has no time for any of us except Michael.

I'm fine, Michael is reassuring her. A little lie to make her feel less horribly upset.

The teachers, Ms. Ladislaw and Mr. Epstein, emerge from along the home trail, looking wrecked until they see Michael in the dawn light.

Mr. Epstein runs up and claps Michael on the back. That's the boy. Knew you weren't an idiot. Take a fucking sat phone next time you run off, will you?

Everyone laughs and understands, and he apologizes for the language. Michael's parents thank him and Ms. Ladislaw so much.

And Ms. Ladislaw is saying she just knew he'd be okay; it's the lunar eclipse next week, and she tried to bet Mr. Epstein one hundred dollars that Michael wouldn't miss that in a million years, but Mr. Epstein wouldn't take the bet because he thought the same.

Dr. Kwong asks Michael's parents if they would like her to get a doctor. No, Michael's father is a physician. He asks Michael if he's okay, Michael says yes, he's fine. Did he have any falls, or bump his head? No. That's good enough for Michael's father.

Michael has a couple of scratches on his face, nothing needing stitches. His father says that Michael probably just needs food, a hot shower, and some sleep. They are pretty low-key with each other.

Dr. Kwong shoos us all off to bed for some sleep before

breakfast, and says, let's give Michael and his parents some time alone together, and we all go.

No one thought to check when people realized Michael had disappeared between 11 PM and midnight, but he had actually written his run down on the track sheet.

88

I am deep inside a dream about having to carefully place small shells and buttons into a container, knowing it is my job to fill it precisely, and noticing some baby teeth and seed pearls in there, wondering if they belong with the buttons and shells or if I have to remove them and start again, when Holly's voice scratches across the strangely worrying collection. "Have you two finally gone lezzer? I knew it had to happen sometime."

I open one eye a fraction of a semi-squint: Annie and Lou are coming out of the bathroom together. Light is soft and low; it mustn't be more than an hour after daybreak.

A wave of thankfulness: Michael got back safely.

A wave of annoyance: Holly.

A wave of exhaustion: I need more sleep. I throw a pillow

in Holly's direction and tell her to shut up, but despite being tired, and wanting to be asleep, I'm pleased to hear Lou biting back.

"Not that I want to talk to you, but no, we are not," says Lou.

"Not that it would be any of your business," adds Annie, tired and grumpy.

"And PS, 'Hol,' my parents are both women," says Lou.

"Two women?" says Holly. "You have two mothers?"

"My mother is Maggie, and my other mother is Biff. It's Elizabeth, but she's always been called Biff, since her little brother couldn't pronounce it. He said 'Liffabiff.'"

"That is gross. Do you even know who your father is?"

"He's my uncle James. Biff's brother. The one who couldn't pronounce her name."

"That's freaking incest," says Holly.

"Wow, you really are almost as stupid as you look. He is not related to my mum. He was their donor. It means I'm biologically related to Biff as well as to Mum, that's all."

"That's sick."

"No, it's bloody not, now shut up," I say.

"Of course you'd defend them," Holly says. "What *were* you two doing in the bathroom?" She really doesn't want to take no for an answer on this one.

"You guys freaked me out so much I can't go in there by myself anymore. Lou stands guard for me," says Annie.

"Against?"

"Maisy and the charcoal man, of course. Who do you think, you idiot?" says Annie, putting a pillow over her head and pulling the duvet up over that.

I need some more sleep before I can figure out how I'll ever be able to make amends to Michael.

tuesday 27 november

We get permission to go on a hike together. Just the two of us. How?

They're so relieved that Michael didn't go and die on them that they've bent the rules? Or maybe Michael's parents have asked them to be lenient. Perhaps they saw his eye tic. Or maybe my mothers asked. Or Merill put in a good word for us.

We go up to Snow Gum Flat, the scene of the infamous party that neither of us went to. We take a picnic. We take our time.

We stretch out between the springy grass and the sky's endlessness. Touch the crisp petals of the everlasting daisies. Hear only birds and swooping dragonflies. Here, only us. Eat. Doze. Read.

Michael says, you know the snow gums?

I know them.

They have to survive such harsh conditions, such extremes of weather, bits of them die. And they are able to grow new wood around the old dead wood. That's how they get to be such strange and beautiful shapes. They are hardier and more complicated than, say, the messmate or peppermint eucalypts farther down the mountain, which are protected by a softer climate.

Thank you. That's a lovely way to think about it, I say.

We look at each other.

I was talking about myself, he says. I was being resilient in the wake of Sibylla's public repudiation, and the ridicule that followed it.

We start laughing. We laugh at our respective self-involvement.

I want to be the snow gum, I say. You need a taller metaphor for your mending heart damage.

My heart will recover; I take the long view.

He picks something up from the grass. It's a dead dragonfly.

Would you like this?

I would love it, I say.

He hands it over, and I tip it gently into a specimen jar

from my backpack. Dragonflies are hands down on my Top Ten list of the most beautiful things in the universe.

I know I'll keep it forever and, looking at it, remember this day. A day on which I felt hope and contentment, and knew sadness was in retreat. A day on which my smile remembered how to work without needing specific instructions. On this day, I will remember, the future woke up, stretched out, and opened its arms to me again. And it felt quite possible to come out of the room of one-day-at-a-time.

I need to cry, because feeling good means I'm taking a step away from you, Fred.

I can cry in front of Michael. I trust him, and so would you.

They're exactly how I imagined fairy wings when I was a kid, I say.

I'm talking about the dragonfly, but Michael knows that is not what's making me cry.

90

I decide it has to be a letter fairly bristling with nine-letter words.

I read it out.

Dear Michael,

Conceding the *hideosity* of my *barbarism* and cruelty, I *haltingly importune* you, seeking your *acquittal* in the *aftermath* of my *abhorrent offending* and *nefarious puerility, expiating* my far from *guiltless maladroit encounter* with *dastardly, dangerous* Holly.

My *execrable fatuosity perplexes* your *cleverest judgement* with its *incaution.*

Pardoning processes, peaceable gallantry will *exonerate* my *harrowing heartsore, providing consoling innocence, steadying stressful suspicion, rewriting poisonous* and *tarnished theatrics* of *toolheads* and *numskulls.*

Primitive, offensive, brainless bullyboys will be *abandoned* with *sharpness,* like a *pocketful* of *spiraling, pixelated pilchards.*

Following this *guiltiest grievance,* may we again find *nobleness, plentiful gleamiest pleasance, suspended tenuously* in the *habitable continuum,* the *indulgent firmament* of *genuinely wonderful compadres*?

I *reimagine* a friendship of *unfailing tomorrows* that *reunifies, reprieves,* and offers *sanctuary, salvaging* a *shattered, sleepless simpleton* (me) from *indignant rejection,* and *nurturing* the *sublimely unequaled nonpareil* (I know they mean the same thing, but that gets *redundant* into the mix) *faultless* (you).

Ihopethis hyperbole is *providing fantasies* of *cordially consoling comebacks.*

Harrowing horsehair suffering of which my *stupidity* is *deserving* will I hope be *suspended* by *lunchtime* (it gets itchy).

Look *pityingly* on my *unhappier prospects, pronounce reparable* my *immediate lowliness,* and *comradely accolades* will be *bashfully enshrined* once again.

We will *luxuriate entranced* in a *merriness ever-green, eschewing senseless secrecies, validated, vivacious*, and *nevermore woebegone*.

Fettucine.

Treasures.

That *completes* my *chronicle*.

Yours, *ultracool, heedfully wrangling vitriolic wildfires* better in future,

SibyllaXX

(*Naturally, plentiful spoonfuls* of *sparkiest nectarine* and *tamarillo sherberts* will be my offering, if your *simpatico surmounts* my *shabbiest desertion*.)

I risk looking up.

He is smiling. "You had me at *hideosity*."

"I took the liberty of a few spelling cheats."

He nods gravely. "That's okay."

I hand his letter to me back to him, resealed in an envelope with his name on the outside. "I didn't read it."

"You can if you like; it's nothing you don't already know," he says. "And you already heard some edited highlights."

I shake my head. "Nuh-uh—it's the one thing I could do to show you I'm your friend."

"I know you're my friend, Sibylla."

I'm floating.

The absence of pain is powerful.

So now if I can just catch up on some work, and figure out where the hell I am with Ben, everything is shaping up kind of okay for the end of term. Because finally, it's countdown time—the last ten days. What I've been hanging out for since day one. It gives me a pang, though, not the spike of joy I would have thought. Seriously, if I'm getting nostalgic...

91

Annie is becoming obsessed with our impending astronomical event, the lunar eclipse.

Someone made the mistake of showing her *Melancholia*, a great movie in which a planet, Melancholia, may or may not be on a collision course with planet Earth. Spoiler alert: Turns out it is on a collision course, and in the last scene Melancholia hits Earth, and it's a giant blinding *ka-boom*, good night, folks. We were crowded around a Mac in Bennett House watching it, and at the end everyone sat in complete stunned silence for a while.

The kid in the film makes a simple instrument to measure and monitor the planet Melancholia's position relative to Earth: a circular wire loop on the end of a stick will, when you look through the loop, show if the planet is getting smaller (farther away) or larger (closer) relative to the circumference of the loop.

So Annie has made her own wire loop-on-stick measuring instrument and is worrying nonstop that the moon is going to crash into Earth.

We have all at different times now during the course of the day reminded her that *Melancholia* is a movie. It's fiction. There is no such planet as Melancholia. The moon is not about to crash into Earth. And so on.

But this is the girl who thought—no doubt secretly still thinks—that dinosaurs are mythological, so it's no stretch for her to think we are bullshitting her about the possibility of the moon being dangerous.

"They thought Melancholia wouldn't crash in the movie, too, for a while, *then it did*. So how do you know that the moon isn't going to crash?" How can you argue when a fictional narrative is offered as evidence?

And she still doesn't get what *literally* means, which doesn't augur well for her future—or current—study of English. When she came back from the exeat weekend with a new haircut, for instance, she told anyone who'd listen, "I literally look like a piece of shit." We tried to explain that this would mean she was like a big brown baguette-shaped thing, with no face or arms or legs. And she looked at us as if we were crazy as we became more and more hysterical and she became increasingly annoyed. "Are you girls on drugs? What does a baguette have to do with anything?"

"Nothing," said Vincent. "They just don't want to say it would mean you'd look like a giant crap."

"You stay out of it. You're disgusting," Annie said. "I wish I could go home now. You literally all make me sick."

"No," Lou started explaining, "we don't 'literally' make you sick—if we did you'd have a temperature, or be vomiting..."

Annie's alarm is growing as her wire loop appears to indicate that the moon is indeed coming closer to Earth, that is to say: looking bigger relative to the circumference of the wire loop.

Michael takes her aside during Elevenses, and as Annie eats two nervous lemon slices, he explains the whole cycle of the moon to her, with diagrams, which is really kind and more involved with a human he doesn't know very well than he would usually get.

He told her that at the moment the moon looks fourteen percent bigger, shines about thirty percent more brightly than usual, but even when it is as close as it ever gets, it's still about two hundred and forty thousand miles from the earth.

"Since when are you so nice to people like Annie?" I ask him. Still privately feeling a rush of relief that he is here. He is safe. Thank you, universe.

He looks at me. "Good question. I technically am not. I did that because Louisa told me Annie was worrying herself into a state of insomnia, which meant Louisa was not really able to sleep, because she is the one in whom Annie can confide her fears."

361

"Lou and Annie are friends?"

"Perhaps not 'friends,' but Louisa is ... sympathetic."

She's nice enough to take the time to talk properly to Annie, and notice when she's freaking out about planet crashes and bathroom ghosts. I used to be that person. But this term I got transplanted into the zone where you just talk to Annie to laugh at her.

92

sunday 2 december

The lunar eclipse, finally.

Sibylla and I are the last ones out, standing in the alien orange moonlight.

There is a line for the telescopes, an orderly procession of nerd-wonder. My name's on the list, too. I want to see the shadow moving away from the moon's surface. There is plenty of time.

The non–science fiends are happy enough to stand around, looking with their naked eyes, and passing around several pairs of binoculars.

Holly is so *cold*, and snuggling up to people. The girlie shit she carries on with annoys me. Truly, if you are cold: get a jacket.

The moon is slowly being obscured by the earth's shadow as the light dims and the stab of each star's light brightens.

As the night darkens further, and everyone else is busy gluing their awe to the sky with *oooh*s and *wow*s, I see Holly tipping her face up toward Ben's.

In the lunar eclipse we, the earth, obscure what is right before our eyes, the moon.

93

Lou and I almost miss it; we were cleaning up the Bennett kitchen after some cake-eating. It's not worth leaving even one sticky fork in the house kitchens; the ants up here are intrepid. They must have read all the school PR material—they make the most of opportunities, take initiative, they are leaders, they work cooperatively together as a group, they enjoy the architect-designed facilities.

Lou and I are sharing a pair of really strong binoculars. Soon she's got a turn booked at the Meade telescope on the oval with the other math nerds. They haven't been overstating things—this is totally awesome. The moon is glowing red-orange, and it's like we're standing on a new planet. I feel a rush of trust and hopefulness that I'll be able to figure stuff out. It's as though I am exhaling properly for the first time in a couple of weeks. Against everything I thought, I have almost survived my time in the wilderness.

I glance around to find Ben, and the first thing I see is Michael enjoying prime telescope time. He and Mr. Epstein are yapping away together in astro-science heaven. Michael comes over to tell us he saw the Copernicus crater, and that the eclipse makes the moon look like someone's taken a fuzzy-edged bite out of it. As the shadow slips farther from the face of the gleaming moon, the light level lifts slightly and I see Ben—I lift my hand to wave him over, but in the half-light and the crowd, he doesn't see me. He's standing next to Holly, tilting his head down toward her.

Jealousy bites; it can make you totally paranoid.

Holly smiles up at Ben. They're just talking. But still I feel a little ping of disappointment—I should have been the one standing next to him.

94

One moment before I wake up at 2 AM, I know it for certain. I know it in the adrenaline rush. I know it in the heartache.

Jealousy bites; it can make you totally paranoid.

Holly smiled up at Ben. They were just talking. Only, as she stepped away from him, she let go of his hand.

Somehow that peripheral picture was there burned into my brain, even though I didn't register it at the time.

Nay, we must think men are not gods.

I catch Ben right before breakfast. And, call me cheap, but I use Holly's trick on him. Unfair? Sure, only I don't care about fairness right now.

"She told you? Why would she do that?" He has the grace to look ashamed somewhere in there with the incredulity at Holly giving the game away. "I don't know what was going on. It was stupid. How come she told you?"

"You agreed not to tell me?"

"Well, yeah."

"You two have so much in common, what with deciding to tell me stuff, or not tell me stuff, assessing my failings as a girlfriend..."

"Okay, fine, get snarky, but can we get over it then? Move on?"

"And *she* kissed *you*, right?"

"Definitely."

"And you kissed her back." I say it firmly, rhetorically, as though I know it to be true, and wait for the blow.

"She told you that? Gee...gotta say, I'm surprised."

"Not as much as I am."

"No, I guess not." He won't meet my eye, and it's just as well, because there's no way I'm letting him see what a sucker punch he has landed.

If I could breathe enough to scream right now, the sound would be gulped down in one mouthful by a black hole of disappointment. I turn away.

He says, "It meant nothing. You know you just have to say the word, Sib."

The word is good-bye.

95

"What? Nothing happened! Who told you?" Holly's eyes are sparkling. I know the look. She's the center of attention. Just the two of us here, but her being at the center is important.

"Who told me 'nothing'?"

"I mean—it meant *nothing*, it was a little eclipse kiss. Little slip of the tongue."

She's making jokes about it? Really?

Seeing as how I already know it's true, I am not quite sure why I want to press it, burning, into my flesh. Mark the betrayal, I suppose. Mark its significance. Make her say the words. "You kissed my boyfriend?"

"Didn't you kind of just tell him you didn't want him anymore? He's basically semi-available, isn't he?"

"He reported our conversation to you, and you thought it was a good time to make a move on him? What else has happened?"

But I realize I don't want to know.

It's time to stop calling this girl a friend.

"It's not like you even really appreciate him, Sib. Be honest."

Be honest? I'm shaking with the honesty of this moment. "Okay. I might not deserve it, but I need a better friend than you. And I feel sorry for you."

I look at her. If I say another word, I'll cry.

It's past time to walk away.

I turn from her, thankful that we have a day of assessment tasks and no one will be in the mood for chitchat; no one will notice that I am walking around with a knife handle sticking out between my shoulder blades.

96

The Mount Fairweather experience culminates in the solo hike. Survival, self-reliance, and new life skills allow each student to take on this significant individual challenge. The "solo" is frequently cited as the high point of the term.

I'm doing it. I hope I don't regret changing my mind.

I pick the closest possible site. If something drastic happens I can run back to school in a couple of hours. I choose the teacher food-drop-off option. I choose the walkie-talkie plus backup-sat-phone option. I am as un-solo as it is possible to be on the solo. But I will be alone, away from Holly and Ben, and as much as I want not to do it, I have to do it. "I'm calling the shots now," trying-to-be-brave me tells wimpy me.

I've brought up a piece of fresh salmon for my dinner. Four minutes on the first side, two on the second. The bliss of not having it overcooked by Priscilla. I eat it with an avocado and tomato and red onion salad, and a fresh roll with lots of butter.

I have a chocolate pudding, and some actual chocolate, for later.

As though they have competing gravitational pull, my big scaredy-cat terror of being alone in the wilderness is keeping my big boyfriend heartbreak and girlfriend betrayal at bay. And the food is a welcome distraction from both.

I eat outside the tent, feeling as brave as a sore-hearted wimp can feel. Which is very scared, because here they are, familiar fears, joining me around the edge of the fire. You can walk as fast as you like, in any direction you like, as far as you like, but they can always keep up with you.

Strange man, or men, rape, abduction.

Crazy anyone, murder.

Drunken hunters, accidental death by getting into the line of fire.

Snake bite, die before help can arrive.

Lose concentration and miss footing while having a wee in the night. Agonizing compound fracture, jagged bone sticking up through skin, fainting, sat phone out of reach. Gnawed by wild beasts (attracted by scent of blood) in the dark. Help arrives too late to save the limb.

Feral cattle stampeding through campsite, kicked in head, die of head injury before help arrives, or worse, live on, able to communicate only via blinking. One eye.

Late-onset asthma. (First time for everything.) Die from attack. No puffer, obviously, having never had asthma until tonight.

Is that it? Are we all here? All finished? Anyone else due to arrive? No? I take some deep breaths, tell the assembled guests that they are all highly improbable, and I don't want to spend the night in their company. Sadly, they don't leave, but at least I said it.

I let myself think about Holly, blinking away the streaming tears.

You were not always like this, Hol.

The summer after grade six you came with us to the beach, we said we'd be best friends forever.

We had three perfect weeks. Dad took us into deep water "out the back" and helped us catch proper waves, and showed us how to read the water. I already knew about rips and stuff, but it was all news to you.

Mom let us not wash our hair. We said we were the wild girls of Santa Casa Beach, and we loved the bushy Hermione Granger effect we got after days of sun and salt and no washing.

We sculpted sand mermaids, with flowing seaweed hair and shell-encrusted tails.

We checked out boys surreptitiously but were unimpressed

with what the tide brought in. Besides, we were deeply in love with Harry Potter that summer, and what living boy could compete with the boy who lived? I did everything I could to try to forget that I was already taller than Daniel Radcliffe.

We stood at the green ocean's edge in soft wet sand, giggling and wiggling till we sank down ankle-deep, shin-deep.

You couldn't believe your luck at our holiday food policy of takeout at least twice a week, and variety packs of the sorts of cereal we were usually never allowed. We were starving at every meal. Reluctant to go home for our two hours out of the sun, but wolfing down our salad rolls. Growling and prowling for our dinner by seven o'clock. Easy to talk my parents into a drive to Queenscliff for after-dinner ice-cream cones.

We shared dreams and secrets in the dark, warm faces close on cool cotton pillowcases in the few minutes before we were sucked under the dark whirlpool of the exhausted sleep that only comes after a day on the beach.

You had fun with us, and I didn't have to compete for your attention. Even Charlotte, who longed to have someone more like you than me for a sister, was with our Sydney grandparents.

When we started back at school, and Tiff arrived, your attention was always half on the group that quickly gathered around her. They were okay, I thought, but too cool for me. And even a little too cool for you till now. Pimples, glasses, zero sophistication, lack of designer clothes, nose that grew before the rest of my face, deathly white skin—still not the right look, despite the vampire books—friends with Michael...wow, I thought I was lucky that you still spoke to me at all.

Now when I look at the kids in grade six, I think, they're babies. But back then, I had this idea that as long as we'd had our perfect summer together, it meant something, and that as long as we'd been so close, at least a kernel of our friendship would remain.

I thought of it as an invisible golden thread that connected us. I never told you that: you'd think it was so sappy. It is sappy. All the other stuff, I let slide. I didn't get offended at my demotions because I really believed in us, and I knew you'd come back.

And you always did.

But, boy, was I wrong about the golden thread.

Nothing connects us anymore.

It's just taken me a little while to figure that out.

To me that summer was magical. To you, it was just the best thing on offer at the time.

I can't feel any sicker about it all.

I can't feel any more afraid of the dark, and what I can't see.

I can't feel any sadder about what I did see.

I have a big, sturdy stick—more of a branch, really—to break over someone's head if I have to defend myself.

I'm not even going to pretend I'm brave. I'm just going to sit it out.

Sometime deep in the hours past midnight, I crawl into the tent and go to sleep. In the new light of a new day, things look shittier than ever.

One more day to get through, and then home.

There is a "last night" tradition here. We get to spend all night in the assembly hall. Boys and girls together. Something that has been totally forbidden all term. Forget the one-foot rule. It seems like a thousand years ago that I was looking forward to spending this night with Ben.

Everyone brings a duvet or sleeping bag and pillows. The hall is soon transformed into a giant squirming seething mass settling into friendship nests. There is a little bit of surreptitious make-out activity, but it's mostly a large and innocent interwoven snuggle.

The screen is set up; the lights are down. There are some awards to give out, a few people have prepared "entertainment," there are movies to watch, and we have "our" song and a slide show of the term. We have argued over and voted on the theme song; it's been a hot issue for some people.

Our song is "Changes." David Bowie has ended up infiltrating and becoming indispensible. And he was the perfect compromise to the irreconcilable argument between hard-core and mainstream mush. Because his fans also happen to be the smart political people, they managed an effective promotional campaign for the song.

The photos show everyone in their respective house groups, dressed in aths gear, in pj's, people dressed up for plays, all of us as human glue following the flour-bomb water-gun fight, people running back down the home trail from the final six-mile run, as "Changes" runs over these bits and snips of our time here.

As everyone watches, we pour our own memories and experiences and emotions into the little gaps between all those pixels, and we choke up a bit and become sentimental about the time here as it winds down. And despite all the words we have written to our parents complaining about absolutely everything expected of us up here, we will, most of us, come to believe that this was a term quite out of the ordinary, a time to grow up and become ourselves a bit more. Breathe the air of a place away from our families. Learn to be independent.

So there are a lot of damp eyes around. As our experience unfolds, revealing itself via this set of color-saturated panoramic dissolving frames, a shot of me and Ben sitting together eating lunch elicits a wave of sighs and *awww*s,

378

a lament at something that no one—except, briefly, the two of us—particularly wanted or endorsed at the time, our aberrant relationship that broke the rules of cool and uncool. But the five-minute nostalgia loop has already tightened around us.

I can't help but look for Ben. He is sitting with his rowing boys, carefully (diplomatically?) not with Holly. He's looking at me, gives me the backward nod, smiles, and shrugs. His look says, *hey, we had some fun. But dudes don't rewind with the sex thing.* Or maybe it is still saying, *you just have to say the word.* As usual, I have no idea.

My look back to him is situated somewhere between neutral and *screw you*, I hope. I fold myself into a thousand pleats to hide the wrenching disappointment—you were my beautiful boy for half a minute.

The lights come up a bit at the end of this digi-digestible mouthful guaranteed to warm parental heart-cockles, and Lou walks onstage. Another song? No.

"I promised a friend who is a filmmaker that I'd do something for her this term that would make her laugh. And so this is for Janie, who is somewhere else."

And the lights are down again.

We're in Bennett House. In stop-motion animation a blob of Blu Tack gathers itself into a ball shape, then a sausage shape, then is followed by a second, smaller ball doing the same thing. Girls appear and disappear in the background of shots, light flickers back and forth from morning to afternoon, but the determined Blu Tack sausages inch, roll, wriggle and squirm their way across the space from the kitchen, along the tabletop, down a chair leg, and across the floor to our sleeping quarters. They are cute; the way they move gives them real character; people are engrossed. As the shapes move along, they pick up bits of fluff and hair and fibers and grass till they finally take on a raggedy, dirty, furry look as they inch up a bedpost and along a rumpled duvet toward a sleeping—Holly? She looks funny, mouth sagging open sideways, a little trail of drool down her cheek, sound asleep. One caterpillar positions itself along the length of her eyebrows, forming a large, grubby unibrow. Now people are really laughing.

I look around to find Holly; she is sitting with Tiff, her face like thunder, till she sees me looking at her. It triggers her response. She has to get on the inside of this joke. Not be the butt of it.

The second, smaller caterpillar now forms itself as a mustache across Holly's top lip, her face twitching and contorting slightly as she sleepily half feels it. The mustache ends curl up.

Laughter is building from bubbles to a roar, and I keep an eye on Holly, who is forced to match her amusement level to that of the room. It's killing her. She hates looking foolish.

Lou's little film ends.

And Lou says, "I have two comments: Beauty is as beauty does. And if you are planning to make a stop-motion film, it takes ten times longer than you think it will. So, be warned."

While Lou is up there, someone asks her to sing.

She sings a wistful song, something about betrayal, and I'm pretty sure she is singing it for me. I look at Michael giving a slow nod to the stage, and I can see he's pretty sure Lou is singing it for him. Holly is staring at Ben, looking hungry, being ignored: the song's working for her, too.

So we're all happy.

A few more people get up and do comedy sketches, sing, play their music, but I've zoned out.

The buses are coming at ten tomorrow morning to take us back to the city, back to civilization, and before that I've got a date to see the sunrise.

98

Lou and Michael and I tiptoe through the all-night tangle of sleeping bags and snores outside into the almost-morning of our last day.

The roof of the assembly hall is wet with dew as we scramble up, but the ridge is wide and comfortable and we can sit here, wrapped around by the mountains, without feeling like we're about to plummet.

Michael smiles his dreamyvague smile, and Lou is wiping happysad tears from her face as the sun slices away the night.

I put an arm around each of them.

friday 7 december

Up on the roof with Sibylla and Michael, and wouldn't you know it, I was sad that it's our last morning despite having frequently and fervently longed for the term to be over.

What an impossible pair we are, quick and dead, two little syllables, never the twain, etc.

When I see the sun split the mountains from the sky on our last day ... I see it with my new friends, and I see it for you, too, Fred.

I won't ever let you die again. You will always be a part of me, and how I see the world.

100

The sky grows lighter too quickly. Time soon to eat our last breakfast and finish packing. As we stand and stretch, ready to climb down, the thought that we won't see each other every day is unimaginable.

"You really should go out with Lou." I am as shocked as the other two to hear the words coming from my mouth. The idea has been building for a while, but...I said that *out loud*?

Michael, better acquainted with my skills at the inappropriate blurt, recovers first. "Louisa won't be giving her heart away for a very long time."

Lou nods in grim agreement.

"Neither will I," I say, thinking of Ben with the stab that happens every time he comes to mind.

"Me neither," says Michael, looking at me.

"So—summer of the lonely hearts club, coming up," says Lou.

We look at each other. It seems like the right thing to scream out to the mountains from the rooftop now that the sun is up.

ACKNOWLEDGMENTS

Heartfelt thanks to Michael Brown, Andrea Claburn, Greer Clemens, Kaz Cooke, Claire Craig, Cath Crowley, Rosey Cummings, Katelyn Detweiler, Debi Enker, Jill Grinberg, Philippa Hawker, Nick Hede, Julia Heyward, Simmone Howell, Penny Hueston, Elizabeth Hunt, Farrin Jacobs (and the team at Little, Brown), Alex Kay, Tessa Kay, Julie Landvogt, Louise Lavarack, Ali Lavau, Violet Leonard, Jo Lyons, Melina Marchetta, Alex McCombe, Olivia McCombe, Cheryl Pientka, Madeleine Ryan, Tom Ryan, Samantha Sainsbury, Jane Sullivan, Penny Tangey, Adele Walsh, George Wood, Zoe Wood, and especially Jamie Wood.

Thanks to Arts Victoria.

Writing this book overlapped with *Six Impossible Things*, and once again I thank Varuna, the Writers' House, for The Eleanor Dark Flagship Fellowship; Iola Mathews, Writers Victoria and the National Trust for the Glenfern Writers' Studios; and the Readings Foundation for the Glenfern Fellowship.